3

Destiny Binds

Destiny Binds

Timber Wolves Trilogy :
Book 1

A novel by
Tammy Blackwell

Just in case the boys turning into wild animals under the light of the full moon didn't make it obvious, this is a work of fiction. All characters and events exist only in the mind of the writer. Any resemblance to real life is a figment of your imagination.

Cover Design: Victoria Faye (www.victoriafaye.com)

Cataloging Information

Blackwell, Tammy
    Destiny Binds/ Tammy Blackwell. - 2nd ed.
    223 p. ; 22 cm.
    Summary : Scout Donovan is a girl who believes in rules, logic, and her lifelong love of Charlie Hagan. Alex Cole believes in destiny, magic, and Scout. When Alex introduces Scout to the world of Shifters, men who change into wolves or coyotes during the full moon, and Seers, women who can see your most private thoughts and emotions with a mere touch, the knowledge changes everything and everyone Scout thought she knew.
    ISBN 978-1460918685
    [1. Werewolves - Fiction. 2. Kentucky - Fiction. 3. Supernatural. 4. Love stories.]

To my YAAPers:
I wrote this one for you

———————

In loving memory of
Rickey E. Blackwell

Chapter 1

John Davis smells like Play-Doh. When we were in elementary school, it wasn't a big deal. I mean, we were kids. Play-Doh was pretty high on the awesome scale. But there comes a time when a guy should stop smelling like crafting supplies and develop a more manly scent, like campfire or gym floor.

I had been roaming up and down the crowded street trying to ditch John and his noxious odor for over an hour, but he was too oblivious for it to work. He followed me to the trashcan, stood in line with me when I ordered a second corndog, and even waited outside the girl's bathroom.

"I still can't believe our senior year is finally here, you know? I feel like we've been waiting for this one year our whole lives." He paused to lift up his NASCAR hat, running his fingers through his hair. My attention drifted as he blathered on about post-graduation plans. I briefly considered stabbing him into silence with the pointy end of my corndog stick, but decided there were too many witnesses. Granted, most everyone was too busy *oooh*-ing and *ahhh*-ing as Jase Donovan regaled them with his *I beat the NCAA's top Point Guard in a one-on-one* story to notice my existence, but I figured the screaming and blood might draw some attention.

I was trying desperately hard to not be jealous that Jase was entertaining the masses, leaving me at the mercy of the only other social outcast within a five mile vicinity. I knew this would happen the moment he suggested heading out to The Strip, a mile long stretch of road that served as Western Kentucky's go-to summer

1

spot. The shops and tourist attractions of The Strip were overrun with vacationing families and tanned locals. It was the second group that mobbed Jase the moment we got out of our car. My brother had taken his rightful place as the center of attention while I was relegated to the Loser's Table with John Davis, who's inability to grasp the fact we hadn't been friends at any time during the past twelve years was truly spectacular.

I was coping by playing a round of Anywhere But Here, imaging myself trekking through Europe with nothing but a backpack and limit-free credit card, when John nudged me back to reality with his elbow. "Do you know them?" he asked, nodding towards two guys sitting on a bench in front of Lynda's Beauty Parlor and Tanning Emporium. They were obviously brothers, both possessing the same chestnut colored hair and aristocratic bone structure. The younger one was sprawled out, a book propped against one knee. I tilted my head, attempting to read the title, but he was too far away to make out the words. I was half-tempted to just go over and ask. The slight smile playing on his lips as he scanned the pages made me think he wouldn't mind the interruption.

In contrast, the older brother looked as though he might be inclined to eat children on occasion. It wasn't just his size; there something about the way he sat, as if he was waiting to pounce on the first person who wandered too close. He scowled at the world in general, and me in particular.

They say a person can get used to anything. Maybe one day I'll get used to being stared at, but I doubt it. According to my mother, people stare because they're intrigued by my "unique beauty." Of course, she's a mother. She has to say stuff like that.

The thing is, there really isn't anything horribly wrong with any of my physical features when taken individually. Hair that is so blond it looks silver? Kinda cool. Pale ivory skin that can only manage to burn and blister in the sun? Appeals mostly to the Goth and Victorian crowds, but not a tragic flaw. Eyes a peculiar shade of

2

icy blue that makes them seem almost translucent? Even those might have looked okay on the right person. The problem occurred when you put all those monochromatic features on a single individual. It made me a freak, a fact driven home by my bottom-rung social status and an endless supply of gawkers everywhere I went.

Depending on my mood, I tend to handle the staring in one of two ways -- either I ignore it or I meet and hold their gaze, knowing that people find it unnerving to have the freak stare back. Thanks to John, I was all kinds of annoyed, which made it a see-if-you-can-make-them-flinch kind of day. I raised my eyes to meet his and waited for a reaction.

He never even blinked.

I didn't realize how tense I was until someone grabbed my shoulder. I reacted to the sudden invasion of my personal space without thinking. Luckily, Jase managed to block my right hook. The sight of my fist trapped in his hand caused my stomach to clench. Had I really just tried to hit my brother? What was wrong with me?

"Do you want to go get ice cream? Yes or no?" Jase asked slowly, as if I was mentally impaired. I heard someone behind him snicker.

Two corndogs and an order of onion rings had more than filled me up, but I ended up agreeing to dessert just as an excuse to stay near Jase and put some distance between me and Bench Boy. The plan had been to stick with the group, but after a few minutes of watching Ellie Davis, John's somewhat skanky little sister, throw herself at my brother, I decided I was willing to risk being on my own. After everyone got their order, I quietly slipped away, heading towards the lake.

"What happened back there?" Jase asked as soon as we were out of earshot. I hadn't realized he followed me, but I was grateful. Although, I could have done without the whole concerned hovering thing he seemed intent on doing since my little episode.

"I wasn't trying to hit you. You just caught me off guard."

3

"I said your name like five times. You were seriously zoning."

He jumped ahead, blocking my path. "Was someone bothering you?"

"It was just some guy with a staring problem."

Jase worked the muscles in his jaw.

"Calm down. It was nothing." I spotted a nice flat rock in the shade and started towards it.

The lake was considerably less crowded than the surrounding shops, restaurants, and attractions A few families splashed in the water, but most people preferred the public pool, since it didn't have the top layer of green slime that may or may not contain byproducts from the nearby chemical plants. We had a large chunk of the beach to ourselves, which suited me just fine.

Despite assuring Jase it was nothing, the incident with Sir Stares-A-Lot had shaken me up. I've dealt with my fair share of jerks, bullies, and weirdos over the years, but none of them had ever affected me like this guy. He hadn't done anything but look at me a whole lot longer than was socially acceptable, yet I was genuinely frightened of him.

I would have driven myself crazy trying to convince myself that he wasn't, in fact, a serial rapist or mass murderer, but luckily I had my brother there to distract me.

"I'm going back-to-school shopping," I said as Jase polished off the last of my banana split, "and I'm going to buy antimatter, baklava, a cyanide capsule, a D&D manual, an Easy-Bake Oven, the *Footloose* soundtrack, a genetically modified goldfish, a harmonica, an imaginary friend, a janitor's uniform, a kidney off the black market, a loincloth, and...medieval weaponry."

"Medieval weaponry?"

I gave a smug smile. Mom introduced us to the alphabet game when we were little with the purpose of keeping us entertained on long road trips. Over the years it evolved from a simple memory game to a contest to see who could come up with the most ridiculous items.

"Okay, then I'm going back-to-school shopping and I'm going to buy antimatter, baklava, a cyanide capsule, a *Dungeons & Dragons* manual, an Easy-Bake Oven, the *Footloose* soundtrack, a genetically modified goldfish named Gabe, a harmonica, an imaginary friend, a janitor's uniform, kidney, loincloth, medieval weaponry for with which to slay, and..." He recited the alphabet under his breath. "N. Nude photos of Betty White."

It was obvious who was winning this round.

"That's just gross."

He threw a hand over his heart and squeezed his eyes shut as if he was trying to hold back tears. "How can you say that about my Betty? She's such a beautiful woman."

He may have gone on, extolling the virtues of naked senior citizens, but I wasn't listening. The guy from the bench -- the big, scary one -- was leaning against a tree about twenty-five yards away.

"Ground Control to Major Spazz. Can you hear me, Major Spazz?"

"Huh? What?" Jase was standing in front of me. I wasn't quite sure when that happened.

"You okay?"

"He's back," I said, my voice a whisper for no good reason.

"Who?"

"The guy with a staring problem." I nodded towards the small cropping of trees.

I knew by the way he called, "I'll be right back," over his shoulder as he took off down the beach that he intended for me to stay where I was. I gave the idea some serious consideration before taking off after him.

"I know the rules," Jase was saying as I approached. "This is our territory. You either fight me now or leave."

Was he insane? This guy could have passed as the Jolly Green Giant's considerably less green and jolly brother. It was entirely possible he could bench press a Volkswagen. Jase would get broken into a million little pieces.

5

"I'm not leaving."

Jase pulled himself up to his full five feet and nine inches, which was less than impressive. "Then we fight."

"Like Hades you will," I said, stepping up beside my brother. "Did you wake up on the stupid side of the bed this morning?"

Jase didn't even look at me. "Go away, Scout. This is none of your business."

"I'm not leaving until you do."

"I think you should go, Scout." I made the mistake of looking up when he said my name. His eyes were an unusual shade of grey, no trace of blue, green, or yellow visible.

"No, thank you."

He stepped over to me and someone made a strange whimpering sound. Oddly enough, I felt certain it had originated from Jase's throat instead of my own. The other guy was less than a foot away from me, and I had to crane my neck to meet his steel colored eyes. Being in such a close proximity caused the hair on my arms to stand on end.

He leaned in so close I could feel his warm breath on my neck. I thought he was going to whisper something in my ear, but instead he quickly inhaled twice through his nose.

Well, I certainly had never been *sniffed* before.

"What is she?"

The question was aimed at Jase, but I took the liberty of answering. "What she is, is offended and quickly becoming angry."

"Leave my sister out of it," Jase said, sounding like a kid telling the bully to give his lunch money back.

Our new friend's eyes flickered quizzically between Jase and me. "Do they know about her?"

Jase didn't say anything, which apparently qualified as an answer. He finally backed away, giving me room to breathe.

"I'm staying," he told Jase is a quiet, controlled voice. "I suggest your people stay out of my way. I'll take out anyone who crosses me." He shot a pointed glance in my direction. "Even her."

Once he was out of earshot, Jase wheeled on me. "Why couldn't you have stayed out of this? What am I supposed to do now?" He yelled out a stream of profanities and kicked a nearby tree hard enough to dislodge some bark and possibly a toe.

"Who was that? What's going on?" My anger matched, if not surpassed, his. "Were you seriously going to fight that guy? He's like three times bigger than you!"

"He's not that big."

"It would have been like The Rock versus Seth Green. Now, tell me who he is."

"I don't know."

Liar.

We glared at each other for a long moment. Finally, Jase stalked off, whipping out his cell phone along the way. I waited until he finished his call to strike again.

"Are you in a gang?" It was the most logical conclusion I could reach. I overheard just enough of his conversation to know he had called Toby, a cop. Convincing his naive young cousin to infiltrate a local gang sounded like the kind of idiotic plan Toby would have.

"Does this look like inner-city Chicago to you?" Jase gestured at the tiny town nestled in the forest. "Do you think the Bloods are doing drive-bys in pick-ups and mini-vans?"

"I think that something very weird just happened. Something about 'territory'. Something that ended with Jean-Claude van Crazy threatening to snuff me out and sent you running to Toby. Did your idiot cousin put you up to something?"

"Can't you just drop it?"

"Not likely."

Jase growled in agitation. "Please, Scout? Just this once? I promise, I won't let him hurt you."

"Can you promise that you won't get hurt?"

"You don't have to worry about me," he said, assuming what must have passed as a tough guy expression in Jase's mind. "I'm made of 100% awesome, totally untouchable."

7

"Promise?"

"Promise."

"Then I'll drop it," I said as I began plotting ways to uncover the truth.

Chapter 2

Just five days before school resumed Ms. Northington resigned her position at Lake County High. Apparently, she met a nice Finnish man on a cruise over the summer, fell madly in love, and was moving half-way around the world. Of this I had been informed. What no one bothered to tell me was that crotchety old Mr. Beck had come out of retirement to fill her position. If someone had mentioned it, I would have changed my schedule. AP Calculus was going to be bad enough without having Satan's right-hand man as a teacher.

One of Mr. Beck's many faults was believing high school seniors should still be forced to sit in alphabetical order, which left me stuck behind the aromatic John Davis. I knew that between Mr. Beck's soporific voice and my brain's insistence on trying to solve the mystery of John's unique scent, I was going to have a hard time keeping focused.

"Scout, do you understand anything Mr. Beck is talking about?" came a frantic whisper from my left.

"It's the first day. He's just going over the class rules and stuff," I explained as quietly as possible.

The tiny girl in the chair next to me nervously gnawed on her nonexistent fingernails while simultaneously bouncing her left leg up and down at about a million miles an hour. Joi Fitzgerald was sweet, but she could make a Tibetan monk anxious. "How on earth did I end up in AP Calc? I'll never be able to keep up."

"You're in AP Calc because you scored 98% on the placement test. You're going to do fine. Stop worrying."

A shadow fell across my desk. "Harper, is there something that you want to share with the rest of the class?"

"It's Scout," I snapped in response to hearing my given name before remembering who I was snapping at. "I mean, my name. It's Scout. You can call me Scout. Please."

"I think we are a little old to be going by nicknames in class." Mr. Beck sneered, which did nothing to help his personal appearance. Of course, there wasn't much that actually would help the man's personal appearance other than a hairpiece and some clothes bought more recently than 1978.

"Th-th-then you can call me Miss Donovan."

"Very well, *Miss Donovan*. Now, if you and *Miss Fitzgerald* are done with your conversation, we can all go back to discussing the grading scale for this course." Mr. Beck turned and began to drone on about how he did not grade on a curve, nor did he give any extra credit or extended deadlines.

I looked forward, waiting for my embarrassment to subside and my heart rate to return to normal. Could I be any more of a dork? One brief exchange with an antagonizing teacher had me shaking like a leaf.

That's when I noticed a pair of familiar grey eyes staring at me. I was so shocked I didn't immediately realize that the face they were peering out of wasn't the same one I had been fastidiously scouring the Internet for over the past three days. The slope of the nose and curve of the jaw were the same, but this face lacked the malice and anger that was so evident on the other.

Jean-Claude's little brother.

Lake County High isn't a big school; my graduating class boasts a whopping one hundred and forty-three students. When someone new shows up, everyone notices. I had been hearing about a new guy all morning. Ashley Johnson was all about the "yummy newbie" who transferred in from Montana. She spent half of our first hour class planning their wedding.

And now the future Mr. Ashley Johnson was turned around in his chair, leaning around John Davis, staring at me.

It didn't take long for my brain to decide that the last thing it wanted was another confrontation and allowed embarrassment to overwhelm me. I dropped my eyes as my face turned a brilliant shade of tomato.

I continued through the rest of the hour with my eyes fixed steadfastly on my desk. I tried to take some notes on what Mr. Beck was covering, but it all basically boiled down to him being a jerk and the class being impossibly hard. I was pretty sure I could remember that without a written reminder.

When the bell finally rang, I quickly gathered my stuff and jumped up, planning to make a quick escape. Instead, I ran directly into the new guy's chest.

"Sorry," I muttered, trying to step around him to get to the door. Instead of moving to the side to let me by, like a decent person would do, the new guy just stood there.

"Excuse me," I hissed through clenched teeth. He finally moved, allowing me clear access to the door, and the blissful anonymity the crowded hallway provided.

***

I breathed a sigh of relief as I sank into the seat next to my best friend, Talley Matthews, in the school's dilapidated theater. The seats were worn and threadbare, the thick velvet curtain had faded from red to a rustic orange, half of the light fixtures were missing bulbs, and a musty, mildewed scent hung heavily in the air. Despite its ruinous state, I was looking forward to the time I would be spending in the old theater taking the school's new Shakespeare class.

"How is your last first day of high school going?" Talley asked, without even a hint of irony in her voice.

"It has sucked, big time. Jase totally hogged the bathroom all morning. Then, he insisted on picking up Nikki Anderson, who made us wait fifteen minutes in the car while she painted on her perfect face. And, of course, Jase then made me ride in the back seat of *our* car so that he could stare at her unnaturally perky boobs as he drove us to school. Ashley Johnson is in my AP English class, and Mr. Beck is a complete tool who refuses to call me Scout. And, remember that guy I told you about from The Strip? Mr. Tall, Dark and Insane? His brother is the new guy."

"There's a new guy?" Talley was always oblivious to the school's latest gossip. "What's his name?"

"His last name is Cole. I don't remember what his first name is though. Some really generic 'A' name. Alan? Andrew?"

"Alex," an unfamiliar male voice replied from behind me. I turned to see the new guy, apparently named Alex, sitting in the second row of seats.

Crap. How long had he been there?

"Should I call you Scout or Miss Donovan?" he asked with a smirk.

I glowered. "Scout will be fine."

"I'm Talley," my best friend chimed in, turning around to stretch her hand out towards Alex. What was she doing? Was she going to shake his hand like they were closing a bank deal or something equally adult and boring?

To his credit, Alex didn't look at Talley as though she was breaking some unwritten high school code, and extended his own hand to her. "Nice to meet you, Talley. Cool name. Very non-generic." His grey eyes seemed to dance their way over to mine. The huge grin on his face revealed perfectly straight white teeth and a pair of honest-to-goodness dimples.

"Thanks," Talley replied, meeting his smile watt per watt. "My mom went into labor with me at O'Talley's restaurant. It was the only thing her post-childbirth drug-addled mind could come up with when they asked her for a name."

"Cool. And how does one become a Scout? Are you like a super cookie salesman?" He was obviously pleased with his own attempt at being clever. I couldn't help but notice that his eyes were still focused intently on my face.

"It's because my name is Harper Lee," I said in the most annoyed voice I could muster.

"And so people call you Scout?" I allowed a condescending smile to spread across my face. I had missed moments like these ever since they assigned *To Kill a Mockingbird* our Junior year.

"Why not Boo?" Alex asked, effectively robbing me of my smugness. Jerk.

My spirits sank even lower as I looked up to see the last batch of students making their way towards the stage. Ashley Johnson practically skipped her way to the seat beside Alex.

"Hi, you must be new," Ashley gushed, pretending she didn't already know exactly who he was. Knowing her super-stalker abilities, she probably already knew what size wedding band she needed to buy him. "I'm Ashley."

Alex finally stopped staring at me to focus on the Bimbo Barbie sitting next to him. I watched as his eyes assessed her, from her super-styled bottle blond hair all the way down to her designer 4-inch heels. Apparently, he liked what he saw. "Well, Ashley, it's a pleasure to meet you. I'm Alex Cole."

I turned back around in my seat so I wouldn't have to actually see Ashley's breasts as they struggled to free themselves from the tiny tank top she had them stuffed in as she leaned over to talk to Alex. Sadly, this didn't stop her grating voice from reaching my ears.

"That's a real interestin' accent ya go there, Alex. Where are y'all from?" Ashley always had a bit of a southern drawl, but she was really laying it on thick.

"I just moved here from Montana," he answered, hamming up his own accent so that he sounded like a member of The Barenaked Ladies.

"How on earth does someone from Montana end up down here in Timber, Kentucky?"

I was actually curious about that myself. Timber isn't exactly a thriving metropolis. Most of the county is covered by Land Between the Lakes, a national forest that is beautiful and mildly entertaining in the summer months, but lacking modern amenities like a Target or movie theater. Occasionally someone would move up from Nashville to escape the city, but most of our families have been here forever. I hadn't even met someone from Montana until three days ago.

I'm not sure if he was being truthful or trying yet again to be clever, but I could tell from the momentary silence behind me that his response of, "This is where the car broke down," wasn't exactly what Ashley was expecting either.

Before Ashley could extract more information from her future groom, or cause my ears to bleed, Ms. Ryder strode onto the stage. The sight of her electric blue legs engulfed in red cowboy boots captured our attention even more effectively than her dramatic recitation of *Richard III*.

The next hour flew by in a blur as Ms. Ryder excitedly went over the details of the course. The class was small, only a dozen of us, and the local art guild was providing funding for a few field trips to see some live performances. I was so excited by the time the bell rang that I almost forgot about Alex.

"So the new guy is kind of a hottie." Talley said from one of the cafeteria's cheerfully colored booths. She was munching on a carrot stick, her latest attempt at going on a diet. I silently predicted that they would be replaced with McDonald's french fires before she made it home that afternoon.

"When did you start using words like 'hottie'?"

"You're avoiding the topic."

"What topic?"

"The hotness that is Alex Cole. Don't pretend you didn't notice."

14

Of course I noticed. I was in possession of two functioning eyeballs and an appreciation of the opposite sex.

"He's one of the beautiful people. God help us all." Talley gave me what I like to think of as her why-the-Hades-do-I-put-up-with-you look. "Don't look at me like that. You know you're the only beautiful person in this school who isn't completely vapid."

Talley learned to quit arguing with me over the fact that she was beautiful long ago. On this one fact I was stubbornly certain. Talley's eyes are a deep blue, set off by her thick, shiny black hair that looks perfect even when she has bedhead. Her skin is as pale as mine, but the sun is much kinder to her. Since it was mid-August, her nose had an adorable scattering of the cutest freckles any human has ever possessed. Couple those features with the fact that she was the kindest and most joyful person alive, and it all added up to a very attractive girl. It was a shame everyone seemed too focused on the fact that she weighed over 200 pounds to notice.

"What about Jase?" Talley asked, looking over my shoulder.

"What about him?

"Don't you think I'm beautiful?" my brother asked, sliding into the booth next to me.

"Of course you're beautiful." Not to be gross or anything, but he actually kind of is. "You're also completely vapid." Which is only partially true.

"Aw. You're just saying that because you know I have no idea what vapid means."

"It means quit eating all my Doritos." I snatched my nearly empty bag out of his hand. "What are you doing here, Jase? Aren't you supposed to be in class?"

"Nope. This is my lunch period."

Talley froze with a carrot stick halfway to her mouth. "No way. How did that happen?"

"Tal, isn't it obvious? Scout and I are mature, responsible Seniors now. Don't be so shocked that the school administration has taken notice."

15

Since an incident in the third grade, Jase and I were separated at school as much as possible. We were never in the same classes or allowed to join the same clubs. It really hadn't been an issue since we got to high school. Jase's interests tended to skew towards athletics while mine had a more academic feel. Yet, I knew for certain the superintendent, who just happened to be our father, still intended for our schedules to never intertwine. Obviously, someone wasn't paying attention.

"You? Me? The same lunch? That's going to be odd."

"Odd?" Jase looked at me, totally confused. "It's going to be awesome!"

It is common knowledge that things have to work a certain way in the world of high school politics. The super-cool, yet approachable, star athlete was supposed to date the prettiest girls, attend the coolest parties, and eat lunch with the rest of the elite, not his socially awkward sister.

"Shouldn't you be holding court with Twiddle-Dee, Twiddle-Dum, and Twiddle-Moron over there?" I asked, referring to a table in the middle of the dining area where three of Jase's teammates - Tyler Burkeen, Seth Roberts, and Jordan Daniels - were hanging all over a cluster of cheerleader types, occasionally tossing a french fry towards the back of James Kiplinger's head.

"I see those guys all the time."

"You live with me. Our bedrooms are roughly five feet from each other."

"Are you trying to say that you don't want to eat lunch with me, Scout?"

"Of course she wants to eat lunch with you," Talley said. "She's just worried that you're going to make her have an actual conversation with someone other than you or me."

That wasn't entirely fair. It wasn't my fault I wasn't as affable as they were.

"You know, they really aren't that bad once you get to know them," Jase said, watching as Jordan managed to get a ketchup coated fry to stick to James' shirt.

"Jordan Daniels is not only a complete jerk, but he's also as dumb as a box of rocks."

"He doesn't still call you Al the Albino does he?"

"No." Not since Jase slammed him into a wall in the boy's locker room and suggested he quit. "That doesn't mean that he suddenly stopped being a half-wit. I overheard him asking one of the secretaries where to put a stamp on an envelope last year."

"Okay, so Jordan is an idiot, but Tyler and Seth are pretty decent, and I think you would like some of the girls if you would just give them a chance."

Sure, we would become the bestest of friends. We could have sleep-overs where we braided each other's hair and talked about how super-cute and hunky Jordan is.

Gag.

I was about to turn back to my table when a pair of steely eyes caught my attention. Alex Cole sat two tables away from us, once again staring. Only this time, it wasn't at me. Instead, he was looking at Jase with an expression which could have easily been interpreted as murderous. His eyes were hard and I could see the muscles in his cheeks jump as he clenched and unclenched his jaw.

I could also see Ashley Johnson babbling on like a ditz beside him. I briefly wondered if she was discussing possible honeymoon locations.

"Earth to Scout," Jase said, pulling my attention away from Alex's table.

"Who are you looking at?" Talley glanced over and smiled. "Ah-ha. The new guy. I should have known."

It occurred to me that it might have been a good idea to have mentioned Alex before that moment.

"What new guy?" Jase looked towards Alex and his face went blank. I was reminded of the time he came home to find that our little sister had decided to make his Star Wars figures "pretty" by coloring on them with a red Sharpie. He had looked at them with this exact same expressionless stare before launching into the biggest temper tantrum ever. Angel had cried for hours.

"His name is Alex Cole, and he just moved here from Montana." Talley said. "He is smart, attractive, funny, and madly in love with your sister."

"What?" Two voices came out in unison -- mine incredulous and Jase's furious.

Talley flinched slightly, but refused to be dissuaded. "C'mon, Scout. You said he was staring at you in Calc, and he was definitely flirting with you in Shakespeare. You could almost see the electricity in the air between you two."

What the Hades was she talking about? I love Talley. Really, I do. But there are times when Talley's world and the real world are two completely different places.

Jase's lips were pressed so tightly together you could barely see them. "Stay away from him. I don't even want you talking to him. Do you understand?"

"Did you seriously just try to tell me what to do?"

Jase narrowed his eyes. "You do realize who he is, right? You remember what the other one said?"

"I remember." Like that was the sort of thing that just slipped your mind. "But Alex doesn't seem so...*intense*. I think he's fairly innocuous."

"I don't care what he is. I promised I'd keep you safe. I can't do that if you're hanging out with one of them."

I could have argued the issue, pointing out that I was perfectly capable of taking care of myself, but I didn't. It wasn't like I actually wanted to hang out with the new guy. "No problem. Really, I can't stand the guy. I would be perfectly happy if I never spoke to him again."

"Good. Let's keep it that way." Jase got up, shooting another glance in Alex's direction. "I'll see you at the car after school," he said, grabbing half of my turkey sandwich.

"What was that all about?" Talley asked, watching Jase as he made his way out of the cafeteria.

"I'm not a hundred percent sure," I admitted. "It has something to do with Alex's psycho brother. I think Jase is involved in something bad. I tried to ask him about it, but he just shrugged me off."

"What are you going to do?"

"I'll just wait it out. Jase will eventually tell me what's up."

"I was talking about staying away from Alex."

"I honestly don't think that's going to be a problem."

Talley looked over at the table where Alex was now chatting away with Ashley. They were most likely going over baby names. I cringed at the mental image of little Ashleys.

"That may be a bit harder than you think."

"Don't be crazy; it'll be a piece of cake."

And it was a piece of cake. I managed to avoid any and all contact with Alex Cole for two whole hours.

**

"There you are, Scout," Mrs. Sole greeted me at the door of my print media class. "Editorial staff is at the table in the corner."

I walked back to the table where Joi Fitzgerald and Meg Jamison waited for me. I took a deep, steadying breath as I sat in the only available seat, next to Alex.

Crap.

"We just keep running into each other," he said as I began to consider becoming a sports writer.

"Yes, it seems karma is intent on us spending some time together. Obviously, I did something horrid in my previous life."

"Or maybe you're my reward for being so good." You would think that grey eyes would be dull and lifeless, but his seemed to glow.

I decided my best response would be silence. Unfortunately, he did not take this as a hint to end the conversation.

"So, I was going to sit by you at lunch, but your boyfriend beat me to it."

"Who? My what?" The boyfriend statement threw me. "Do you mean Jase?"

Joi, who had been listening intently to our conversation, looked even more shocked than Talley had earlier. "You and Jase have lunch together? But I thought that there had been a royal decree that the Donovan Twins weren't allowed within 500 feet of each other on school grounds since the Ms. Tubbs incident."

Good grief. So you make one teacher have a mental breakdown in elementary school. Was it really that big of a deal?

"Twins?"

"Jase is my brother."

"No, he's not," Alex said with absolute conviction.

I was about to tell Alex exactly what I thought about him and his presumptuous arrogance when Joi decided to be helpful.

"Oh, we just call them twins. Jase's mom married Scout's dad when they were babies. They don't look anything alike, and Jase is technically a couple of months older, but they act like twins."

"Five weeks to the day," I corrected automatically.

"That's quite the distinction, Scout, " Meg said. After watching an episode of *Law and Order* in the fifth grade, Meg Jamison decided she wanted nothing more in life than to be a lawyer. She had been speaking like one ever since. I tried imagining her using "hottie" or "yummy newbie" to describe Alex, but my imagination wasn't that good.

"Do you have any siblings, Alex?" she asked, steering the conversation away from Jase, who she loathed with a passion since a brief stint as his flavor-of-the-month last year.

I eventually came to know that Alex's brother was named Liam, and he served as Alex's legal guardian. ("He's two years, ten months, and four days older," Alex told me with a wink.) They moved from Libby, Montana, a town about 75 miles from the Canadian border, to Kentucky the first week in July.

There was no mention of Liam's habit of terrifying random strangers for fun.

It quickly became apparent that Alex was one of those naturally outgoing people that could coax even the most aloof individuals into a group discussion. Thanks to him, the entire class was debating the best zombie survival tactics when school was dismissed for the day. I was so intent on making sure he understood the advantages of owning a blimp I never considered how Jase would react to seeing the two of us strolling through the parking lot together. It was, without question, one of my more remarkable errors.

Chapter 3

My senior year was off to a spectacular start. I had Beelzebub as a Calculus teacher, half of my classes came with first day homework, and the new guy had managed to completely disrupt my peaceful, structured world. I was so distracted by the time I got home, I didn't notice the boy sleeping in my bed until I almost sat on him.

Charlie Hagan isn't handsome in the classic sense - his features are a little too sharp and his lips a little too full - but he was unmistakably attractive. It's not so much his physical appearance as his personality. Although, his athletic body, piercing green eyes, and curly hair with natural high-lights aren't to be ignored.

I wanted to go lie down next to him. I wanted to feel his arms wrapped around me and discover what his lips taste like. I wanted to tell him I had been secretly in love with him since I was two years old. So, I did the only thing I could do. I hit him in the head with Guido, my sock monkey.

"Ow, Scout." He yawned and stretched out, causing the bottom of his T-shirt to ride up and reveal a sliver of bare stomach.

I seriously considered passing out.

"Charlie, what are you doing in my bed?"

"Jase's room smells funky and Angel's room is too pink. Your bed, on the other hand, is just right."

Well, if he felt that way about it...

No, Scout. Bad. Think of something else.

"Shouldn't you be home packing?"

Charlie was Jase's best friend and paternal cousin. He lived with the rest of the Hagan clan near the Army Base, but spent as much time at our house as possible. On Friday, he was going to break my heart by moving three hundred miles away.

"Pack, shmack. I'll do it later. I wanted to see how your first day of school went."

I plopped down on the bed. Although my heart accelerated slightly at being so close to Charlie, I knew that he thought nothing of it. To him I was just like a sister. Or, at least, a cousin.

"School sucks. I'm dropping out and becoming a truck stop waitress. I think I'll change my name to Flo and get a really bad perm. Flo the truck stop waitress with a bad perm doesn't need high school. She lives off the knowledge of life."

Charlie reached over and put a consoling arm around my shoulders. I had trouble hearing his words over my pounding heart. "Was it Goat Girl? Do you need me to kick her ass for you? I mean, I don't normally like the idea of hitting girls, but I'll make an exception."

Goat Girl was what Charlie and I called Ashley Johnson. It was because when you actually took the time to look at her face, she really did look like a goat with her little mouth, long face, and oddly placed eyes.

"No," I grumbled. "She's not the problem. Although, having two classes plus lunch with her doesn't add up to happy, happy fun."

"Then what is the problem?"

Before I could answer, my bedroom door swung open and in marched the very definition of a little girl: pink skirt, pink top, pink sandals, and a pink bow keeping her bouncy, blond curls pulled back from her little, round face.

"Found him!" Angel yelled at the top of her lungs. "He's in bed with Scout!"

My parents adore my six year old sister, positive that she is the most perfect child to have ever been born. Jase and I mostly just manage not to kill her.

"Why are you in bed together?" Angel asked, shooting Charlie and me a disapproving look.

"Because it's the most comfortable place in the room to sit," I explained, refusing to feel guilty.

"Why is his arm around you?"

"Because my first day of school sucked."

"You shouldn't say 'sucked'. It's a bad word."

"I'm seventeen. I will say 'sucked' if I want to."

"I'm gonna tell Mom."

"Go ahead. See if I care." These little talks with my sister always brought out the best in me. We could have gone on for hours, but Jase came into the room with a plate of Oreos and a glass of milk.

"Good work, Munchkin," he said, handing the snack over to Angel. "Here's your reward. Now, why don't you go eat it in your room?"

She looked like she was going to protest, but saw something on Jase's face that made her comply. Maybe it was the dried blood.

"What happened to you?" Charlie asked, surveying the damage. Jase's face was starting to swell around his nose, and the area around his eyes was turning purple.

"Wasn't paying attention in gym. A football hit me in the face."

"That's pretty good. Excellent delivery. Your parents are sure to buy it. Now, tell me what really happened."

"Scout's new boyfriend punched me."

All of the zen-like calm Charlie's presence had created immediately vanished. "He's not my boyfriend, and you swung first."

It was the ultimate in high school drama. When Alex and I got outside, I had tried to shrug him off.

"Well, Jase is parked over by the gym, so I'll see you later."

It was stupid of me to think he would let me off that easy. The boy couldn't seem to take a hint.

"That's where I'm parked too," he had said with his ever-present smile before walking with me towards Jase, who was leaned against our little Mazda, engaging in some slightly embarrassing PDA with Nikki Anderson. We were still about three cars away when Jase pulled back from Nikki.

"What are you doing here?" Jase asked Alex as rudely as possible.

"Well, I was walking to my car." Alex motioned towards an old red Toyota in the next row.

"I meant here at this school, in this town."

In retrospect, Alex must have been purposefully trying to provoke Jase. Maybe he was more like his brother than I thought.

"We thought it would be a nice place to settle down." One corner of Alex's mouth pulled up as his eyes locked with mine. "I had no idea it would be this nice."

The next series of events went so quickly I can't be exactly sure what happened. Jase took a swing at Alex, but it didn't connect. I don't know if Alex managed to duck out of the way, or if Jase's aim was just really off. I do know he meant business because it really hurt when my shoulder accidentally got in the way and I fell to the ground.

The next thing I knew, Tyler Burkeen and Seth Roberts were holding Alex's arms, and Jase's nose was dripping blood.

"Stay the hell away from my sister," Jase spat out, red droplets flying from his lips.

Alex ignored him to look down to where I was frozen on the ground. "Scout, are you okay?"

"I'm fine." Sure, I was going to have a bruise on my shoulder, and there were a few scrapes on my palms, but I could hardly complain with Jase spouting blood.

"Don't talk to her!" Jase looked ready to get even. I found myself worrying about Alex. Obviously, he could throw a good punch when he wanted to, but Jase was strong. And surrounded by friends. And seriously pissed off.

"Go home, Alex," I said, picking myself up off the ground.

"Scout--"

I was curious as to what sort of explanation he could have given for the fisticuffs, but I refused to let him finish that thought. "Please, just go home. You've done enough." I pulled some tissues out of my purse and attempted to wipe some of the blood from Jase's face.

After one final look in my direction, he walked away. Jase and I rode home in complete silence.

"That was incredibly stupid," Charlie said, bringing my thoughts back to the present. "Do you have any idea what could have happened? What could still happen?"

The room was still and silent as an unspoken exchange occurred between them. Despite my feelings about my brother's behavior, I automatically defended him.

"It's no big deal. There were no teachers around, and no one is going to rat out Mr. Basketball himself. There's no way this will affect his position on the team or scholarships. It's all good."

"Good to know I don't have to worry then," Charlie said, never relaxing or taking his eyes off of Jase. For the first time it occurred to me that Charlie may have been in on whatever scheme Toby had conned Jase into.

Charlie repositioned himself so that he was turned towards me. My shoulders felt naked without his arm covering them.

"So, what's the deal with you and this new guy? Do you like him?"

Like the typical teenager I am, I rolled my eyes. "No, I don't like him. Good grief. He's on the newspaper staff, and we have a couple of other classes together. We were just talking. Quite frankly, I think he's arrogant and rude."

Charlie chewed this over for a minute. "But he has the hots for you?"

"No, he doesn't," Jase interjected. "It's Scout, for Pete's sake. He's obviously playing her to get to me."

I recoiled as if I had been slapped. It's not like I actually thought Alex liked me. Guys that looked like him only asked girls

26

like me out to win some sort of stupid bet, and that only happened in cheesy teeny-bopper movies. I knew all those dazzling smiles weren't really meant for me. And I didn't care. I didn't want Alex Cole to like me, but to hear my brother dismiss me like that hurt. A lot. I felt tears welling up.

"Scout, he didn't mean it like that." Charlie reached towards me, but the last thing I wanted was pity.

"Get out of my room." I closed my eyes to keep the tears trapped.

"I'm sorry—"

"Please just leave me alone for a minute," I managed to get out without my voice breaking.

Charlie, as always, came to my rescue. "Let's go, man. C'mon."

As soon as I got the waterworks under control I stomped into the bathroom that connected Jase's room to mine and began digging through the medicine cabinet. I was being overly emotional and moody. A double dose of Midol was definitely in order.

I must have been making a lot of noise, because there was a tap at the door, and then Charlie's voice asked, "Can I come in?"

Instead of answering, I reached over and turned the knob. Charlie was leaning against the door frame, looking more tempting than anyone standing two feet from a toilet had a right to.

"Your brother feels like shit."

"Yeah, well I wouldn't be surprised if his nose was actually broken."

"That's not what I meant, Smarty Pants."

I closed the medicine cabinet and caught my reflection on the mirrored door. There were big red blotches creating a striking contrast to my fair skin. My eyes were puffy and gave off an eerie glow. There was even a little bit of snot along the edge of my nose. Nice.

How could I blame Jase for pointing out the truth?

"I'm not mad at him," I said, getting a tissue for my nose. "It's okay. No big."

I hadn't seen Charlie move from the doorway, so I was startled when I felt his arms pulling me into an embrace. I instantly regretted not being one of those tiny little girls who can snuggle into a guy's chest when they need to be comforted. Instead, I had to make do with leaning my forehead against his.

Actually, that was pretty awesome too.

"If you want my personal opinion, Jase is wrong." Charlie's breath smelled like cinnamon. "I'll bet you batted those long lashes, gave a rare Scout giggle, and the boy turned to mush."

Yet another ridiculous tear made the short trek from the corner of my eye to my chin. Charlie pulled back and wiped it from my cheek. It was a very tender and sweet thing to do, which was why I was completely unprepared for what he said next.

"That means it's even more important for you to stay away from him. He can't be trusted. It's not a question of if but when he hurts you. We just want to keep you safe. So, please, don't encourage him. Okay?"

I stepped back, moving to the other end of the tiny room. "I'm not some mindless ditz that tries to hook up with every cute guy that notices she exists —"

"Scout..."

"And I don't take orders from you or Jase —"

"We're not —"

"And I don't like being the only one in the dark here. Tell me what's going on, Charlie.

He scratched the back of his neck. "I don't know what you're talking about."

"Yes, you do. What's up between you guys and the Coles? I feel like we've suddenly stepped into the middle of *The Outsiders*."

"It's complicated."

I crossed my arms and cocked my head to assume what Jase and Charlie had always called my teacher stance. "Well, Charles, I believe history has proven that of the three of us, I'm the smart one.

So, why don't you go ahead and tell me what is going on. Maybe I can uncomplicate it for you."

I mentally prepared myself for a fight. After the day I had, I was hungry for it. I wanted to scream and yell and let out all of my pent up frustrations, so I was more than a little disappointed when Charlie didn't take the bait.

"Sorry, kiddo." He really did look sorry. Of course, calling me "kiddo" didn't exactly endear me to his cause. "This isn't the sort of problem that can be figured out with those complex equations or thick books you like so much."

"Don't be so sure. The answers to all of life's problems are out there. It's just a question of finding the right book." My desire to have a throw down was slowly subsiding, but that didn't mean I was ready to give up. "Lucky for you, I've read lots of books. So, if you'll just explain the 'sitch..."

"The 'sitch? Did you watch that *Kim Possible* movie again? You know it only makes you sad that you don't have a hairless mole-rat of your very own."

"One, I've been watching *Buffy*, not *Kim Possible*. And two, it is so not fair that Dad won't let me get a Rufus when he lets Angel keep that stupid turtle."

Charlie came across the room to gather me once again into his arms. He was being uncharacteristically touchy-feely. It was kinda nice.

"God, I'm going to miss you," he said, giving me a peck on the forehead. For the record, my forehead was very happy. The rest of me, however, was realizing this was goodbye.

Yes, he would be home on the holidays and maybe the summers. We would still text, email, and talk on the phone, but I knew things would never be the same. After seventeen years of growing up together, this was the first giant step towards growing apart.

"I'm going to miss you, too." I was also going to completely dehydrate if I didn't stop crying.

Fifteen minutes later, I heard Jase and Charlie pulling out of the driveway as they headed off to a farewell game of pool at Randy's. I sank onto the bed, left alone with my thoughts and Guido.

Chapter 4

There's an old adage about everything looking better in the morning light. I'm guessing that whoever thought of that had never been punched in the face.

Jase woke up the next day with two black eyes and a huge, bulbous nose. Mom, a registered nurse who surprisingly bought the rogue football story, thought he should go in for X-rays. Jase brushed it off by telling her, in a somewhat nasally voice, that a crooked nose would help him to look tough.

I countered that no one ever described Owen Wilson as tough.

When we got to school everyone was talking about the "major throw down" that had gone on the day before. There were at least a dozen different rumors going around as to the cause. It was about a girl. Basketball. Money. Drugs. Gay love. Pirates versus ninjas. (Okay, so the whole pirates versus ninjas one came from me, but how was I supposed to respond to all the people who kept asking me what happened?)

The most prevalent theory, however, had to be that Alex Cole had been misguided enough to flirt with Scout Donovan. Some versions even had me delivering the first punch after a confession of undying affection. I overheard Ashley Johnson shooting down that theory in AP English.

"Oh come on," she said when one of her plastic friends mentioned it. "Have you seen Alex Cole? He's hot. Like Johnny Depp hot. The fact that he would even speak to Scout is mind boggling. He was just being kind to her because he's, like, a super-sweet guy. It's probably some sort of Freak Outreach program or something, y'know?"

"I guess it's some type of Whore Outreach program that makes him talk to you." It was the first time I had spoken to her in over a year. I knew I should feel bad about calling her a whore, it wasn't very Christianly of me, but at that moment I really didn't care. The last thing Ashley made me feel was godly.

All of the interchangeable girls sitting around Ashley looked aghast, but the witch just narrowed her beady eyes. "Are you actually climbing down off that high horse to speak to us, Scout? If so, maybe you could enlighten us all as to why your brute of a brother was picking on the sizzlin' new guy."

Sizzlin' new guy? Who talked like that?

"What? You didn't know? It was all about you." All of the bitterness I had been carrying around since last summer weighed heavily in my words. "Alex said he heard that you were a backstabbing skank that would screw her best friend's boyfriend. Jase was just trying to defend your honor. He really is quite fond of you."

Of course, Ashley is exactly the kind of skank that would sleep with one of her former best friend's boyfriend. She would even be so skanky as to do it in my own bed.

As for Jase, he would happily beat her to death with her own arm and she knew it. Mostly because he had told her as much.

"You are so self-righteous. What makes you think you're so much better than the rest of us?"

"I'm not better than everyone," I said honestly, "just you." I turned and walked away without waiting for her reply.

My high from putting the back-stabbing ho in her place lasted exactly fifty-eight minutes. I was trying to avoid the unidentifiable sticky black substance that clung to one of the legs of my desk in Mr. Beck's room when I felt him standing by me.

"Hey," Alex said softly. I noticed several pairs of curious eyes flicker in our direction. John Davis brazenly turned around in his seat to witness the action.

Great. Confrontation with an audience. With Ashley I had been thinking of what I would say to her for fourteen months. I had played the scene over and over in my head and was just waiting for the right moment. This was different. I didn't know what I was going to say or even why I was saying it.

"What do you want?"

The room was small and cramped, forcing him to stand too close to me. The angle made him look very tall. "I just wanted to say that I'm sorry."

"It's not my nose that's broken." Although, I did have a fairly wretched bruise on my shoulder, but that was mostly Jase's fault.

"Yeah, but you're the one I really don't want to be mad at me."

As messed up as it was, I wasn't mad at Alex. It wasn't his fault his brother needed some serious psychiatric help, and that mine was a tad bit over-protective. I wanted to tell him it was no big deal, but instead I did what Jase and Charlie had asked me to do.

"Alex, let's be clear on something. You and me? We're not friends. We're not going to be friends. If you could just leave me alone from now on, that would be awesome."

Apparently I had caught him off guard. It took him a minute to respond. "Is that what you want, or what your brother wants?"

"It's what I want," I lied. "Now, if you could please just go sit down and start pretending like I don't exist, my life would be perfect." Or, at least, it would be normal.

"I'm sorry I bothered you then." Taking my advice, he went to his desk and proceeded to ignore me for the next several months.

***

It didn't take long for a monotony to overtake our senior year. Every Tuesday there was a "surprise" pop quiz in AP English, and on Fridays we did a lab in AP Chemistry that never actually worked. Mr. Beck consistently assigned at least two hours worth of homework every night. Even the Shakespeare class had fallen into a pattern: read a play, watch the movie, write a paper.

Every day during lunch, Jase would eat with Talley and me in a corner booth before going to hang out with his friends. Talley and I would then usually shuffle off to the library to spend the remainder of our break hunched over text books. We both decided four AP classes may have been a bit much.

I was so busy with the mountains of homework I had to move on a daily basis that I didn't have time to notice Alex Cole. I didn't notice the way he would click his pen when he was really trying to concentrate. I didn't notice that he only seemed to own five T-shirts, all of which hinted at the lithe, muscular body underneath. I didn't notice that he had a habit of licking his lips before he spoke, or that his left dimple was more pronounced than the right one. I certainly didn't notice (or care) that he took Ashley to Homecoming.

Okay, so maybe I did notice a little.

And, to my chagrin, Talley noticed my noticing.

"You know she asked him, right?" Talley asked, sitting a bowl of popcorn on my bed. It was the night of Homecoming, which meant Talley and I were having our traditional school dance night sleep-over. Usually Joi joined us, but she had a date, with John Davis of all people. We were enjoying a night of junk food and geeky movies.

"Who asked who what?" At this point in the movie there were only a couple of hobbits and some scruffy old guy that was supposed to be, but in my opinion totally wasn't, attractive. No girls to ask anyone anything.

"Ashley asked Alex to Homecoming," Talley said as if we had just been talking about him, instead of avoiding that topic for weeks now. "I heard Tinsley Henson telling Molly Eastwick that she had to practically beg him to take her."

Talley looked at me expectantly as I tried to figure out where this conversation was heading. "Well, you know our Ashley. She will do whatever it takes to get what she wants. Remember when we were in the sixth grade and she ate nothing but lima beans for a week so that her dad would get her a puppy?" I took a thoughtful bite of Funyun. "That never did make any sense whatsoever, but Lima was a cool dog."

"Wow. You would really rather reminisce about Ashley than talk about your feelings for Alex? You are seriously repressed."

I squirmed. "I don't have any feelings for Alex, other than annoyance."

"Of course you don't. I'm just imagining that you're always looking at him when you think no one will notice. And I'm sure there is some totally unrelated reason as to why you always start chewing on your bottom lip every time he gets within ten feet of you."

I ran my tongue over the inside of my bottom lip, which seemed to be missing most of its skin.

Crap.

I flopped back onto my bed and threw Guido across my face. Loyal sock monkey, always there to hide my humiliation.

"Okay. He's kinda cute, mildly intelligent, and slightly charismatic. If Jase didn't happen to be the President and Founder of the I Hate Alex Cole Club, and his brother wasn't a raging psycho, I might be half tempted to have a tiny crush on him."

Instead of gloating over the fact that she was right, Talley sat strangely silent for a long while. Then, in a voice that was way too serious for my comfort level, she said, "Jase can only fight fate for so long."

I was about to ask her what that was supposed to mean, but at that moment Orlando Bloom's face appeared on the screen, distracting Talley's thoughts for the rest of the night.

As for the interaction between Alex and Jase during those months, it was virtually nonexistent. After that first day, Alex no longer spent his lunch in the cafeteria. I had a feeling it didn't have as much to do with the mystery meat they served as avoiding Jase.

The only time their paths crossed was one night when Jase and I took Angel to dinner at Dairy Queen. Mom was working an afternoon shift and Dad had a school board meeting, which left us with the little monster for an entire evening. We bribed her into being on her best behavior with the promise of a kid's meal and dipped cone. Neither of us had been informed that the DQ had a new employee.

My stomach wound into knots as we approached the counter where Alex waited. I said a silent prayer that we could get our dinner without causing a scene.

"Can I help you?" Alex asked, eyes locked on Jase. Even in the ridiculous fast food uniform he looked like the embodiment of physical perfection.

"Number five with a Mello Yello," Jase said sharply. "Scout?"

Alex didn't even look at me while I ordered for Angel and myself, nor did he feel the need to acknowledge my presence when he handed me our tray of food. I tried to ignore the tiny bit of disappointment I was feeling almost as hard as I tried to ignore the tiny spark of hope I felt when Angel later announced that the pretty boy behind the counter kept looking at me. Of course, the snarl that escaped from Jase helped with that second endeavor.

Mostly, though, those autumn months were uneventful. Alex Cole lived his life, and I lived mine. We shared a state of peaceful coexistence.

And then Mrs. Sole changed everything.

"I've had the best idea," she announced as she attempted to perch herself on the end of the table that served as the editorial staff's office. Mrs. Sole is a 5 foot tall 65 year old woman who is rather round and has a unusual fondness for double knit pants. She really should not try to perch onto anything ever. "I want to do a series of articles where we have two writers giving opposing views on a topic."

"Like a point/counterpoint type thing?" I asked, liking the idea.

"Kind of," Mrs. Sole said, "but instead of two separate articles I want it to be more like a conversation." She dropped her head as though she were confessing to some big secret. "I got the idea from reading a transcript of my favorite podcast."

Mrs. Sole knew what a podcast was? That woman was always full of surprises.

"Sounds cool," I said.

She looked relieved. "I'm so glad you think so, because I want you and Alex to write it."

The lights in the room suddenly got much too bright and the oxygen, which had been plentiful just moments before, went thin.

Okay, so Alex definitely has some writing talent. Two weeks ago he wrote an article on the lack of support the academic team received that almost made me want to go to a meet, and I hated watching those when I was actually on the team. I could see why she would choose him, but Meg would have been a much wiser choice than I was. She had placed in the state debate finals last year, and her writing was flawless.

"Me?" I asked, trying not to look in Alex's direction.

"The two of you have such similar writing styles and cadences that I think you will play nicely off of each other." Mrs. Sole slid rather ungracefully from the top of our table to the floor. "I need one thousand words by Friday on socialized medicine. You can decide who is pro and who is con."

She walked away, leaving me in a state of absolute panic. A thousand words by Friday? It was Wednesday!

Then, my biggest concern spoke up.

"What do you know about socialized medicine?"

"Ummm...they have it in Canada?" I looked up to see that, for the first time since August, he was smiling at me. Well, one corner of his mouth was turning up. It was at least the beginning of a smile.

"We're being punished for something, aren't we?"

I considered the possibility for a moment. "I heard that my dad is pushing her to retire at the end of the year, so that is probably how I ended up on her bad side. Teachers just love taking out their aggressions against my father on me." It was true. My dad's relationship with Mr. Beck was part of the reason he was so awful to me. "What did you do to deserve such a fate?"

Alex grinned for real this time. "I ran over her car."

"No, you did not!"

He shrugged and dropped his gaze. "The brakes on my car aren't so good. There's just a tiny dent on that huge boat of hers, but she has been out to get me ever since."

"You hurt the Caddy," I teased. "It's a miracle she didn't try to kill you."

"I think Mrs. Sole is more of a torture kind of woman. Murder would be much too gauche."

Personally, I didn't find homicide nearly as gauche as telling a girl that you considered spending time with her torture.

I reluctantly made plans to meet him after school. How was I supposed to work with someone that obviously wanted nothing to do with me? I was angry at him for being so blunt, at Mrs. Sole for putting me into this situation, and mostly at myself for wanting him to like me. I knew better than to care what someone like Alex Cole thought of me. I tried to talk some sense into myself that afternoon as I drove to the center of town.

Our public library is my absolute favorite place on earth. Several years ago, the Methodist church relocated to a larger building on the outskirts of town, and the library moved into the old, gothic building on the court square. All of the wood, stone, and stained glass gave the place a majestic feel.

Of course, my little sister didn't care about the splendor of the building, or the fact that I felt like I was going to puke.

"Can't we go to the park and swing first? Pretty, pretty please?" she asked as I pulled into the tiny parking lot. Jase had basketball practice every afternoon, so I was stuck with baby-sitting duty on the days Mom worked.

"Sorry, Munchkin, but I have to work on a homework project. But it's Wednesday, so Emma will be here for you to play with."

Angel immediately perked up. Emma was Miss Nancy, the librarian's, niece. On Monday, Wednesday, and Friday afternoons she stayed at the library while her mom went to aerobics. She was in the third grade and Angel's idol.

Angel ran up the stone steps and through the heavy front door before I could get everything gathered from the back seat. I hurried after her to ensure that she was not causing a ruckus. Miss Nancy preferred to keep her library as peaceful as the sanctuary the building previously housed.

I spotted Alex sitting at a table tucked into the reference section, but it took forever for me to work my way through the library. First, I had to stop and help Mr. George, a grouchy old man who hated everything except for the gaggle of animals with which he shared a two room apartment. I fixed his "broken" computer by turning the monitor back on. Then, Miss Nancy gave me a stack of books I requested and talked endlessly about the debate her blog had sparked over the importance of Holden Caulfield in modern society. I thought I was home free after that, but a hand came out of nowhere, grabbing my elbow and pulling me towards a rack of comics.

"Scout, look what just came in!" The hand and voice belonged to Bruce Parker, a rather unfortunate looking guy. He works as the assistant manager at MovieMart, an accomplishment he is extremely proud of. When he isn't extolling the genius of Guy Ritchie to the locals, he can be found bumming around the library. I would have found it pathetic if I wasn't there as often, if not more often, than he was.

"Is that a new manga? I've never heard of this series." I took the book and flipped through the pages. The artwork was fairly unambitious, but Bruce usually had a good eye for graphic novels.

"It reminds me of Kishimoto's work."

"The guy who does *Naruto*?"

"Yeah, it's huge in Japan right now. You want it when I'm done?"

"No thanks. I'm more of a *Death Note* girl." I was already moving towards the back corner where Alex waited, regarding me with a bemused expression.

"Sorry you had to wait," I said, sitting my things on the table.

"No problem." He looked like he was suppressing a laugh. "You had your many fans to attend to."

I felt my cheeks turn red. I must have looked like the Queen of Geeks, talking to everyone in the library as I came through. "I come here while Jase is at basketball practice. We live pretty far out in the county, so it doesn't make much sense to drive home and then back into town again."

"Oh, I figured that you were the kind of girl that hung out at the library. I'm somewhat surprised that you're into manga, though. I guess that explains all the angst."

"You found me out," I deadpanned. "I'm a closet emo. Not all of us can be a ray of freaking sunshine like you."

"You think of me as a ray of sunshine?" His smile effectively proved my assessment, lighting up the normally dark library.

"Yes, and I'm a little black rain cloud. Now, can we please get down to business so that I can go home, change into my My Chemical Romance inspired wardrobe, and write poetry on my arm with a Sharpie?"

"I'm one step ahead of you, Amy Lee," he said, handing me a couple of reference books. "This is everything the library has on socialized medicine."

An hour later we had combed through the books Alex had found, plus some articles we came across online. It was all making my head hurt.

"God, this is boring," I said. My eyes were glazing over as I stared at the computer screen. "I don't even see why this is an issue. Who would want the government making decisions on what kind of medical treatment they receive?"

"You think it's better for the insurance companies to make that call?"

"No, I think that it's for a doctor and patient to decide."

"Like that is how it works." Alex looked like he was ready to go on a tirade, so I frantically started digging through my bag.

"Wait a sec." I finally found what I was looking for and sat it on the table. "Okay, now go."

Alex looked questioningly at the machine I had produced from my bag. "What is that?"

"A tape recorder." It was pretty obvious.

"Why do you have a tape recorder?"

"My mom brought it home for me when I joined the newspaper staff last year. She said that all reporters needed a tape recorder."

"And we need it now because...?"

"Because we're going to argue this out now, I'll type it up tonight, and tomorrow you will turn it into a journalistic masterpiece. You cool with that?"

Alex replied by pushing the record button and going off on the current state of our healthcare system. We were really on a roll when we were interrupted by my sister's tear streaked face. I reached over and hit pause on the recorder. "What's wrong, Angel? Are you hurt?"

Angel threw herself onto me and stared bawling. I pulled her into my lap and wrapped my arms around her. She might be a brat, but she's still my baby sister. It almost caused me physical pain to see her so upset.

"Emma said I was a baby," she sobbed into my shoulder. "She doesn't want me to play with her any more."

I never did like that Emma kid.

"Somebody thought *you* were a baby?" Alex leaned back in his chair and looked Angel over. "What are you? Like eight or nine?"

Angel turned her head to peek through the curtain my hair provided. "I'm six and a half."

I had to admit that Alex was a pretty decent actor. I almost believed that he was really shocked. "Six and a half? Man, you seem a lot older than that to me."

Angel sat up and brushed the hair and tears from her face. "I'm very manure for my age."

I had to bite my lip very hard to keep from laughing at her word confusion. Alex didn't even flinch.

"You are. Why would you want to play with that little kid for anyway? You should stay here and hang out with us."

Angel looked up at me, eyes huge. The only time she ever got to hang out with the big kids was when Talley was in a particularly generous mood. I had never seen her look so hopeful.

"Yeah, we could really use your help," I said, wiping the last remnants of tears from her face. "Do you think you could hold the tape recorder while Alex and I argue?"

Angel eagerly nodded her head in agreement before casting a glance in Alex's direction. "You should know that Scout is a really good arguer. She always wins against me and Jase."

"Is there anything your sister isn't really good at?"

I was surprised that Angel had to actually think about it. "She sounds like a dying cat when she sings," she finally concluded. "And she always sets off the smoke alarm when she tries to cook."

Alex tried to look serious, but his dimples got in the way. "Well, I'll have to remember not to ever let her sing lead on Rock Band or make me dinner."

By the time we left, Alex had managed to wrap my little sister around his finger. She was defenseless against his charm and infectious laughter. I was horrified to realize that I wasn't as immune as I had hoped.

Chapter 5

"I have a new friend," Angel announced at dinner that night. I was carefully trying to extract all the bell peppers from my spaghetti sauce, and therefore not paying much attention to the conversation. "He's really nice and funny and cute."

Dad reached over to peel a noodle from the side of Angel's face. "Is he in your class?"

"Nope. He's Scout's friend. He let me help him and Scout work on their homework because I am so manure."

"I think you mean *mature*, Sweetie," Mom corrected.

Crap. I hadn't had a chance to tell Jase about the newspaper assignment yet. And by *hadn't had a chance to tell him yet* I meant *hoped that he would never find out*. I had to distract the Munchkin before she said anything else. "Hey, Angel, could you hand me the cheese?"

Of course, like any good little sister, she never did what I wanted her to do. "Is Alex going to be at the library again tomorrow?"

There was a loud clanking noise as Jase dropped his fork onto his plate. "You were at the library with Alex Cole?"

"It was no big deal..."

"Don't tell me it was no big deal! I told you to stay the hell away from him."

"Jase Stewart Donovan," Dad said in a voice that can only be achieved by someone that has been both a father and a teacher. Normally hearing any of our full names spoken in that tone would have all three of us cowering under the nearest piece of furniture. Jase was unmoved.

"I asked you to do one thing. *One thing*, Scout. Are you trying to get yourself killed?"

"Sweetheart --" Mom began, but Dad cut her off. "Do not yell at your sister."

Jase's volume dropped a few decibels, but the emotion of the yell was still there. "He's not what you think he is."

"It was a school assignment," I said, emphasizing every word so they would sink into his hard skull.

"Sure it was."

I was gripping my fork so tightly the edges were biting into my skin. "Just because Liam is a —"

"Liam!?!?" Jase was turning an impressive shade of reddish purple. "You're on a first name basis with that one now, too?"

Dad slammed his hand down on the table, causing water to fly out of my glass. "That is enough. I want to know what is going on right now."

"It's none of your business," Jase snapped.

Everyone at the table completely froze. I'm not sure I was even breathing.

"What did you just say?"

Jase didn't reply. He just sat there trying to make my head explode with the power of his stare.

It may have been working.

"I think maybe you need to go to your room and cool off, son."

Jase stood up and thrust his chair back under the table. "I'll go," he said as he walked out of the dining room, "but I'm not your son."

My mouth literally hung open in shock. Jase and Dad had their fair share of disagreements over the years, but he had never said anything that cruel before. No, my dad wasn't Jase's biological father, but since Jason Hagan died in a hunting accident before his son was born, Dad was the only father Jase ever knew.

"I'm sorry. I didn't mean to do anything bad. " Angel's voice was small and timid. I found my heartstrings being tugged by her sad little face for a second time that day.

"You didn't do anything wrong."

"Did you?"

Had I? I knew Liam was dangerous, and I fully intended on keeping my distance from him, but why should that automatically extend to Alex?

"Nobody did anything wrong."

"Then why is Jase so mad?"

Three pairs of eyes were focused on me, eager for the answer. "Jase doesn't like Alex. He doesn't trust him or something."

"Is Alex a bad person?"

Why was she asking me all of these impossibly hard questions? Had I not been the ideal big sister all day?

"Honestly, Angel, I don't know what kind of person he is."

"That doesn't sound like Jase," Mom said. "He wouldn't just dislike someone without having a good reason."

I seriously considered telling them everything - about our creeptastic encounter with Liam, about Jase's odd reaction, about my suspicions.

"Maybe he does have a good reason, but he's not sharing it with me."

"This Alex kid, he hasn't been inappropriate towards you, has he?"

Good grief. "No, Dad. I barely know the guy."

"You know, honey, if you are feeling threatened physically, emotionally, or *sexually*..."

Oh dear God. "You know what, I think I should go talk to Jase now," I said, getting up from the table and away from the horribly awkward place this conversation was heading.

"Scout, if you find out what's really bothering him, you will tell us, right?" Mom asked.

I leaned over to kiss the top of her head as I walked by. She looked so worried that I had to try and make her feel better. "Sure. Don't worry, Mom. It's probably just some weird boy thing."

Of course, I didn't stop at Jase's room. I knew better than to try to deal with him when he was upset. Instead, I slinked off to my room to distract myself with homework. I was in the middle of trying to figure out exactly what an antiderivative was when my phone rang. My heart leapt when I read the caller ID.

"Chuck! How goes the college life?" True to my prediction, communications from Charlie had been growing more and more infrequent as the semester progressed.

"This school stuff is hard work. You would love it - tons of books to read, long papers to write, impossibly hard tests to pass. I wish you were here."

And I desperately wished I was wherever he was. "Sounds like heaven."

"How are things back home? Writing anything good for the paper?"

Leave it to Charlie to be subtle. Jase must have called him to tattle.

"Not really." I hoped he could hear the flatness in my voice through the phone.

"Funny, your brother said that you were working on an article with Alex Cole."

"I am, but it's on socialized medicine. That is pretty much the opposite of interesting."

The rush of air from Charlie's sigh sounded like static on the phone. "Scout, I thought we talked about this. I thought you understood."

"I never understood. I agreed to not be friends with him, which I'm not, but you never explained why." I was starting to get annoyed again.

"I told you, it's complicated."

"And I told you that I am smart enough to keep up."

There was a long pause. "I can't tell you. I'm sorry, I just can't." His voice got quieter, and I knew that I was not imaging the added emotion there. "I couldn't stand it if you got hurt. You know that, right?"

"I know." I also knew that my insides felt like Jell-O. "It's just an assignment. I'll keep it purely professional."

"Promise?"

"Promise."

It turns out that some promises cannot be kept, no matter how hard you try. I had every intention of keeping Alex at a distance because Charlie, who couldn't bear to see me hurt, asked me to. Really, I did.

What I had not considered when making that promise was Alex himself. Mrs. Sole loved the article so much she decided to make it a weekly feature. That meant Alex and I were spending more and more time together. At first, it was just the after school library sessions to work on the articles, but it didn't take long for the gulf that existed between us at school to close up. Soon, Alex was chatting with me before Calc and sitting with Talley and me in Shakespeare. Some days we would even find him milling around the library at lunch.

It was a rainy November afternoon when were at the library working on our homework for Mr. Beck's class. The topic of that week's article had been changing the legal drinking age to eighteen. Just for fun, I took pro and Alex argued the con. We had enough material on tape in five minutes.

"So, I have a Calculus related question," Alex announced.

I stopped beating my forehead with the eraser of my pencil and looked at him to indicate that he should proceed.

"Have you ever noticed that John Davis smells funny?"

Well, I supposed that since he sat between us in that class it was somewhat Calculus related. "The aroma du Play-Doh that he emits is overwhelming. You would have to be missing a nose not to notice."

"Play-Doh!" It was as if a cartoon light bulb went off over his head. "I knew that it was a familiar smell, but I just couldn't place it." Alex stared off into space and started clicking his pen. "But why does he smell like Play-Doh?"

"I don't know," I said, leaning towards him as though we were discussing something horribly important, like global warming or brown sugar cinnamon Pop-Tarts superiority over the iced strawberry variety. "I have sat behind him for thirteen years and he has always smelled like Play-Doh. Do you think he rubs it behind his ears like cologne?"

"Maybe he eats it," Alex speculated. "There was this kid I went to Kindergarten with that was always eating random things -- crayons, glue, pocket lint."

"That is so gross."

"Hey, I was five. I didn't know any better."

"I thought we were talking about some kid you went to Kindergarten with."

Alex shifted awkwardly in his seat and ran his fingers through his hair. I was momentarily distracted by the sight of his tongue on his lips. "I meant to say that *he* was only five and that *he* didn't know any better. Not me. *I* wasn't some crazy lint eater."

"So, what does pocket lint taste like?"

Alex narrowed his eyes. "Scout, I've got lots of homework to get done. I wish you would quit distracting me."

I made a big display of zipping my lips and punching some numbers into my calculator. He did the same, but our quiet time didn't last long. I found that studying with Alex was almost impossible since the more I talked to him, the more I wanted to talk to him. Mrs. Sole was right, we played really well off of one another. It was as if the cadences of our personalities were as similar as our writing styles. I lied to myself, saying that I was just enjoying his friendship, until one day in Shakespeare I had to admit how bad my little crush had become.

We were prepping for a run through of *The Taming of the Shrew*. I had been assigned the role of Katherina and Alex was playing Petruchio. I was channelling my inner Julia Stiles when Ashley slid up between Alex and me.

"Hey, Alex," she said with her pink, glossy bottom lip gutting out like a pouting child. "You haven't called me lately. Where have you been?"

Alex smiled apologetically. "Sorry, I've been really busy with work and school and stuff."

I felt as though something rather large and misshapen, like a professional wrestler, had taken up residence in my stomach. A quick fantasy flashed through my mind of delivering a right hook to Ashley's stupid, goat-like face.

"Well, if you get a free night sometime soon, we should make plans." She leaned her whole body against him to whisper in his ear. Judging by the blush that crept up his neck and onto his face, it had something to do with exactly what those plans would entail.

Alex coughed nervously. "O-o-okay. So, I'll...ummm...talk to you later."

"I look forward to it," she cooed. She was practically caressing him with her breasts. I couldn't decide if I would rather puke or beat her to death with my shoe.

Alex stepped back and almost tripped over a wooden sword. "Yeah. Okay...so, yeah. Later."

"Well, I'll let you guys get back to practicing then." She turned her attention to me, her expression condescending. "Scout as the Shrew. I guess Ms. Ryder is a big fan of typecasting."

I was glad I was wearing a pair of tennis shoes. She would die much too quickly and not suffer nearly enough if I were to beat her with my boots.

"Her boobs are fake, you know," I said after she was gone. "She also wet the bed until the seventh grade and wore a robe to school every day for three weeks when we were ten because she thought middle school would be just like Hogwarts."

Alex just stood there and stared at me as if I had grown a second head.

"Sorry," I said. "I know you guys are dating or whatever. I was being rude."

For some reason, Alex was smiling. He was probably laughing at my idiotic behavior. I would be if I were him.

"I'm not dating Ashley Johnson."

"You're not?" What was he talking about? Of course he was dating Ashley. Or maybe they didn't do "dating" in Montana.

"Nope. She's not my type." He was in full-on dimple mode. His eyes were even doing that sparkly dancing thing.

"But you took her to Homecoming."

"I just did that to try and make someone else jealous."

He liked someone else. Great. My mind started going through the possibilities. Molly Eastwick is pretty, and I had seen Alex talking to her a couple of times in the hallway. Jase recently broke up with Nikki Anderson, who looks like an MTV backup dancer. Every male in a five county radius was trying to be the rebound guy. I shuddered at the thought of how Alex dating Jase's ex would play out.

"Did it work?" What I was really asking was if he was dating someone else already, because nothing feels quite so good as pouring salt in an open wound.

"I didn't think so at first, but it looks like I might have been wrong."

It was not until the blush returned to his cheeks I even considered hoping that he was talking about me.

He was running his hand through his hair again. Did that mean that he was nervous? Was *I* making him nervous?

"So, are you doing anything over Thanksgiving break next week?" Alex asked, apropos of nothing. He also seemed to be very interested in his shoes. While they were cute - some well worn Adidas Gazelles - they were far from fascinating.

"I have to go to Washington to spend the holiday with Senator and Mrs. Harper."

"Senate Majority Leader Senator Harper? Why?"

Because my life sucked. "He's my bio mom's father."

"Senator Harper is your grandfather?" Alex sounded impressed.

"Technically."

I only see my mother's parents once a year. They always fly me into DC for Thanksgiving break. For four days I get attacked by stylist and posed in different activities with the Harpers to ensure there are enough pictures of their All-American Family for the next campaign.

The eyebrow plucking and itchy sweaters are nothing compared to the painful conversations I have to endure. Mrs. Harper can wax on for hours about how I am nowhere near as pretty as my mother, while the Senator likes to lecture me on the responsibilities that came with being a politician's granddaughter and the necessity of applying myself. The whole thing made me a little wrist-slitty.

My distaste for the whole situation must have shown on my face.

"You aren't exactly fond of your grandparents, are you?"

"My grandparents blame my mother's death on my father. They see him as a murderer, and me as his weapon of choice. They have never acknowledged my birthday or sent me so much as a Christmas card. The only time they contact me is when it benefits them in some fashion. So, no, I'm not fond of them. It's hard to like someone that hates you for being born."

Alex studied my face as I tried to appear nonchalant about the whole ordeal. "So, why do you go see them over Thanksgiving? I'm sure there are better things you could be doing."

There were about a million better things I could be doing. I could go see Dad's mom, who makes the best Derby Pie on the planet, or his dad, whose Derby Pie comes in a close second. I could go to Rebecca's family's Thanksgiving where everyone played cards and board games until the wee hours of the morning. I could go down to the Base and have Thanksgiving with Jase's bio dad's parents, who have always treated me like family. That one was extra tempting because it involved seeing Charlie.

But I wasn't going to do any of those things. I couldn't.

"I go because she would want me to."

Somehow Alex managed to get the whole story out of me. I told him about how the doctors had realized there was a problem in her second trimester and suggested she terminate the pregnancy for her own well-being; about how she decided that my life was worth risking her own; about how she held my tiny body and told me she knew she made the right decision; and about how she died with me in her arms. I told him how I found it necessary to excel in everything I do so she will be proud of me. I confessed to worrying I would never be worthy of her sacrifice.

I spilled my guts in a way I never had before. I'm not sure what compelled me to do it. He just kept asking questions, and I kept answering them, a bit too honestly.

So much for my business only relationship.

"And that's my sad story," I said. I had run out of steam and was feeling slightly embarrassed and exposed, not unlike those dreams where you show up to school without your shirt on. "Now, what's yours?"

"What makes you think that I have a sad story?" Alex started picking at the threads sticking out from a hole in his jeans.

"You live with your brother, right? So, where are your parents?"

"Car accident. I was eleven. I don't like talking about it." He continued picking at his jeans, never looking up in my direction.

I had the urge to smack his hand away from those stupid threads. I had just bared my soul to him and he was going to brush me off with an *I don't like to talk about it*? I was about to explain the unfairness of the situation when the bell rang. Alex was up and out of the door before I could even collect my thoughts.

I didn't see him at lunch that day, and I didn't have a chance to talk to him in Mrs. Sole's class. When he disappeared before the end of day announcements, I was certain he was avoiding me.

I felt utterly humiliated. First, I had spewed out a fountain of Ashley Johnson hatred that even the most clueless guy would recognize as a jealous fit. Then, I prattled on endlessly about my dead mother, dysfunctional grandparents, and insecurities. Worst of all, I had managed to convince myself he was interested in me. He probably picked up on that. Of course he was avoiding me. He probably felt bad for leading on the freakish, emotionally unstable girl.

Talley tried to cheer me up that afternoon with a generous helping of french fries and milkshakes, but it didn't work. I was embarrassed, my ego severely wounded. The only thing I was certain of was that I never wanted to see Alex Cole again.

Chapter 6

The best part of holiday breaks, other than the absence of Calculus, is that people tend to come back to school in a happier, less neurotic mood. At least, that was the case for Alex and me. The days before Thanksgiving were strained and awkward, partially due to my habit of running away every time he got anywhere near me. Monday, however, saw the return of our comfortable, if somewhat unsatisfying, friendship.

"So, you're kind of orange," Alex said as I pulled up recent articles on immigration laws.

"Holy crap," I exclaimed, examining my arms. "How did that happen? Thank you so much for pointing that out. I never would have noticed it on my own."

I had returned from my DC trip looking like a Fraggle. Mrs. Harper, in her latest attempt at making me a bit more photogenic, drug me to an exclusive salon in Virginia where I was forced to strip naked inside a space-age capsule that sprayed a sickly sweet smelling powder onto my entire body. They had promised that I would emerge a sun-kissed beach blanket beauty.

They were liars.

Mrs. Harper got a full refund and an apology. I got the honor of looking even more bizarre normal. Fortunately, it was fading rather quickly. I figured another week of taking a morning, afternoon, and evening shower would have me back to my normal shade of freak.

"Scout got a really fancy tan because she gets to be in commercials on TV. Her grandpa is famous," Angel said, looking up from her coloring. Although she and Emma were on speaking terms again, Angel preferred to stay close to me on the afternoon Alex joined us at the library.

"Scout is a walking cartoon character, because her grandparents are sadists," I corrected.

"I want a fancy tan."

I supposed that if I had a third eye in the middle of my forehead she would want one of those too. "You don't want a fake orange tan, Munchkin."

"Yes, I do," she insisted. "It's pretty."

Alex was amused. "Oh, I think so too. Very pretty *and* informative. I have always wondered what the female Oompa-Loompas looked like."

I kicked his shin under the table. "Don't make me whip out my mad ninja skills." I really didn't mind Alex teasing me about my tan gone wrong. It was, after all, the most ridiculous thing anyone had ever seen. Plus, the way he was looking at me at that moment gave me butterflies in my stomach, and I was not one to complain about happy stomach butterflies.

"You're not a ninja anymore." It had been thirty whole seconds since Alex had paid any attention to Angel, so she had to say something.

"You were a ninja?" Alex's eyebrows raised up under his long bangs.

"Yeah, but I had to quit. The whole wearing black from head to toe thing was getting old."

Angel, who had yet to completely understand the concept of sarcasm, felt the need to correct me yet again. "Only your belt was black. Your pajamas were white."

"Tae Kwan Do?"

"The first couple of years," I said. "Later we started cross-training. By the time I had to quit we were mostly doing mixed martial arts."

"So, theoretically you could kick my a..." Alex's eyes flicked over to Angel, "butt?"

"It's not so much theory as fact."

Okay, not really. I was way out of practice, not to mention Alex had some very nice looking muscles peaking out from the sleeves of his faded Abercombie t-shirt and a good three or four inches of height on me.

"Is that an invitation to throw down, Donovan?" Alex's smile was positively wicked.

"Name the time and place, Cole."

His mischievous smile was interrupted by my "Across the Universe" ringtone. I quickly snatched up the phone, petrified Miss Nancy had heard. She had some very strong feelings about cell phones and kicked people out of the library for using them on a regular basis.

"What's up, Charlie?" I asked quietly, turning around so my back was to the circulation desk and Alex. For some reason I found talking to Charlie in front of Alex unappealing.

"Same as always. You know how this rock star life of mine goes," Charlie replied. "Champagne breakfasts every morning and lobster dinners every night. I'm actually meeting up with Bono later to cure AIDS, and then we're hitting the club scene. I hope the Edge comes along this time. That guy is a seriously awesome wing man."

"And here I was thinking you would be sitting around in clothes that should have been washed a week ago, eating Ramen noodles, and spending your evenings studying until your eyes bled."

Charlie's laugh seemed to reach every cell of my body. "Damn you and your psychic powers. Although, you're a little off. Ramen noodles gross me out. I'm on a strict cereal and microwave popcorn diet."

We bantered back and forth for a few minutes before I managed to steer the conversation to the pragmatic reasons for Charlie's unexpected call. Once I told him how to find tangent, relayed the capitals of several South American countries, and explained how most of this information could be found on Wikipedia, I ended the call and turned back around to apologize to Alex for the distraction. I was surprised to find Angel sitting alone, Alex and his stuff gone.

***

The day after Alex's disappearing act our Shakespeare class headed down to Nashville to watch Vanderbilt University's production of *The Taming of the Shrew*. I was going to ask Alex about what happened and attempt to make up for lost research time on the drive down, but Ashley immediately claimed the spot next to Alex in the back seat. I tried not to think about whether or not it was the first time that they had found themselves in the back seat together as Talley chatted away with Ms. Ryder from our seats in the front.

It was raining by the time we got to the city and, as fate would have it, we had to park more than a mile from the theater. I cursed myself for not wearing my raincoat or bringing an umbrella. I had been out of the van for less than a minute and was soaked. Talley looked ridiculous, but dry, in the odd rain-suit type thing she had packed in her bag.

"Did you not watch the weather this morning?" Alex asked, moving his umbrella so it covered the both of us.

The gesture was appreciated, but I still had an ax to grind. "I was too busy searching for my co-writer. He disappeared while we were supposed to be working on an article yesterday afternoon. I think he must have fallen through a portal to a magical, cell phone free world, since he never called to explain."

Alex had the good sense to look guilty. "Sorry, it was getting dark, and I didn't think you would notice."

57

"It was getting dark?" I snickered. "Are you afraid of the Boogey Man?"

He scowled. "I'm not afraid of anything. I *am* the Boogey Man."

I was laughing so hard I almost didn't hear Ms. Ryder as she doled out tickets and instructions, begging us to act like mature, cultured individuals.

We had to wait for the ushers, who were an even bigger embarrassment to society than my classmates, to finish their flashlight enabled lightsaber duel to actually go into the theater. When Darth Vader finally found the time to lead us to our seats I was pleased to find myself sitting between Talley and Alex.

"Now, remember ladies, we're here to watch a theatrical performance, not to socialize. I do not expect to hear any chit-chat between you two after the lights go down," Alex said in what would have been a perfect imitation of Ms. Ryder if it hadn't had been for a giant yawn at the end.

"And we don't expect to hear any snoring from you, Mr. Cole," Talley chided.

"I don't know if I can promise that," he said. I thought that he was probably telling the truth. He looked like he hadn't slept at all. What was it with guys and insomnia? Jase seemed to be operating on little to no sleep half the time.

Once the house lights went down and curtain came up, it didn't take long to understand why Vanderbilt was known for its medical program and not its drama department. By the third act I was in as much danger of falling asleep as Alex was. When I looked over to see if he had nodded off yet I was surprised to find him looking at me.

"This sucks," he mouthed.

I could only gawk and nod in return. The low lighting did amazing things to his features. The line of his jaw seem more pronounced, his lips fuller, and his eyes were like two silver dollars shining back at me.

I realized I was staring at him and quickly looked away, my heart pounding. I could feel my cheeks growing warm and hoped desperately it was too dark for him to notice. I caught a flicker of movement out of the corner of my eye, but didn't realize what was happening until I felt him take ahold of my hand.

Alex Cole was not the first boy I ever held hands with. That honor went to my third grade boyfriend, Jeremy Rande, who bought me a chocolate rose for Valentine's Day and then moved to Illinois the next week. Over the years there had been others - including Dalton Riley, the asshat Ashley had done the nasty with - but none of those times had felt like this. With the other boys it had merely been skin on skin. I remembered how they always squeezed my hand too tightly or too loosely, how their palms had always been too dry or too sweaty.

Alex's hand was perfect. His skin was soft and warm. He held onto me gently, but with confidence. My own hand felt small and delicate wrapped around his.

I was, at that moment, in possession of the world's happiest hand.

I was also in possession of the world's reddest cheeks. I could hear my heart pounding in my ears; the air I drew into my lungs sounded shaky. I couldn't tear my eyes away from his.

"Hi," he whispered.

"Hey," I squeaked out, slightly louder than I intended. I had yet to fully regain control of my oxygen supply.

Talley jabbed me in the ribs and shushed me under her breath. I dragged my eyes away from Alex and tried to focus on what was happening on stage. While my eyes resolutely stayed trained on the play, my mind remained transfixed on Alex, who held my hand until the house lights came back up.

"Dear, sweet Jesus, that was awful," Talley said, hefting herself out of the tiny theater seat.

"Did they totally skip the fourth act?" I asked. I couldn't remember Tranio tricking Hortensio into no longer courting Bianca.

"The fourth act in which Lucentio's accent changed at least twelve times? The fourth act in which Kate actually tripped over Petruccio's foot and fell onto the stage? The fourth act which drug on *forever*? That fourth act?"

"Ummm...I must have fallen asleep or something," I lied weakly. Alex choked out a laugh behind me, causing my cheeks to go up in flames again. I playfully elbowed him in the stomach, enjoying the tingling sensation that raced up my arm when I made contact.

Talley indulgently nodded her head in agreement. "I'm sure that was it. You were *asleep*."

"Shut up." I pushed Talley towards the door, blissfully aware of Alex behind me.

The first thing I noticed as we exited the theater was how much colder it was than when we arrived. The second thing I noticed was how slick the sidewalk was. I didn't notice that it was snowing until I was sprawled on the pavement.

"Scout! Are you okay?" Alex's face loomed above me.

"I think I broke my butt."

"Impressive ninja moves," Alex chuckled as he reached down to help me to my feet. I was about halfway up when he lost his footing, and we both tumbled back onto the ground.

"Yep, my butt is definitely broken," I said through gritted teeth. Judging by the way Alex was doubled over with laughter, he managed to escape without any serious injuries.

By this time the entire class had gathered around to watch as Alex and I clumsily helped each other up. Once we managed to have our feet planted somewhat firmly on the ground, Alex wrapped his arm around my waist. "We don't want you doing any permanent damage to that butt," he informed me.

I wasn't so sure I hadn't already. Falling onto concrete, tailbone first, cannot be good for you. It helped that Alex's proximity was having an anesthetic-like effect on me. I could feel the heat of his body, despite the fact that we were both wearing thick coats.

Ms. Ryder walked gingerly up to the spot where we had congregated. "Okay, guys, as Abbot and Costello have so nicely demonstrated, it's slick out here. Mr. Donovan has informed me that there have been several wrecks in the past hour and most of I-24 is closed." She took a deep breath before continuing, as though she was less than excited about whatever it was she was about to tell us. "He believes that for our safety we need to stay the night in Nashville and drive home tomorrow, after the temperature rises again. The school has already made reservations for us at a hotel about three miles from here, so please call your parents and let them know that you will not be home until tomorrow afternoon."

A dozen voices started speaking at once. The class seemed evenly divided. One half was thrilled to be spending an extra day in the city and out of school, while the other half had other places to be and things to do.

As for me, my spirits were somewhere beyond the stratosphere. Beautiful, fat flakes filled the air, I had been granted a two day reprieve from Mr. Beck, and I now had an entire afternoon and evening to spend with Alex and his perfect hands. Could life get any better?

"Ms. Ryder, I have to go home now," Alex said. He sounded even more upset than Ashley, who was terrified she would have to spend the night at a Motel 6.

Okay, maybe it would work out a little better if Mr. Perfect actually wanted to spend the day with me too.

"I'm sorry, Alex. There's really no way that I can get you home safely in these conditions." Ms. Ryder emphasized her point by taking two steps before falling into James Kiplinger, who managed to accidentally feel her up as he caught her. Given James's propensity to spend the majority of his time playing *Magic: The Gathering* instead of bathing, I felt fairly certain he had just experienced his first contact with boobs ever. The painfully humiliated, yet somewhat ecstatic, look on his face helped confirm my suspicions.

I was so busy watching James and Ms. Ryder (and feeling somewhat embarrassed for the both of them), I hadn't noticed Talley slide up beside Alex.

"I can't stay here," Alex said to her as she gripped onto his elbow for support.

"I think you have to," she said slowly. Apparently she could feel the tension in his body as well as I did. Whatever it was he needed to get home to, it was important to him. I took comfort in the fact Ashley was with us. At least I could rest assured that he wasn't running off to go out on a hot date with her.

"I'll call Liam. He'll come and get me," Alex said, already retrieving his phone from the pocket of his coat.

Talley's eyes grew wide and her grip on his arm visibly tightened. "No, you can't do that. It'll be okay. Promise. But you have to stay here. Please don't call your brother."

I mentally seconded Talley's assertion. I planned on living the rest of my life without seeing Liam Cole again.

Alex was reluctant, but eventually agreed it wouldn't be wise to have his brother drive in bad weather. I carefully made my way back to the van while Alex helped Talley, whose attempt at walking on her own reminded me of Bambi crossing the frozen pond. Occasionally, the wind would sweep fragments of their conversation up to me. It sounded like Talley was still reassuring Alex that the world was most certainly not going to fall apart just because he had to stay overnight in Nashville.

I tried not to take his desire to flee personally.

The streets of Nashville were like an ice skating rink and the huge flakes were falling so quickly that there was near zero visibility. It took us over an hour to drive the three miles to the hotel were Dad had made reservations. To Ashley's horror, it was indeed a Motel 6.

Ms. Ryder's nerves were so shot by the time we checked in she didn't really care what we did with the rest of our day. In fact, she disappeared into her room shortly after our arrival, and didn't emerge until the next morning.

After a brutal snowball war, I ended up hanging out in a room where a group was watching a *Harry Potter* marathon. I realized that I didn't find Daniel Radcliff quite as attractive with Alex's hand once again intertwined with mine.

Alex was uncharacteristically taciturn all evening. He obsessively checked the time every few minutes. Despite my repeated attempts to figure out why he so desperately needed to get home, I was still in the dark.

We were about halfway through *The Goblet of Fire* when I became aware something was wrong. Alex's hand was sweltering in mine and his breathing didn't sound quite right.

"Are you feeling okay?" I asked as two girls sitting on the other bed had a very heated discussion as to the exact hotness level of Rob Pattinson.

"Ummm...sure. Yeah. I'm fine." Alex seemed to be having trouble focusing on anything going on in the room around him.

"You look awful," Talley pipped up from beside me. "Maybe now would be a good time for you to go to bed."

Alex looked again at the clock sitting on the bedside table. It was 5:00, the sun was just starting to set. Normally I would think that it was way too early for someone to call it a night, but Alex was obviously sick.

"I'm fine."

"No, you're not. You need to go to bed, and you need to go to bed *now*." Talley was being unusually assertive, sounding shockingly like her mother.

"You're right. I could use some sleep." As Alex got up to leave a shiver went through his entire body.

"Are you sure you're going to be okay? Maybe we should get Ms. Ryder or a doctor." Every muscle in Alex's body seemed to be twitching.

"I'll be fine once I get some sleep. Don't worry about me." Alex stood in front of me awkwardly for a moment, running his fingers through his hair. "Thanks for today, Scout. It's been really great."

I could feel everyone in the room watching our little exchange. The embarrassment killed a bit of my buzz, but not much.

The evening drug on after he left. Harry couldn't hold my interest, even when he drug poor Cedric's dead body back to Hogwarts, which normally made me shed at least a tear or two.

Eventually we all grew tired of vending machine food and walked a block down the street to Taco Bell. I paused outside Alex's door on our way back.

"Do you think he's hungry? Should I ask him if he wants me to go get him something?" I asked Talley.

"I think he needs to sleep. C'mon, Scout. You'll survive not seeing him until tomorrow."

I looked around to make sure no one else was in earshot. "I really like him," I confessed.

Talley's superior expression was mildly annoying. "I know. I have been trying to tell you that for months."

She was turning into such a know-it-all.

"Do you think that he might like me too?" I was unable to meet her eyes.

"I *know* he does."

I wished that I could be that confident. I leaned against the wall by the door to our room and watched the flurries dance in the glow of the street light as Talley dug for the room key.

"Jase hates him, you know."

"I know."

"Do you know why?"

After four attempts at swiping the room key, Talley finally got the door open. Stale cigarette smoke and bleach burned my lungs.

Instead of answering my question, Talley began the long, complicated process of extracting herself from the rain-suit. By the time she managed to free one of her legs from the ridiculously cheerful yellow vinyl, my patience was running thin.

"You know, don't you?"

"Know what?" she grunted out. She was struggling as she tried to force the garment to release its death grip on her thigh.

"You know what's going on with Jase and Alex. Tell me."

Talley stretched out on the bed, having finally defeated the rain-suit. "Do you honestly think Jase would tell me and not you?"

Yes.

Well, maybe.

Okay, probably not.

"What am I supposed to do, Tal?" I looped my arm through hers and leaned my head on her shoulder. Her hair smelled of the same baby shampoo that she had been using since we were kids.

"I don't know," she said, kissing the top of my head. "We'll figure it out, though. I promise to make everything okay."

I flipped open my phone to set the alarm, and realized I had missed a handful of messages from Charlie.

How do you feel about hippos?

Large animal. Likes water.

Let me know asap

I was slightly confused, but texted back that I held the majestic beast in high regard. I really didn't have an opinion on hippos, but it seemed like the right thing to say.

"Who was that?" Talley asked. "Did Jase text to check up on us?"

"No, it was Charlie." I crawled into the bed and pulled the covers up over my head. I was suddenly not feeling so well. Maybe I was coming down with whatever Alex had. Or maybe it was the Mexican food.

"So, what does it feel like to be in love with two guys at the same time?"

I flipped the covers down so that Talley could see my face as I responded. "I am not *in love* with anyone. I have a crush on Alex and Charlie is... Charlie is Charlie."

Talley's expression was pretty easy to read. It said "BULL CRAP" in big, capital letters.

"I am not in love with anyone," I repeated.

"Be sure and let me know when you realize that you're wrong about that, okay?" Talley said as she reached over to turn out the light. "I would hate to miss another opportunity to say 'I told you so'."

I spent the next few hours tossing and turning, despite the nighttime pain reliever Talley had given me for my sore butt. I have never slept well in a bed other than my own without Guido, and all the inner-turmoil certainly was not helping the situation.

I dozed off for a short time and awoke feeling deeply unsettled. Snippets of a dream floated just outside my consciousness. All I could remember clearly was Alex, Charlie, ice cream, and the sensation of being ripped in two.

The thin sheets scratched my arms and legs as I listened to the heater's choleric rumble and Talley's deafening snore. When the walls began to close in on me I realized I could not stay in that room one moment longer. I got up, putting on my coat and shoes as quietly as possible before slipping out the door.

The night was silent and beautiful. The snow storm had ended, leaving the sky clear enough to see hundreds of glittering stars and the bright, full moon that reflected on the pristine newly fallen snow.

I spotted the electric glow of a gas station and developed an intense craving for stale snack cakes and super-sweet hot chocolate. If I followed the sidewalk to get there I would have to pass in front of Hank's Hangout, a bar whose chipped pink paint job was certain to attract only the most reputable clients. Instead, I opted to cut through the wooded area behind the motel.

Thanks to my NyQuil induced brain fog and the shadows provided by the trees, it wasn't until I was a few feet away that I noticed a man standing at the bottom of the hill. I froze as I recognized the telltale signs of a street person - multiple layers of dirty clothes, unkempt hair, unwashed skin, and the unmistakable air of desperation.

He had picked something up off the ground and was examining it. It was just a plain black coat, but something about it bothered me.

I cautiously moved closer. There were more articles of clothing scattered around the old man's feet. It looked like some jeans, a shirt, a sweater, and a pair of shoes. The man picked up one of the shoes and held it in the moonlight.

The soft, wintery world froze around me. Even from a distance I could tell that it was from a pair of Adidas Gazelles.

Adrenaline pumped through my veins and I acted without thinking.

"What are you doing?" I demanded, stumbling down the embankment. "Where did you get those? What have you done to him?"

The man wheeled around to face me. I was close enough to smell a mixture of body odor and alcohol as he disturbed the air.

"These things are mine. I found them." His words were slurred, but his movements were quick and jerky, like a wild, skittish animal.

Or a homeless guy hopped up on meth.

"Those are Alex's clothes. Where is he? What did you do to him?" I frantically looked around, terrified I would see his dead, naked body frozen on the ground.

"I didn't do nothin' to nobody. I found these things. They're mine." He started gathering up all the clothes. I noticed that the T-shirt was a retro Spider-Man shirt, the one that Alex wore every Tuesday. I reached out and snatched it away.

"You can't have these things! These are Alex's things! Give them back!" I reached for the pants, but the man grabbed my arm with a surprising amount of strength.

"I told you, I found these," he said, pulling me towards him so that our faces were almost touching. The smell was overpowering. His eyes had a manic glint. "I told you they were mine."

He suddenly shoved me backwards, throwing me to the ground. The intense pain from falling yet again on my backside caused me to black out for a few seconds. By the time I recovered the man was on top of me, his knees on either side of my hips. A knife appeared out of nowhere and pressed against my throat.

"I don't like bein' called a liar, girl. Ya hear me?"

I couldn't respond, paralyzed by fear. I knew I should try to fight back, that I should do something other than just lie there, but I couldn't. My body seemed incapable of movement.

He rubbed himself against me, his bloodshot eyes roaming up and down my body. "You're not a very pretty girl, are you? Don't worry, though. That's alright with me. I never did like pretty girls anyhow."

My brain finally managed to get through to my body. My right hand came up and wrenched the knife away from my throat as my left delivered a sharp punch to his midsection. I tried to roll my body to get out from underneath him, but he anticipated the move. He pressed himself even more firmly against me and grabbed my arms, pinning me to the ground.

"Don't be that way, sugar," he said with a laugh. My stomach turned at the realization that he was enjoying himself. "We're gonna have us —"

His next words were cut off by a feral growl that sliced through the night and reverberated in my bones.

"What the hell?" I heard him mutter just before something flashed above me, knocking him backwards.

I should have been terrified by the scene that was playing out, but it was too surreal. I sat up to find the man sitting on the ground, the knife outstretched in his hand in an attempt to keep the wild animal standing before him at bay. The animal, which appeared to be a large dog, was crouched down, hair standing on ends as a litany of snarls and growls erupted from its throat. There was no doubt that his razor sharp teeth would have no problem ripping the homeless man to shreds.

They could just as easily have done some rather unpleasant things to my fragile flesh, yet I couldn't seem to make myself be frightened. Instead, I was fascinated by beauty of the creature before me. His thick coat was a blend of white, reddish-brown, grey, and black. A part of my brain determined that it was a wolf, while another part of my brain realized that I might have been experiencing some sort of trauma related shock.

The standoff finally ended when the man lunged at the animal with his knife, causing the wolf to jump back. He had just enough time to get back on his feet and run. The wolf gave chase, gaining on him as they disappeared into the night.

I pulled myself off the ground. A quick inventory of my moving parts determined that aside from a broken tailbone, some wet clothes, and possible mental scarring, I was okay. I forced any thoughts of the horror I had just experienced from my mind and focused on what needed to be done.

I knew that I was supposed to leave everything just as it was so the police could gather evidence. I watched *CSI*, I knew how murder investigations worked, but I couldn't do it. I couldn't walk away and leave his clothes laying there. It would be admitting that he was gone, and I couldn't do that just yet.

I was attempting to fish one of his shoes out of the creek when I realized I wasn't alone. One the opposite bank, mostly hidden by the brush, the wolf sat watching me.

I choked back a scream and remained very still. At least, I tried to be very still, just like those Discovery Channel shows always say you should when encountering a wild animal. Unfortunately, I couldn't stop my body from trembling or my breath from coming in loud, ragged gasps.

I was debating on whether I should run, scream, or just hope to die quickly when my eyes locked with the decidedly human eyes of the wolf.

"Alex?" It came out as a whisper, but he heard me. The wolf bolted, running back towards the spot where the creek wound its way around the hill and out of sight.

"Alex!" I called out, louder this time.

I would have been able to convince myself I was wrong. I could have rationalized that the shock of the evening was causing my eyes to play tricks on me. I would have believed I was suffering from post-traumatic stress or temporary insanity. Any of those options would have been so very easy to accept if he hadn't turned and looked at me once again with those familiar grey eyes before disappearing into the night.

Chapter 7

Sleep was pretty much a lost cause. My body was exhausted, but my brain was on hyper-drive. I was shocked, scared, confused, and ashamed. Snippets of everything that happened kept playing in my head like an avant garde film whose sole purpose is to leave the audience bewildered and jittery. I was terrified of how much more I would see if I closed my eyes.

I was curled up in the room's only chair - a surprisingly comfortable overstuffed blue and yellow stripped monstrosity - watching the light in the room turn pink with the approaching dawn. There were so many thoughts and questions screaming for attention, I couldn't concentrate on any single one. Instead, I focused on the way the light moved across Talley's sleeping face and the throbbing ache I felt from the multiple bruises slowly forming all over my body.

When I first heard voices, I thought they were just part of the chaotic noise in my head. It wasn't until I heard someone say his name that I realized people were arguing just outside my room.

I pulled back the edge of the heavy curtain and breathed a sigh of relief. Alex was there, alive. Unharmed. Human. His clothes were beyond dirty, despite my most valiant efforts in the Mapco station's smelly bathroom, but he looked good. Better than good, actually.

Getting out of the chair was a bit difficult with the pain that radiated from my tailbone. I wrapped the fuzzy blue hotel blanket even more tightly around me, casting a quick glance at the heater where I had left my clothes to dry. I could have tried to put them back on, despite the fact they were still damp, but I didn't. The need to speak to Alex, to see if he was really okay, outweighed my inhibitions. I inched the door open, inviting in an arctic breeze that caused an outbreak of goosebumps.

"We're leaving now," Liam was saying. "You know what happens if they find us. I can't believe you would risk that, risk everything, for some girl."

"This isn't about 'some girl'! It's about —" Alex looked up and noticed me standing in the doorway. "Scout."

"Hey," I said, closing the motel room door behind me. The intensity with which Liam regarded me made my knees threaten to give out, but the joy I felt over the fact that Alex wasn't dead or walking around on four legs kept me from slinking back into the room.

Alex pushed past Liam to get to me. "Are you okay? Where are your clothes?"

I regretted not taking the time to put them on. The expression on Liam's face was not doing stellar things for my self-image. I adjusted the blanket so the only things sticking out where my fingers and head.

"They're wet," I mumbled, staring at the site of my bare toes on concrete.

"You've got five minutes," Liam said to Alex with all the love and warmth I expected, "then we're gone. Understood?"

I watched in relief as Liam crossed the parking lot and climbed into a battered old Jeep Cherokee. The moment we were alone, I started becoming increasingly aware of my unbrushed hair, make-up free face, and near-nakedness, which is why I just blurted out, "You're a werewolf."

Alex shifted his weight back onto his heels and fixed his gaze on the foot of sidewalk between us. "You noticed that, huh?"

Yeah, I'm just crazy observant that way.

"I don't understand." I took a deep breath and tried to get my nerves under control. It was one thing to suspect someone of being a monster and another thing all together to have them confirm it. I was tempted to run back into the hotel room and bar the door, but my desire for answers outweighed my fear. "How is that even possible?"

"Can we not have this discussion right now?" His eyes kept flickered over to the spot where his brother sat watching us.

"Okay," I said. Even I could hear the edge of hysteria in my words. "So, how about this weather?"

I mean, really, where was the conversation supposed to go after, *Hey, aren't you some sort of mythical creature?*

Alex chuckled. "It's cold. Too cold for you to be out here without shoes or proper clothes on."

"The cold doesn't really bother me."

"Is that why you were out last night in the freezing snow?"

I shrugged. "I needed to go for a walk."

Alex took a step forward and cupped my face in his hand. Any discomfort I may have been feeling due to the frigid temperatures quickly vanished as a glowing warmth spread from the place where his flesh touched mine to every inch of my body. Despite everything, he was still Alex and I still felt giddy at his touch.

"Scout, I'm so sorry," he said in a whisper. "I thought you had gone to bed. I went to hunt and didn't even realize you were outside until I heard you scream."

I resisted the urge to reach out and smooth away the creases in his forehead. "Don't be sorry. You saved me. If you hadn't got there when you did..." My voice trailed off, unable to put the horror of what might have happened into words.

Alex's thumb gently traced along the edge of my cheekbone causing a shiver to run through me. "Don't worry. He's never going to touch you or anyone else again." His hand trailed down my face before resting on the back of my neck. I could hear him pull a deep breath into his lungs as he slowly licked his lips and inclined his head towards me.

At that moment I no longer cared that Alex turned into a wolf and might possibly be a murderer. The only thing that mattered was that he was going to kiss me.

And then the horn of the Jeep blared, causing Alex to jerk away as if he had been electrocuted.

"I guess that's your cue to leave." For some idiotic reason, I was giggling.

"So it seems."

Liam honked the horn again, and Alex immediately took off across the parking lot. "I've gotta go," he called over his shoulder. "Tell everyone that I got sick and had to go home, okay?"

I just nodded mutely. He was nearly to the Jeep when I realized what I forgot to say.

"Alex," I called out. He turned to look at me. The motion was eerily the same in his human form as it had been the night before. "Thanks. You know, for being my hero and all."

He waved one last time and then climbed into the Jeep. I watched it pull out of the parking lot before returning to my room.

Talley was awake and waiting for me on the other side of the door.

"Did you just walk outside in nothing but a blanket? What happened to your clothes? Where is Alex going? What happened? Are you okay?" Talley's questions came out in such rapid succession I had trouble picking out any single one.

"Slow down. My brain is too sleepy to work that fast."

Talley looked me over, taking in my puffy, bloodshot eyes and slow, stiff movements. "You haven't slept at all," she said. "What happened?"

Oh, you know. Not much. I got in a fight with a cracked-out homeless guy, which I lost, by the way. No worries, though. Alex came by in just the nick of time. Hey, did you know he turns into a wolf during the full moon? I do, because there just happened to be one of those last night. Incidentally, he's a pretty hot wolf.

"Nothing."

74

"Then why are your clothes covered in mud and not on your body?"

"I went for a walk because I couldn't sleep and fell down." Which was basically the truth. I was just leaving out a few minor details.

"And what were you doing outside with Alex just now?"

What was it that Monty Python used to say about not expecting the Spanish Inquisition?

"His brother came to pick him up because he's sick. He just stopped by to say good-bye before he left."

"You're lying to me," Talley said. "Scout, it's okay. You can tell me, whatever happened."

I could. I could also end up with a nice padded room of my very own.

"Believe what you want, Tal," I said walking into the bathroom. "I'm taking a shower."

I was pleased to discover that after two sessions with the cheap bar of hotel soap my skin had faded to a nice jaundiced yellow. I twisted my hair into a french braid and attempted to get as much of the dirt off my clothes as possible, but still looked like death warmed over when I arrived at the McDonald's Ms. Ryder had designated as our gathering spot.

Talley was obviously still upset with me over our earlier conversation. She hardly said three words to me after I got out of the shower, which must have taken a great deal of effort on her part. Usually she was a regular Chatty Kathy in the mornings. After we got breakfast, she sat with Jane Potts, leaving me at a table with James Kiplinger.

I was tearing off bits of biscuit and rolling them into tiny little balls when Ashley Johnson sashayed into the restaurant. While the rest of us had spent our afternoon throwing snowballs and watching mind-numbing television, Ashley had put her daddy's credit card to good use. The members of our Shakespeare class were pretty easy to pick out in the crowd. We were the ones who had obviously slept in our clothes and were lacking basic beauty products. Of course, that would never do for Ashley. She was decked out in a Vanderbilt University sweat-suit, complete with a baseball cap to hide her unstyled hair. She looked like a freaking recruitment poster.

"James, how nice of you to share your breakfast with a poor, destitute street person," she said, stopping at our table. "Oh wait. Scout, is that you? My bad."

I was too exhausted to put with her crap or deal with Talley's silent treatment. Not to mention, the sight of James's greasy hair and the faint sour smell that accompanied him was turning my stomach. I decided sitting with the creepy Ronald McDonald statue outside would be preferable to keeping my current company. I got up to dump my uneaten food in the trash.

"God, would you look at her," Ashley said as I passed by. "No wonder poor Alex had to go home. I would probably need hospitalization if I was forced to spend time with that."

I snapped.

The look on her face when my fist connected was priceless. She staggered back into a table, her eyes filled with tears.

"You bitch!" she shrieked. "You broke my jaw!"

"No, I didn't." I had hit her in a spot that would, at best, leave a bruise, though my fun-filled night hadn't left me with enough strength to do even that much damage.

"Just wait until the school administration finds out. My dad will make sure you get expelled over this."

"You're not telling anyone," Talley said from my left.

A blob of ketchup fell from Ashley's new sweatshirt as she resumed an upright position. "And why is that, Porky?"

Jane managed to grab me around the waist and jerk me backwards before I could break her jaw for real.

I expected Talley to cry or, at least, look deeply hurt and embarrassed. The sardonic grin that spread across her face put Ashley and me both on edge.

"Because while everyone else seems to have forgotten who you were before your step-mom performed her magical make-over, we haven't," Talley said. "We have enough stories and pictures for a new humiliation every single day between now and graduation."

"Like I care," Ashley said. It was fairly obvious, however, she very much did.

"Fine then. Scout, you still have those pictures from your thirteenth birthday party, right?"

"You bet." That was the night that Ashley decided we needed to "prepare" ourselves for our lives as teenagers. There were pictures of her in my mom's lingerie, the top stuffed with toilet paper, making out with a poster of Zac Efron.

Of course, there were some equally embarrassing pictures of Talley and me, but no one is going to see those. Ever.

"You know, if you wanted, I could probably make sure that at least one or two of those pictures made it onto *All Around the School*," said Jane, who was was the student director of our televised morning announcements. I was taken aback by her support. Jane is a nice girl, but we've never exactly been friends.

"I don't even know what you guys are talking about," James said. "From what I saw Ashley tripped and fell into that table."

If Jane's assistance was unexpected, then James' was downright startling. It was generally his goal to speak as infrequently as possible, and he never did so voluntarily.

"Fine," Ashley spat at me in a quite literal fashion. I had to wipe the moisture from my face. "You and your little freak friends get your way this time, but I swear that I will pay you back, Harper Donovan. And that moment when I do? You're gonna wish I had just broken your ugly face."

It wasn't intentional, but it turned out that yawning was a fairly appropriate and awesome response.

As was typical with local weather patterns, an hour later the temperature was racing past 40 degrees, turning the ice incrusted streets into tiny rivers and the picturesque snow covered landscape into a muddy mess. Once Ms. Ryder finally showed up and downed two large cups of coffee we were on our way back home.

I got a second wind as we trudged along the Interstate and had a very long and animated discussion with Jane about our favorite singers. It was nice to find someone else who knew more about Damien Rice and Regina Spektor than the Lady Gaga. I practically came unglued when she showed me where Ryan Adams had scribbled "To Pottsie - Try the tacos, Love Ryan" on a napkin after she met him at a Mexican restaurant in Atlanta.

Talley offered to give me a ride home once we finally found ourselves back at school. The sun shining through the windows had created a greenhouse effect in her car. The gentle warmth, coupled with the hum of tires on pavement, acted as a lullaby. I was more asleep than awake when Talley cut off the engine in front of my house.

"I'm sorry I got upset with you this morning," she said. "I just want to help. You know you can talk to me about anything, right?"

"Of course." I could tell Talley anything. Just not this. I couldn't tell her about the homeless man and what he was going to do to me. I couldn't tell her about how I had panicked and almost let it happen. I couldn't tell her how afraid and humiliated I was. And I certainly couldn't tell her about Alex.

Talley leaned across the gear shift to give me a hug. I leaned in and rested my head on her shoulder, embracing the security and comfort she offered.

There were tears in Talley's eyes when she finally let go. "Are you sure you're alright?"

I shook my head, unable to speak. I should have asked her if she wanted to come in. I really needed to thank her for giving me a ride, but I felt an ocean of tears threatening to spill over.

I went directly to my bed, crawling in without bothering to take off my soiled clothes. No matter how furiously I fought against it, the tears came with an accompaniment of sobs that shook my entire body.

It took longer to fall asleep than I would have imagined, but eventually exhaustion took over. I expected to dream of violent encounters in snow filled woods and four-legged beasts stalking their prey. Instead, I dreamt of a boy with grey eyes and dimples.

Chapter 8

I'm not really much of a dreamer. Most nights when I go to
sleep that's all I do, sleep. My brain doesn't turn into some big,
bizarre movie theater the moment my eyes close. If I do dream, I
rarely remember details.

This dream was different. I remembered everything. I
remembered how the air smelled of honeysuckle and dirt. I
remembered the green of new leaves, the yellow of a hundred
daffodils, and the murky brown-blue color of the lake. I remembered
the feel of the breeze tickling my neck. I remembered the way he
looked as he leaned against the gnarled trunk of an old oak tree,
arms and ankles crossed, head cocked so that his bangs hung down
over his right eye.

The lake was less than fifty feet wide here, so I was certain
Alex was watching me from the opposite shore. I raised my hand in
an awkward wave.

"Hi," I said, feeling like a complete dork.

Alex looked over his shoulder as though he was expecting
there to be someone standing behind him. When he realized he was
alone, he looked back at me, startled. I saw his mouth move, but was
unable to hear anything he said.

"I can't hear you," I called back.

Again, I saw his mouth move, but heard nothing.

"Alex!" I yelled as loudly as I could manage.

He was shaking his head as he continued trying to talk to me. I
could tell he was yelling, but all I could hear was the splash of the

water on the shore and the tree branches as they rubbed against one another.

I don't know how long we stood there, struggling to be heard by the other, but my throat was growing sore, which bothered me. I had figured out that I was in a dream already, so wasn't I supposed to be impervious to pain?

Eventually, Alex had enough and tried another approach. I watched as he tore off his shoes, socks, and shirt. His hands hesitated at the waist band of his jeans. I was ashamed to realize I felt disappointment when he decided to leave them on.

The world had been very peaceful until the moment Alex put his foot in the water. In the blink of an eye, the sky turned black and the wind grew violent, tangling itself in my hair and thrashing my body with my clothes. The lake churned and swelled, pulling Alex under.

My scream was lost in the thunder.

I was about to do something really stupid, like jump in after him, when his head popped up out of the water. As a wolf, he was able to swim against the current, back to shore.

The storm continued to rage on around me. Debris flew in the air as a nearby tree came crashing to the ground. Something jabbed me in the back, just above my right hip. The pain was so sharp I let out a yelp.

My eyes flew open. It was dark, and it took me a few calming breaths to realize the figure standing by my bed wasn't Alex.

"That is one nasty bruise," my brother said, flipping on the lamp by my bed. A soft, white light burned into my retinas. "Did you and Talley get into it over who was going to get to marry Billy Lomac again?"

In first grade Billy Lomac was the epitome of cool. He wore his hair in spikes and always shared the candy bar his mom tucked into his lunch box with whomever was his girlfriend that week. The only fight Talley and I ever had occurred when he dumped me for her.

By the ninth grade, he was the school's most notorious pothead and roughly resembled Phillip Seymour Hoffman. I'm pretty sure the only way I would fight Talley over Billy Lomac was if she tried to date him.

"I told her, he was mine first," I said, pulling my shirt down so the bruise was covered. I vaguely remembered feeling a rock embed itself into my hip when I was thrown to the ground.

"No, really. How did you manage to come back from some boring play looking like one of those refugee people from the news?"

I sat up on the side of the bed, cringing as pain radiated from one spot to the other. Jase watched with concern etched on his face.

"I fell down. You know me, always a klutz."

"You've never been a klutz. You were the first toddler in history that didn't toddle. Our entire martial arts class had to spend months learning ninjitsu because Sansei liked your grace."

"Well, this is one ninja that never learned to walk on a solid sheet of ice in a pair of three-inch heeled Marc Jacob wanna-be boots." Or to actually use her ninja skills when she was in trouble. This ninja sucked.

"Thank God I'm a boy," Jase said, commandeering my computer chair. He swung it over to the edge of the bed before straddling it backwards. "There's no way you could get me to strut around in a 3-inch heeled anything."

"I seem to remember it taking very little to get you in a pair of ruby red stilettos. And you didn't strut, you pranced."

"Scout Donovan, what did I tell you that I would do to you if you *ever* mentioned that?"

I looked as angelic as possible. "I fell down. Hard. I may have even broken my tailbone."

"So?"

"So, my big brother doesn't fight people on the injured list."

That managed to get an eye-roll. I only referred to Jase as my big brother when I wanted something or was trying to get out of trouble. I mean, five weeks hardly counts as older, and the inch of height he had on me was pretty much moot as soon as I put on a good pair of shoes.

"Yeah, just remember this conversation when I give you a proper ass kicking the moment you're back to one hundred percent."

Now it was my turn to roll my eyes. "I'm looking forward to watching you try." I might not be able to fight off a homeless man, but Jase was easy. It wasn't so much that I was stronger than him, because I wasn't, but he was very predictable. It was like fighting a robot.

Jase and I sat talking for a long while about absolutely nothing. Despite its lack of substance, our conversation managed to erase some of the tension that I had been carrying around for the past twenty-four hours. He even managed to distract me from the whole werewolf freak out that I should have been having.

When Angel heard that I was awake she came into my room, bringing a turkey sandwich to guarantee her admittance. I didn't realize how hungry I was until I took my first bite. I was famished by the time I popped the last piece into my mouth about ninety seconds later.

"That was so good I think I'll go get another one," I said. "And maybe some chips. And cookies. We have cookies, right?"

"But you're gonna take a shower and put on clean clothes first, right?" Angel asked. She was snuggled up to my side. I got the feeling that she had missed me while I was on my impromptu overnight trip. Since I was actually letting her sit like that I must have missed the Munchkin a little bit too. "No defense, but you stink."

This, of course, made Jase nearly fall out of his chair from laughing so hard. I felt embarrassed despite the fact that I had seen the other two people in the room walk around in dirty diapers.

"Thank you for that helpful bit of information, Angel Dear," I said. "And it's 'no offense' not 'no defense'."

"But offense is when our team has the ball."

"Yes."

"And defense is when the bad guys have the ball."

"The other team isn't really 'the bad guys', but yeah."

"So, it's no defense," Angel said as if she had just made the most stellar closing argument in the history of litigation.

There is no logic quite like kid logic.

"Makes perfect sense to me," Jase said. "And the other team is 'the bad guys'. Especially if we're playing those arrogant jerks from Marshall County."

Well, Jase logic and little kid logic are pretty much synonymous.

My brother and sister were almost overly-attentive all evening. Angel insisted on making my second (and, to be completely honest, third) sandwich. She maintained that sandwich making was the same as cooking, which I was not allowed to do under any circumstance. Jase had recorded last week's episode of the newest angsty-upper-class-teens-with-major-issues show we were both hooked on and the three of us piled onto his bed with a bag of chocolate chip cookies to watch it.

On a normal day, I might have found all the attention annoying, but I was grateful for the distraction. Thanks to my siblings, I hardly had time to think between Jase's assertions that he only watched the show for the hot chicks (and his long diatribes on the latest plot twists), and Angel's nearly three hundred questions that ranged from "Why is your favorite color white instead of pink?" to "What are you going to be when you grow up?".

That night I once again had a vivid, in living Technicolor dream of Alex and the lake. He kept calling to me, but I still couldn't hear him. It didn't take long for me to grow bored with that routine, so I yelled, "Just tell me at school tomorrow," and walked off into yet another dream, which may or may not have had something to do with dancing hippos.

Despite my five hour nap and early bedtime, I still managed to oversleep the next day. Jase threatened to make me walk as I stood in front of my mirror, trying to pick an outfit.

I fidgeted the entire way through English class. What was I going to say to Alex when I saw him? Would he really talk to me about the werewolf stuff? And what was going on between the two of us? As impossible as it seemed, it looked like Alex might actually like me too. I didn't know quite how to handle that.

At first, I was relieved that he wasn't waiting for me in Mr. Beck's class, but relief quickly turned to concern when he failed to make an appearance by the end of class.

"Where do you think Alex is today?" I asked Talley when we were supposed to be working on our written reviews of the *Taming of the Shrew* performance that seemed like a million years ago.

"I guess he's still sick," she said, working diligently on her assignment as if there was something to say other than, "It sucked."

"He's sick?"

Talley looked at me as though I was missing something obvious. "Remember the whole having a fever and his brother coming to pick him up in Nashville thing?"

Oops.

"Oh yeah. I meant that I can't believe that he's *still* sick. He thought it was only like a twenty-four hour bug or whatever."

"I guess he was wrong," Talley said, returning her very focused attention back to the criticism and away from me.

I leaned back and thought about all the reasons Alex could have for not being at school. I guess it was possible that he was actually sick. Of course, it seemed more reasonable that he was trying to avoid me because either (A) he didn't want to discuss the whole werewolf issue or (B) he deeply regretted the hand holding and almost kissing stuff.

I found myself rooting for the "he actually got sick" option, which was so not cool of me.

***

"Scout, I need to talk to you about the immigration article," Mrs. Sole said as I slumped into a chair beside Nicole later that day.

"We're not quite done with that yet," I said. Of course, by *not quite done* I meant *haven't even started.* "Alex got sick before we could get much accomplished, but we'll work on it tonight and have it ready by tomorrow."

"I was afraid of that," Mrs. Sole said. "Do you think you could write a thousand word op-ed piece to fill the spot?"

"Sure, but I really think Alex will feel up to working on it this afternoon." Especially since he was never actually sick in the first place, unless being a werewolf is considered an illness. Maybe it's a virus.

"I'm afraid that isn't going to happen. I got an email from the office this morning informing me that Alex was transferring schools."

"He is what?" There was an edge of hysteria to my voice. "Are you sure?"

Maybe she misread the email. Maybe it was a different Alex. Maybe Mrs. Sole was developing Alzheimer's. Maybe...

"His brother signed the papers yesterday afternoon. They are moving back to Montana to live with a relative."

Mrs. Sole may have said more, but I didn't hear it. My brain totally checked out for the rest of class.

After school, I bummed a ride home from Talley so I wouldn't have to come back to pick up Jase. Once home, I spent an entire hour sitting on my bed, clutching Guido, staring resolutely at the wall, and trying desperately hard not to be such a girl about the whole situation.

Okay, so Alex was gone. Like, gone forever, never to hear from him again, gone. But the world wasn't ending. Sure, I was left with a million questions, but he didn't owe me anything. If anything, I owed him. He was the one that saved me, after all.

So, why was I so pissed he hadn't so much as called to say good-bye? Why did I feel so hurt and betrayed? Why was I having to bite my lip so hard to keep from crying?

When I could no longer handle listening to all the voices whining and griping in my head, I got up and got busy. I knew the only way to keep my thoughts away from Alex was to keep occupied. I started by trying to catch up on my Calculus homework, but gave up when I realized that I was spending more time remembering the way he *always* knew the answer when Mr. Beck called on him class than actually doing logarithmic differentiations.

Staying busy and trying not to think about Alex became my entire existence. Life was an endless stream of studying for finals, Christmas preparations, and finishing my college applications. Every time my thoughts threatened to shift towards Alex, I worked harder, forcing myself to focus on the task before me.

When I was decorating the tree with Mom and Angel, I didn't wonder where he was or if he was putting up a tree of his own. When Jase and I began our No Cats for Angel campaign (Jase is allergic; I'm terrified that they will suck out my soul), I didn't remember how Alex hated cats too. When I helped Miss Nancy with the annual Deadly Christmas Murder-Mystery fundraiser for the library, I didn't think about how Santa's dead body was slumped over our table. And I didn't look at every single face in the crowded stores of Nashville and Paducah trying to find him.

Or, at least, I tried really hard not to do those things.

The only time I would allow myself to really focus on Alex was at night. That is when I would lock myself in my room and research werewolves.

I checked out everything our library had, and read anything I could find online. Since that kept me occupied for less than a week and didn't answer any of my questions, I got Miss Nancy to find me a bunch of things on Inter-Library Loan. Stacks of books on all things lupin were crammed into every space I could find in my bedroom and closet, out of Jase's sight. The information I found ranged from interesting to horrifying to downright stupid. There were several books from a library in Ely, Minnesota, that I found the most helpful. They were so fascinating, in fact, I sent an email to the librarian there to compliment her on the collection.

Her replying email simply reminded me of the due date.

The number of legends surrounding werewolves was a bit overwhelming. It seemed that every culture from the dawn of time had their own version of the man who transformed into a wolf-like animal. I automatically rejected any that spoke of huge, hulking creatures that looked like a cross between man and beast, and focused on those that referenced wolves with human eyes. Some stories painted the creatures as victims, others demons.

Every evening I would rush home from whatever holiday cheer task I had to endure so I could read stories of myth and legend. I was becoming a werewolf expert, and it was affecting my sleep. My once peaceful nights were now filled with brilliant dreams. Sometimes I would find myself running from a pack of wolves. In others, I would transform into one myself. Occasionally, I would dream of the lake, but now Alex was always in his wolf form on the opposite shore.

Despite all my research, I still had more questions than answers.

How did Alex become a werewolf? (Being bitten or scratched by a werewolf was the most popular theory.) Did the change hurt? (Judging from Alex's pre-change condition, and by virtue of logic, I was thinking that was a definite yes.) Was the change affected by the full moon? (There was a full moon that night in Nashville, so I thought it was likely.) Was Alex conscious of who he was and what was happening when he was in wolf form? (Most of the things I read said no, but Alex seemed to be trying to protect me, and he seemed to remember everything the next morning.) Do werewolves really kill people or was that all just propaganda that was spread out of ignorance and fear? (I was really hoping for the latter.) And how much did Jase know and how did he know it? (I was leaning towards him being a cross between the Winchester boys and Buffy.)

For most of the questions I had no way of getting answers. I could read books and come up with theories, but without asking Alex directly, I would never know.

Jase, on the other hand, I could get information from.

Of course, I couldn't just walk up and say, "So, Alex is a werewolf. What do you know about that?"

But I was nothing, if not resourceful. I had a plan. It wasn't a fool-proof plan. It wasn't even a good plan. But it was a plan. And on Christmas Day, I was going to put my plan into action

Chapter 9

Christmas is a time of family gatherings, which sounds great unless have more sets of grandparents than clean socks. It took two days and endless patience to get through our multitude of family celebrations that included each of Dad's divorced parents, Mom's ever-expanding family, and an evening with Talley and her mom, who were considered family since Mrs. Matthews had baby-sat Jase and me since we were babies.

On Christmas morning, Angel woke everyone up with screams of, "He came! Santa came! Scout! Jase! Presents!" at six o'clock in the morning. I hoped he had brought her a watch and sense enough to let me sleep. After ripping open our ridiculously large mound of presents (including Angel's new kitty, Elf, that promptly hissed at Jase and attempted to claw out my eyeballs), Jase and I headed down to the Base for the Hagan Family Christmas.

My spirits lifted the moment I stepped through the door of the quaint log cabin tucked into the woods. Part of it was due to the delicious smell that wafted from the kitchen, making my stomach completely forget the abuse from the previous two days and growl as if I hadn't eaten in weeks. Part of it was the magical atmosphere created by hundreds of twinkling lights and decorations that covered every inch of the house. Part of it was the sound of Christmas carols being played on acoustic guitars. But mostly, it was because of the boy who gathered me into his arms and spun me around the room.

"God, I've missed you," Charlie said, setting me on my feet. He held me at arms length, looking me over.

"Well, do I pass inspection?"

Charlie screwed his mouth up to one side, which made him look ridiculous and adorable at the same time. "I thought you were supposed to be orange with a splattering of black and blue."

For once in my life, I was grateful to be a whiter shade of pale. "It's all faded away, except for a rather spectacular spot on my bum that has turned an unnatural color of greenish yellow."

I regretted the words the second they were out of my mouth, but only because that was the moment Gramma Hagan decided to shuffle in from the kitchen. Jase was trying so hard not to laugh that he had tears rolling down his cheeks by the time she finished lecturing me on appropriate conversation topics for proper young ladies.

Later, when we gathered around the tree, Charlie placed a small blue package in my lap. I eagerly ripped through the paper to uncover a vintage looking necklace. The pendant was in the shape of a hippo decked out in a tutu and toe shoes.

"Do you like it?" Charlie asked, sweeping my hair over my shoulder. "I bought it at one of those hipster-cool stores down by campus. I can't walk into one of those without thinking about how much you love that sort of stuff."

I fingered the tiny piece of metal as he secured the clasp. "I love it. It's perfect." And it was. It was funky and cool without being ostentatious. I didn't plan on ever taking it off.

Jase managed to score the latest gaming system from his grandparents and a nice stack of new games from Uncle Charles and Aunt Diane. Jase and Charlie immediately went to set it up in what Gramma Hagan called "the back parlor" and everyone else referred to as "Uncle Charles's old room".

At first I took turns racing cars through candy-colored landscapes and engaging psychotic bunnies in some fairly inane competitions with Jase, Charlie, and Layne, Charlie's somewhat demented twelve year old nephew. Eventually, though, Layne got tired of not getting our jokes and went to do something infinitely more Layne-ish, like torturing small animals. I soon after remembered how much I hated video games and tapped out. Jase and Charlie pretended to be disappointed, but really they were just excited to tear into the new two-player shooting game they had both been drooling over since Jase opened it.

I spent the majority of the evening snuggled into Charlie's side on the love-seat, watching as they valiantly attempted to defend the world from...something.

"I'm confused," I finally admitted. "Are they aliens or zombies?"

"They're obviously zombified aliens," Jase said as he shot one between the eyes, causing brain matter to splatter on the screen.

"Zombie aliens are the number one risk to truth, freedom, and the American way," Charlie informed me. "There's a special government task force to address that very issue."

"And the clowns?" I asked as a grenade blew a mime to smithereens.

"Clowns are just evil," said Jase. "End of discussion."

I watched the carnage unfold on the screen for a few more minutes before reluctantly hefting myself away from Charlie.

"Where are you going?" he asked, pulling his eyes away from the television for the first time in over an hour.

"I need some Tylenol. All this brain rottage is giving me a headache." I grabbed my bag from the corner and began making an oral inventory of its contents. "Gum. Sunglasses. Phone. Sour Patch Kids. Tissues. Angel's pink plastic puppy. Alex's pen. Huh, guess that one is mine now. Wallet. I have a Tootsie Roll from the Bush administration, but no Tylenol. Great." I sat my bag down between Charlie and Jase. "I'm going on a pain medication scavenger hunt. Anyone need anything while I'm gone?"

"Mello Yello," Jase automatically responded.

"Make that two," said Charlie. "And some of those cookies with the red raisin things in them."

"And a ham sandwich on one of those rolls with some hot pepper cheese and mayo," Jase added.

"Oh, I want one of those, too. And a piece of pumpkin pie with the whipped topping that comes out of a tub, not the weird stuff from a can."

The sad thing was, neither of them were kidding.

I grumbled to myself the entire way to the kitchen, resolving to only take back drinks. Charlie's older brother was leaned against the counter, eating the last of the Snickers Salad directly from the bowl.

"Hey. What's up?"

"Harper," he mumbled, the only indication I got that he noticed my presence.

I was rummaging through the cabinets for some glasses the boys wouldn't accidentally crush into a million little pieces when I heard someone behind me. I jerked to the left, barely escaping the blow aimed at my head. My feet were immediately swept out from under me, sending me face-first into the counter. I rolled, my leg arching through the air until it made contact, sending my assailant into the pie safe. My fist shot out, but he managed to catch my wrist and pin me back onto the counter.

"You're getting rusty, Scout," Toby chuckled, letting me up.

I rotated my shoulder, certain I would have a new bruise in the morning. "Sorry, Sensei."

Of course, it might have been more appropriate for Toby to apologize since he was the one that attacked me for no good reason. Not that I was going to hold my breath for that one. Toby wasn't big on the whole admitting he was wrong thing. It's not that I dislike Toby. Really, I admire him in many ways. After knocking up the head cheerleader in high school, he joined the Army so that he could support his new family while making the old one proud. After serving two tours of duty in Iraq, he came back home and joined the police force. When his child-bride left him a year later, he took on the job of raising Layne by himself. And he managed to do it all while still looking like a rock star.

On the other hand, he was a bit arrogant, somewhat moody, and excessively sexist. Toby had always helped out at Uncle Charles's martial arts school when he was around and pretty much took over when he got out of the Army. He always expected Jase and Charlie to excel at every move. He pushed them hard, and was very expressive with his disappointment when they didn't live up to his exceedingly high expectations. If I managed to do well in any way the only emotion he ever managed to show was shock.

Toby's biggest insult? "You fight like a girl."

His biggest compliment? "That's showing you've got balls."

Imagine how proud Mom was when an eight year old Scout asked her what balls were and why it was good to have them.

"If you wanted a real fight you should've ambushed one of the boys," I said with more than a little sass in my voice.

"A lot of good that would've done me. You're the one with all the talent."

Well, that was unexpected.

"You think I'm talented?" It was still entirely possible that this was some big set up with my girly fighting skills serving as the punch line.

"Are you kidding?" Toby asked through a mouthful of pie. "You're not as strong as Charlie or as fast as Jase, but you're the single best defensive fighter I've ever seen. It's like you can see the punch coming before your opponent even decides to throw it."

He was complimenting me? Really? Perhaps a zombie alien apocalypse was rapidly approaching after all.

I was grateful though that Toby had given me the perfect opportunity to bring up something that I had been thinking about for a while. I gnawed on the inside of my lip and focused my eyes intently on a water stain shaped like Abraham Lincoln on Gramma's ceiling. "I want to start training again," I finally mumbled.

I was nervous as to Toby's reaction. Toby was as abrasive and mercurial as Charlie was calm and consistent. I fully expected him to either laugh at me or complain about my attempt to waste his time.

"Really?"

"I've been thinking about it for a while." Since a snowy, icy day in November to be exact. "Do you have a class I could join?"

"No, I don't." My heart sank. "But I wouldn't mind giving you private lessons once a week." My heart soared. That was even better than I had hoped.

We worked out a time that would fit both our schedules as I made a couple of ham sandwiches.

"Thank God, I'm starving," Jase said, relieving me of half my load when I returned to the back room.

Charlie quickly grabbed the other half. "This white stuff is from a tub, right? You know I hate that can stuff. It tastes like metal."

At some point I should have gotten used to their lack of gratitude, but I hadn't. What did they think I was? Some sort of personal servant eager to meet their every whim and desire?

Ummm, no. I don't think so.

"Wow, thank you so much, Scout," I said sarcastically, repositioning myself between my brother and Charlie. "That was so sweet of you to fix us something to eat."

"Thank you, Scout," Charlie said, leaning over to plant a kiss on my cheek. "You're the best."

Okay, so maybe I was somewhat wiling to meet Charlie's every whim and desire. "Is it good?"

Charlie took a big bite of his pie. His eyes got big as he struggled to swallow. "It's great."

Charlie has always been a wretched liar.

"What did I do wrong?"

"Nothing. It's great. Different, but good different."

I grabbed the plate from him and took a big bite, which I immediately spit out. "That Cool Whip is rancid!"

Jase leaned over and scooped a big glob of creamy white vileness onto his finger and plopped it into his mouth before I could stop him.

"Excellent work, Paula Deen," Jase laughed. "I'm sure pumpkin pie with a nice sour cream topping is going to be all the rage at next year's holiday gatherings."

I took a tentative taste and realized he was right. I had mistaken sour cream for whipped cream. At least Angel wasn't around to gloat over my disastrous culinary skills. "Sorry," I muttered. "I'll go get you another piece of pie."

Charlie grabbed the plate out of my hand. "No, you won't. I told you, I like it."

"You don't have to--"

"Scout, please shut up and let me eat my pie."

He ended up eating the whole thing, sour cream and all. He tried to act like he was enjoying it, but I could tell he was just doing it so my feelings wouldn't get hurt. Charlie really was a good person and one of my best friends. He would do absolutely anything for me and trusted me implicitly. Which is why I felt really guilty as I dug into my purse when I was back home, sitting in the middle of my bed.

I grabbed the earbuds off of my iPod as the tape recorder rewound. The last thing I needed was for Jase to catch me.

The first thing I noticed when I pushed play was that my purse only slightly distorted the quality of the recording. I breathed a sigh of relief. My planning would have been for nothing if I couldn't hear what they said while I was out of the room.

The second thing I noticed was how loud and abrasive my voice was. Did I always sound like that? If so, how on earth does anyone manage to have a conversation with me?

The third thing I noticed was that boys can go a really long time without talking. I was just about to give up when one of them spoke.

"Why in the hell does she have that mongrel's pen in her purse?"

Yes! I made a mental note to thank Mr. Brenner for all of the useful information he taught us in our section on basic human psychology.

"I told you, she was working on that newspaper stuff with him," the other voice said. I was pretty sure that one was Jase. It was somewhat surprising how much they sounded alike. *"I'm sure she borrowed a pen from him and didn't give it back. It's no big. Seriously."*

"I told you to keep an eye on her." Was that really Charlie?

"I was." Well, that was definitely Jase.

"Not good enough." Okay, that had to be Charlie, although I wasn't used to hearing him speak so gruffly towards anyone, especially Jase. *"I swear, if he touched her..."*

There was something on the tape that almost sounded like a growl. At first I thought it had come from Charlie, but then I remembered they were playing the stupid zombie alien game.

"Speaking of people keeping their paws off of my sister."

"My paws have been over 300 miles away from your sister ever since August." Yep, definitely Charlie. And definitely not happy. *"I waited until Tuesday to come home just so I wouldn't be anywhere near her. I didn't want you to worry your pretty little head even though you know I could never do anything to hurt her."*

I glanced over at the calendar on my desk. Friday had been Charlie's last final. I had assumed he waited until Tuesday to come home so that he could celebrate all weekend. It appeared I may have been wrong.

"That's not what I'm talking about and you know it." The music from the video game was adding a dramatic edge to the conversation. Well, that or the pounding of my heart. *"You know how she feels about you, man."*

He did? Oh God, no. No, no, no, no, no.

"And you know how I feel about her."

How did he feel about me? I didn't know how he felt about me. Shouldn't I be the one with that knowledge?

"She's my sister." Even though his voice was slightly distorted, I could tell that Jase was talking through clenched teeth. It didn't take much imagination for me to visualize the hard look he was sure to have on his face. *"Anyways, don't you already have a girlfriend?"*

Charlie had a girlfriend? Since when? And what did that have to do with me?

This wasn't exactly the sort of information I had been seeking, but I found it infinitely fascinating. And humiliating. And confusing.

There must have been a noise that the recorder hadn't picked up, because one of them asked, *"What was that?"*

"Toby and Scout." That was Charlie's voice. *"Toby is trying to convince her to start training again."*

"How? By throwing cookware at her?" Well, that wasn't too far off the mark.

"Who knows with Toby, but he'll do whatever it takes. He thinks it's his job as Pack Leader to keep her safe. I'm surprised he hasn't assigned someone to guard her 24/7."

Pack Leader? Huh? And guard who? Me? From what? Alex? Did everyone know he was a werewolf?

"Well, he can back off now. The Coles are gone."

Yep. They were talking about Alex. I wondered if I was the last person in Lake County to know about his split personality.

"Are you sure?"

"Positive. I went over to their place Monday night and the scent has almost completely faded. They've been gone a full cycle. We are once again the only Shifters in Western KY."

I sat, not breathing. My eyes were still frozen on the calendar. I had been unable to look away from it since I realized Monday had been a full moon. Charlie waited until after the full moon to come home.

Because he was a werewolf. Charlie and Jase were werewolves.

I pulled a long, shaky breath into my lungs. This was crazy. My brother was *not* a werewolf. I would have known.

I walked over and tore my calendar off the wall and began flipping through the pages. This theory was going to be very easy to dispel. All I had to do was remember seeing Jase, fully human, on a night of a full moon. No big.

Or, it should have been no big. But of the twelve nights we had a full moon over the past year, I couldn't remember doing anything with Jase on any of them. On the contrary, I could specifically remember *not* seeing him on several of them. In February, he missed a basketball game and spent the entire night in his bed, deathly ill. In April, he had been on a camping trip with Charlie during the full moon. September's full moon coincided with the night he spent at Gramma Hagan's after she had a short stay in the hospital. Monday night he had went to do some last minute Christmas shopping in Nashville and spent the night at the Base.

Still, that didn't prove anything. I was not going to accept that my brother had a secret identity as a supernatural being without something a bit more concrete.

I grabbed a stack of books from underneath my bed and began thumbing through them, acting more out of habit than anything else. I was just about to grab another stack when something caught my eye. On the inside cover of a local library book was a plaque that read, "In loving memory of Jason Anthony Hagan."

Donating books to the library in honor or memory of a loved one was a common practice in our small town. Miss Nancy encouraged people to do it as a way to keep the library well-stocked, despite the county's flimsy budget. When someone in Lake County passed on, their family would almost always purchase a book by an author or on a topic with which their dearly departed had a special connection. It was like sharing a piece of that person with the community.

Jason Hagan's book was *The Voice of the Coyote* by J Frank Dobie.

The pieces started to slowly slide together and click into place.

I turned on my computer, grateful I had the foresight to dig it out from under a pile of Jase's dirty clothes when we got home. After a brief debate with my morals, I managed to hack into the library's newspaper database.

The first thing I found was the obituary. It solemnly stated that Jason Hagan passed away on November 23. He was survived by his mother, one brother, and his wife, Rebecca Lowery Hagan. It did not mention that she was two months pregnant with his son at the time.

I finally found what I was looking for a few pages later. The headline read, "Local man dies in an early morning accident." Below was a picture of a man decked out in camo, displaying the rack of a large buck. Although I never met him, I could imagine the way his green eyes shone with pride. Mom always said that Jase was a carbon copy of his father.

"Jason Hagan, 30, of Timber was fatally wounded in an accidental shooting at 4:36 am Tuesday morning in a wooded area approximately 15 miles north of Princeton," the article stated. "Royce Pearlman of Fredonia states that he saw what he believed to be a coyote approach his deer stand. It was not until he reached the place where he thought the animal had fallen he realized his grave error. Hagan was pronounced dead on the scene."

Click, click, click went the pieces of the puzzle in my head. Of course a large pack of wolves would draw attention running around Western Kentucky, but not coyotes. Coyotes were a dime a dozen. Just last summer Dad swore that he saw a huge one in our back yard.

Oh. That was probably Jase.

Of course.

And it explained the animosity between Jase and Alex. According to all of my extensive research, coyotes and wolves aren't exactly BFFs.

So, my brother had a habit of turning into an animal once a month. I already knew some people had a tendency to do that. It hadn't changed my opinion of Alex that much. If I was being completely honest with myself (which I wasn't totally fond of doing), Alex's werewolf status made him sorta sexy.

But being a were-coyote did not make Jase and Charlie sexy. It made them foreign, different from the boys I thought I knew. It was as if I had been betrayed in some deep, irreconcilable way.

How could they keep a secret like that from me?

I was getting angry, as was my usual emotional response to being hurt and confused. I don't know what I might have done if I had been left to my own devices, but it wouldn't have ended well. I imagine it would have involved me screaming some wild accusations at my brother in the wee hours of the morning. In fact, I was on my way to do just that when my phone vibrated.

Chapter 10

I stared blankly at the bedside table. Who would be calling at 2:47 AM?

I checked the caller ID, but didn't recognize the number. Panic started to bubble up inside me. Someone knew that I knew. They had been keeping tabs on my computer and realized I finally figured it out. Now I was going to be eliminated for knowing. Or, maybe I would be carted off to some juvenile delinquent facility for computer hacking. I would have to share a cell with one of those scary metalhead chicks with all the piercings and tattoos.

I nearly jumped out of my skin when the phone in my hand beeped. I flipped it open to find a text message that read, "It's snowing."

Weird.

I went to the window, cupping my hands around my face to peer into the darkness. The night was pitch black, but I could see a few tiny flakes blowing underneath a utility light.

I could also see the boy who stood underneath it, looking up at me.

Thankfully, I took the time to throw on a coat and boots before racing into the wintery night air. Of course, if I had known I was going to be hiking through the woods, I might have taken the extra thirty seconds to make sure they were actually mine.

Alex had yet to say a word, his only greeting a heart melting smile. When he took my hand and began leading me down a well-worn path that wound through the forest, I let him. Since I'm not a complete idiot, I understood that sneaking off into the woods in the middle of the night with a known werewolf was not the best idea I ever had. Somehow, though, I couldn't be bothered to care. It probably had something to do with those hormones my mother was always warning me about.

"Where are we going?" I asked, breaking the silence.

He stopped walking and looked around, staring in the direction of my house for a long time before declaring, "Here's good."

"Here" was a patch of forest that looked identical to every other patch of forest we had walked past. At least there was a giant log I could sit on. My feet ached from trekking up and down hills in Jase's boots.

"So" I said, plopping down on a sturdy looking brach, "to what do I owe this visit? Was no one in Montana up for a snowy midnight stroll?"

Alex sat on the trunk opposite me, close enough that our knees brushed against one another. "Don't know. I never made it that far."

"You couldn't make it to Montana in a month? What was your mode of transportation? Horse and buggy?"

"Burrow, actually. Damn thing wouldn't go any further than Effingham."

I waited for that sentence to make sense. "Ham? Is that the name of an actual place, or do I need to access my urban dictionary app?"

Alex laughed. "Not f'ing ham. Effingham. One word. It's a town in Illinois whose singular claim to fame is a 198 foot tall cross."

"So, you got bored with your ginormous cross and thought, 'Hey, I bet Scout will be awake. Maybe we could go for a walk?'"

"Close. I finally convinced Liam into giving me what I wanted for Christmas."

"What was that?"

"To come home," he said. "We just got into town a couple of hours ago. I had some business to take care of on this side of town, but then I saw your light on and got distracted." He was staring at his feet again. I noticed he was still wearing the same pair of Adidas shoes, despite the fact that their little swim in the creek left them a bit worse for the wear.

"You had business to attend to at three in the morning?"

"I can't really talk about it."

"Because it's werewolf business?"

"Yes, it's werewolf business."

We sat in silence for a few moments. Once again, I questioned the logic of being alone in a darkened forest with a werewolf. Amazingly, I still wasn't afraid. It was Alex Cole, for Pete's sake. The boy couldn't go more than five minutes without flashing a million watt smile or cracking up over some stupid thing I said. He wasn't going to hurt me.

Probably.

"I don't suppose your werewolf business has anything to do with my brother being a were-coyote, does it?"

That certainly got his attention.

"He told you?"

"So, Jase really is a were-coyote?" The look on his face was the only confirmation I needed. "Is that why you guys can't get along? Are werewolves and were-coyotes mortal enemies or something?"

My assessment seemed to amuse Alex. "I think 'Shape Shifter' or 'Shifter' is the politically correct term," he said. "I'm not sure 'were-coyote' is even a word."

My eyes narrowed. "You know what I mean."

"It's true that my kind has a little trouble getting along with our cousin species, but that's only part of the problem. When the local pack found out we were here, they sent a few delegates over to talk to us. A treaty was agreed upon, allowing us to stay. If we failed to keep up our end of the bargain the Hagan Pack has the right to challenge us."

"What did the treaty entail?"

"Liam and I must stay within a predetermined boundary during the full moon. Also, we're to have no contact with those under Pack protection, especially you."

I was under Pack protection? Okay, so I guess I already knew that from my super spy mission, but still. What made me so special? Why was I being singled out?

"What delegates?"

"The Pack Leader, Jase, and Charlie." Alex ripped off a piece of decaying bark and began turning it into sawdust with his thumb. "You already knew your boyfriend is a Shifter too, right?"

"If you're referring to Charlie, then yes, I had already guessed that he was a *Shifter*. But he isn't my boyfriend."

"Are you sure Charlie knows that?"

After the intel I got from Jase and Charlie's earlier conversation I found I didn't really know how to answer. I kept opening my mouth, but nothing came out. Luckily, Alex was too immersed in dismantling the tree to see my fish out of water routine. Finally, I managed to get out, "Charlie has a girlfriend. I mean, he's dating a girl who isn't me."

"That didn't stop him from getting you that for Christmas," Alex said, jerking his chin towards the hippo that peeked out from the top of my coat.

"How do you know it's from Charlie?"

Alex, who had been leaning on his elbows towards me, pulled back, and shifted his knees shifted away from mine. "I can smell him on it. Either he gave it to you, or he's been wearing your jewelry."

"You can *smell him on it*?"

"Did you know that a wolf's sense of smell is one hundred times greater than a human's?"

"Actually, yes. I did." I didn't mention that was because I had read everything I could find on wolves over the last month. "I just didn't expect that you would be able to do that when you were, you know, a biped."

"Not always. I can only do it now because we just had a full moon a couple of days ago. The closer we are to a full moon, the more wolf-like we are. As the moon waxes, our hearing, sense of smell, physical strength and all that wolfy stuff gets stronger, more sensitive. When the moon begins to wan, the extra-sensitive senses go with it, until we're almost wholly human during the new moon."

Interesting. "So, the day of the full moon...?"

"I can hear every heart beating in a classroom and smell a pizza from a mile away."

And impressive. "It's like you have super-powers."

"You mean other than being able to turn into a wolf?"

"Oh, like that makes you special," I said with mock ease. "Everyone I know can change into a dog of some sort."

A growl emitted from Alex's throat. "Dog?" he snarled. I caught a glimpse of predatory eyes as he lunged for me. My heart and breath both abandoned me as I prepared for the impact of teeth and claws. I managed to grab him as his body slammed into mine, using the force to flip us over as we fell back so I landed on top. I quickly leapt to my feet.

The body on the ground shook all over. I might have been able to best Alex in human form, but there was no way I could take on a wolf. I contemplated whether or not I could run fast enough to make it to the house before the transformation was complete.

"That will teach me to attack a ninja," Alex said between gasps.

Laughing. He wasn't changing into a wolf, he was laughing.

"You jerk!" I roared. "I thought you were going to turn into a wolf and eat me!" I gave into temptation and planted my foot in his ribs.

"Ouch. Hasn't anyone ever taught you not to kick a man when he's down?"

"Hasn't anyone ever taught you not to scare a girl to death for no good reason?"

"I thought ninjas eschewed fear." Alex sat up, brushing twigs and grass from his hair. "And, for the record, I can't Change unless the moon is full. I'm not a Dominant."

"A Dominant?" My curiosity overpowered my agitation.

"Shifters, like natural wolves, have a hierarchy based on strength. The stronger the wolf, the higher their social standing. But with Shifters, it's based on more than the ability to smack down all the other wolves. You have to have control over your animal. Every Shifter has to Change during a full moon. Whether they want to or not, they're on four legs from dusk to dawn. Dominants, though, can change other nights."

Alex sat on the ground, a la criss-cross-applesauce, and I paced in front of him. "You say that like it's an enviable quality. Why would someone want to Change?"

"Besides the dominance issue?" I shook my head. "It's hard to explain. Being the wolf is... It's amazing. It's more than the strength or the super-powers. Running through the woods, being part of nature in some primitive way humans can't manage, it's liberating. Intoxicating." His entire body became animated. "And the chase. You wouldn't believe how thrilling the chase is. The moment you finally close the distance between yourself and your prey is the single most satisfying thing you could imagine."

I could see delight written all over his face. The mere memory of it seemed to make him giddy.

I felt nauseous.

"You enjoy killing," I managed to choke out. "It doesn't bother you that you're taking away someone's child or brother or mother..." My voice broke over the last word.

"You think I kill people?"

Instead of answering, I decided to gnaw a hole in my bottom lip.

"How can you think that about me?" He bounded off the ground in one graceful move and began pacing along the forest floor. "What about Jase? Do you think he's a killer too?" He stopped directly in front of me. I shifted my body, ready to fend off an attack. "And what the hell do you think you're doing out here with me if you think I'm a murderer?"

I gritted my teeth and forced myself to meet his steely gaze instead of cowering, like I really, really wanted to. "Are you a murderer?"

"That depends, are you one of those animal activist that believes meat is murder?"

"No." I was born and raised in the rural south. Hunting is practically a religion.

"Then, no, I'm not a murderer."

"So, when you were talking about the chase and your prey..."

"Rabbits mostly. Occasionally Liam and I can take down a deer together."

"Rabbits and deer?"

"Rabbits and the occasional deer."

"Never a person?"

"I'm not a monster, Scout."

"What about homeless meth heads?"

"What about them?" He started to move away, but I grabbed onto his shirt. It smelled like Waffle House, that unique blend of smoke and grease.

"Did you kill him, Alex?"

He brushed my hands away. I watched him walk back over to our original spot and sag back onto the trunk of the fallen tree. "Does it matter?"

I thought about how it felt to trapped on the ground, the body of my attacker on top of mine. "Please, tell me what happened."

"I chased him as far as I could. Once he got into the more populated areas, I had to let him go. Anyway, I needed to make sure you were okay. I didn't mean for you to see me. I just wanted to be certain that you hadn't been hurt. I was watching so closely for some sign that you were about to fall apart I forgot I was supposed to be hiding." His grey eyes bore into mine. "How did you know it was me?"

"It was the eyes." I would know those eyes anywhere.

"You really are amazing, you know."

He would have to settle for a blush as a response.

"Anyway, after I left you, I went back and tracked his scent. Liam got into town just before dawn to find me slinking around the tent city near Centennial Park, which made him furious. He tried to force me into the Jeep, but I wouldn't budge.

"He had to wait almost thirty minutes for dawn to come so I could Change and tell him what was going on. Liam went to take care of things while I recovered. By the time I could walk, it was clear he would never be able to hurt anyone again."

"What did Liam do?" My voice sounded foreign, as if it was coming from another place, another person.

"Liam didn't attack first."

"What did he do?" The alien voice was devoid of emotion.

"I'm not a doctor, Scout. How am I supposed to know?" My mouth opened to repeat the question for a third time. It seemed, though, that he was as unwilling to hear it as I was. "His right hand was crushed. His arm, nose, and collarbone all looked broken, too. He was coughing up blood, so there was probably some internal injuries. I don't think it was anything fatal, but, like I said, I'm not a doctor."

My shoulders slumped in relief. "How did Liam get to you before dawn? Isn't he a werewolf too?"

"Of course he's a werewolf. It runs in the family."

"But you said that you had to stay in wolf form from sunset to sunrise on the night of a full moon."

"The rules don't really apply to Liam," Alex said with a wry smile. "He has an amazing amount of control. He made his first successful non-full moon change when he was fourteen. By the time he was sixteen, he could change at noon on the day of a new moon." Alex's words were saturated with admiration and envy. "It's not even supposed to be possible, but neither is changing back to human during a full moon."

The fact that Liam was such a good werewolf wasn't really surprising. It was clear that he was different than Alex. More other. More wolf.

Alex casually reached over and placed my hand in his. "You're cold," he said, misinterpreting my slight tremble. "Maybe we should head back."

Like Hades we would. "I'm fine. I've got a million burning questions to keep me warm."

"A million burning questions, huh?" He tried to appear put out, but I could see a rogue dimple.

"At least a million, and I'm prepared to stay out here all night if that is what it takes to get answers. I mean, unless *you're* too cold..." Growing up with Jase and Charlie taught me one truth about boys - the best way to ensure they do what you want is to question their masculinity. I could tell by the set of Alex's jaw he was no exception.

"I'm not cold. This is balmy compared to Montana."

"So, you'll stay and answer all my questions?"

This time the weariness on his face was real. "I'll try."

That was good enough for me. "So, being a werewolf or Shape-Shifter or whatever is inherited, right?"

"Yes."

"So, Jase's kids will all be able to turn into a coyote during the full moon?"

"Jase's sons will start changing sometime during adolescence. It's one of the perks of puberty, like a deeper voice and chest hair."

"Only boys? Girls can't be were-whatevers?" That hardly seemed fair.

"It's rare for a girl to be born with the gene. Most of the ones that do, don't survive the first change, if they last that long."

Something about they way he said "if they last that long" didn't sit right with me. "Why wouldn't they make it to puberty?"

"The childhood mortality rate amongst female Shifters is abnormally high, most likely due to the body's inability to accept the physiological changes associated with being a Shifter," Alex said as though he was reading aloud from a text book. He often did that when we were debating issues for our newspaper articles. It meant that he didn't believe a word of what he just said.

That bothered me. Why would he tell me something he didn't believe? And if it wasn't some sort of allergic reaction to being half-wolf (or half-coyote) that caused little girls to die, what was? Not knowing was going to drive me crazy, but pushing the issue might make Alex less inclined to answer the rest of my questions. Reluctantly, I moved on.

"Does it hurt? Changing, I mean."

Alex's loosened his vice-like grip on my hand. "In the beginning. The first time I Changed I thought I would die before everything got in the right place, but you get used to it. Now it's more uncomfortable than painful."

"How does it work? It's not like wolves and humans have the same physical make up. I mean, they have more teeth than we do, and smaller internal organs, and a tail, for Pete's sake. And coyotes are tiny compared to people. Where does Jase's extra 100 pounds go when he's Coyote Jase? Or is he the world's biggest coyote?"

My mini-rant managed to illicit nothing more than a laugh from Alex.

"What's so funny?"

"You want me to explain magic?"

Of course I did. "In the most scientific terms possible, please."

He gave me one of those full-force smiles that made my heart skip a beat. "I thought you might feel that way," he said, reaching into the pocket of his coat. "That's why I have this."

"What is it?" I stared at the package he placed in my hands.

"Your Christmas present. I wrapped it myself."

No kidding. Only a boy would require half a role of Scotch tape and five feet of Pokemon paper to wrap a single present.

"I thought you didn't plan on seeing me tonight."

"I didn't."

"So, you were just carrying this around in your coat pocket in the off chance you ran into me in the middle of the night?"

Alex ducked his head and peered up through his lashes. "Promise not to freak out on me?"

"No."

His laugh echoed off the surrounding trees. "Will you promise to *try* not to freak out on me?"

"I will put forth a valiant effort," I conceded.

"I was going to sneak into your room and leave it." His words came out so rapidly it took a minute for me to realize what he said.

"You were going to break into my house?"

"You live ten miles outside of Timber, Kentucky. I was going to walk through the unlocked front door. That hardly constitutes breaking in."

Illogically, the thing bothering me most was that my room was trashed. There were probably bras and panties sitting out in plain view.

"It's a good thing that plan didn't work out," I said. "Jase's room is next to mine. You would've totally been busted."

"Actually, I was coming to talk to Jase, to let him know we were back in town. I was going to say I ended up in your room by mistake." Obviously, he thought he was very sly. I, for one, felt certain that Jase would have easily seen through such a weak lie, but I allowed him to believe his little fantasy.

"There is no gift tag on here," I noticed. "How was I supposed to know it was from you?"

"Open it."

It took some time to get through all the tape, but eventually I was looking at an old, yellowed paperback. The cover had a beast that looked like the illegitimate love child of Chewbacca and Lassie and read, "*Werewolf Autopsy* by PJ Smith."

He thought an ancient pulp novel was going to sate my curiosity?

"In 1955 George McPhearson, a werewolf, turned himself over to a scientist at Cambridge University. After two years of observations and experiments, Dr. Smith presented his findings, and was subsequently laughed at by every academic institute across the globe. Maybe it would've been different if he could have offered proof, but George conveniently disappeared right before the study went public. Eventually, Smith was only able to get his findings published as fiction with only one limited press run. You may well be holding the only copy of the only book that tells the truth about werewolves."

"Where did you find it?" If it was as rare as he said it was, which I fully believed, he must have searched everywhere for it, or got really lucky on eBay.

"It was my dad's. I guess that technically qualifies as re-gifting."

In the back of my closet there is a box filled with some of my mother's things - her favorite albums and books, some pictures, a few pieces of jewelry, and her wedding dress. None of the items would bring much at an auction, but they're my most prized possessions. I couldn't bear to part with any of them.

"I'll take good care of it," I said, turning the pages with care, as if it was an invaluable holy document. My eyes skimmed the pages, pausing on words like muscular regeneration, skeletal fusion, and passionate embrace.

Passionate embrace?

"This is all real?" I asked as I quickly read a paragraph detailing the trials and tribulations of kissing with fangs.

Alex looked over my shoulder. "Well, not that stupid love story stuff. The publishing company added all that crap in, but the pages upon pages detailing werewolf anatomy and the Change in 'as scientific terms as possible' is as real as it's going to get."

I was holding all the answers I had been so desperately seeking for the last month. Ever since the moment I realized what Alex was, my world had been off balance. I found comfort in logic and reasoning. Werewolves defy both. Alex gave me a way to turn the impossible into something that could be explained and studied. Tears stung in my eyes. "Thank you."

"I'm glad you like it," he said. "Does this conclude the interrogation portion of our evening?"

"That depends." I gently placed the book in my lap, gathering up every ounce of courage I had to reach over and grab his hand. "Does Dr. Smith also cover the science behind vampires?"

"Vampires? You think vampires are real? Seriously?"

"The *werewolf* is asking me if I believe in vampires?"

Alex's smile only widened. "Point taken."

"So, there are no vampires?"

"As far as I know, vampires are just a legend."

"How about faeries? Ghosts? Witches? Zombies? Unicorns?" He squeezed my hand and moved in closer so that we were leaning against one another. My heart rate kicked up a few notches and my brain threatened to shut off completely. "Or, you know, gnomes. Maybe gnomes are real. Are gnomes real?"

"Gnomes? I don't think so." We were sitting so close I could feel his warm breath on my cheek. "I've never seen a ghost, but I wouldn't discount the possibility. There are women with supernatural senses, but they're called Seers."

"Seers? Like precogs?"

"There are a few very powerful Seers that can catch a glimpse of the future, but it's extremely rare. They come in different varieties. Some are dream walkers, Seeing things that have happened in the past or something going on a thousand miles away, but only when they're asleep. Some Seers can See your thoughts, emotions, or deepest secrets just by touching you. The Seer that served my father's Pack could See everywhere an object had been when she held it in both hands."

"*Served* your father's pack?" It's not like I'm a don't-shave-your-legs-in-definance-of-our-patricarical-society type feminist, but things like a woman *serving* a pack of men made my skin crawl.

"I didn't mean in a sexual way."

Oh gross. I hadn't been thinking that, but I was stuck with a searing visual and queasy stomach anyway. "How did you mean it?"

"Seers are honored, exalted members of the Pack. Like lycanthropy, it's an inherited trait, but it's a recessive gene. When a werewolf has a son, he knows that one day he will be a werewolf too, but the daughter of a Seer doesn't necessarily have the gift. The ratio of Seers to Shifters is probably less than one to ten, yet they are important for our survival."

Alex paused and looked at me expectantly.

"Important how?" I didn't want to disappoint.

"While their other talents vary, all Seers have the ability to communicate with us in our animal form They can warn us if someone is coming too close to our hunting ground, or tell us if one of our brothers is in danger. It's a bit more effective than the howl and growl system Liam and I use."

"Seers are telepaths?" My world was beginning to look like a cheesy made-for-SyFy movie.

I was partially right. It turns out that Seers minds can only link with Shifters when they are in wolf (or coyote) form. They can also link to the Alpha Female, no matter how far away she is.

"I guess you want to know what an Alpha Female is now?" Alex asked with a dramatic sigh.

"No, thanks. I already know what an Alpha Female is."

"Really?"

"Really."

"Would you mind enlightening me then?" He eyes were filled with little sparks of laughter.

I raised my chin and said with absolute certainty, "The Alpha Female is the wife of the Pack Leader."

"I'm sorry. That answer is incorrect."

What? No, it wasn't. I had read like a million books on werewolves in the past month. I knew what an Alpha Female was. "I'm wrong?"

"You're wrong." He seemed to take great pleasure in this fact.

"So, are you going to tell me what she is?"

"Are you going to ask nicely?"

He was so annoying. "Alex, darling, could you please explain to me exactly what an Alpha Female is?"

"Certainly, sweetheart." The next ten minutes consisted of a lecture on Pack social structure conducted by Professor Alex Cole, Werewolf Extraordinaire. In simple terms, it breaks down like this: newer, weaker Shifters; older, stronger Shifters; Pack Seer; Pack Leader; Alpha Pack; and then the Alpha Male (a Shifter) and Alpha Female (a Seer) shared the top spot.

"So, where is Shifter HQ?" I asked once we came to the question and answer portion of the class. "Do the Alphas run their kingdom from the Bat Cave under 1600 Pennsylvania Avenue?"

"It's more like Wayne Manor, and it's in Romania."

"Romania?"

"The Alphas control all the Shifters in the world, Scout. They have a house in almost every country with a Shifter population, but the main house is in Romania."

"The werewolves have chosen the home of Dracula as their base of operations?"

"The irony is not lost on me."

"Well, at least they can't really have much influence on what happens here," I said. "They probably don't even know that there are a bunch of Shifters running around Lake County, Kentucky. Heck, they probably don't even know Lake County exists."

"They know where almost every Shifter and Seer in the world lives," Alex said, face tight. "The Alphas are all about micromanagement. For example, if Liam or I were to break our treaty with the Hagan Pack, they would have to file a petition with the Alpha Pack before they could seek recourse."

"Seek recourse how? Like chase you out of town or fight you?"

He hesitated before answering. "The Alphas set the terms. If it was a boundary dispute, they would set up a Challenge between the Pack Leaders. When a treaty is broken, the guilty party faces either banishment or death."

Death? Alex and Liam would be killed for crossing a boundary line or hanging out with me?

"The Hagans aren't killers. They wouldn't do something like that."

"The laws about this sort of thing are very clear, and Shifters have to follow the laws. If they didn't comply, they would face their own executions. The Alphas don't allow disobedience. Anyone they view as insubordinate or a threat ends up dead or on the run for the rest of their lives."

"Why did you come back here, then? Why risk it? Couldn't you find a place where you wouldn't have any other Packs to deal with?"

He cupped my face in his hands, his thumb gently brushing a snowflake from my eyelashes. "You know why I came back."

My heart started beating against my ribcage as if it was trying to break free. "The fried chicken they serve at The Farmhouse?"

"I came back for you, Scout."

I had to say something. Something clever. Something dazzling. Something to make this moment perfect.

"I hope the snow sticks."

That was not it.

Alex laughed nervously. Or, maybe it was my ears that were nervous. Every other part of me was.

"It's going to clear up soon," he said. "Zero accumulation."

"That's a pretty cool super-power. I didn't realize wolves were so in tune with the weather."

"Oh, did I forget to mention the werewolf's natural born ability to watch the Weather Channel?" For the record, Alex's dimples were clearly visible when he smirked. "It's our most prized talent."

I am an idiot.

"Are you pouting?" he asked when I chose not to respond.

"No," I lied. I couldn't bring myself to look at him, so I tilted my head back and watched as glittery white flakes tumbled down from a black sky. My eyes rested on a clump of greenery wound around a high limb just seconds before Alex asked, "What is that?"

"What is what?" I could feel every nerve in my body buzz to life and hoped he hadn't notice my hands were shaking. I felt ridiculous for letting a ball of weeds get me so riled up.

"That green stuff. Is it..."

"Phoradendron serotinum?"

"...mistletoe?"

"Yes. Mistletoe." It was only two words, but it took all my mental facilities to get them out.

"Are you sure?"

I nodded my head in confirmation.

"Mistletoe on a snowy Christmas night." Alex gently grabbed my chin and tilted it so I was looking at him. "It seems I'm under a certain obligation here."

I just sat there like a statue, too nervous to breathe. Alex leaned in slowly, pausing once our noses were in tickling distance. "I'm going to kiss you now, Scout, unless you do something to stop me."

I leaned in.

His kiss was soft, tentative, and way too short for my liking. It sent electrical jolts through my body that left me wanting more. My lips reached out for a second kiss and his eagerly complied, moving against mine until I was lightheaded.

"Hi," Alex said, his forehead resting against mine as his hands explored my face.

"Hey," I replied before giving him a quick peck on his upper lip. "I'm glad you're back."

Chapter 11

The remainder of my Christmas vacation was uneventful and frustrating. I knew Jase had been made aware of the Coles' return when he became grouchy and sullen. Charlie spent a lot of time at our house, but I rarely saw him. He and Jase spent most of their time locked in Jase's room. On more than one occasion I heard the undeniable sounds of a quiet argument through my bedroom wall. I tried to listen in, even attempting the old hold-a-glass-to-the-wall routine, but never heard anything of interest.

When school finally started back, my reunion with Alex didn't go quite how I imagined it. He didn't stride into Mr. Beck's class, give me a slow smile, and tell me he missed me. In fact, he didn't look at me at all. Of course, we were supposed to be flying under the radar. He couldn't exactly wrap an arm around my waist and lead me to the theater for our Shakespeare class. So I was okay with fact that he talked to everyone except me, explaining that the situation with his relatives hadn't worked out. I wasn't jealous that other girls could hug him and say how happy they were he was back. It was cool. I could handle it.

However, I could not handle seeing Ashley Johnson pressed up against him, her finger trailing slowly down his chest.

That was not cool.

What the Hades was he doing? How could he just stand there with her like that after everything we shared? After the way he kissed me? It had been over a week and I could still remember the way he tasted. Had Christmas night meant more to me than him?

"What's your problem?" Talley asked, situating herself in the seat beside mine.

"What makes you think I have a problem?" I rooted furiously through my purse for a writing utensil. All of my pens and pencils apparently had been spirited away by goblins.

"You normally don't terrorize poor Tori just for fun."

"All I did was ask her to move."

"You told her to get the hell out of your way and looked at her like you would enjoy ripping her still-beating heart from her chest. I think she may have wet herself."

I looked over where Tori Alyson stood clustered with a group of her artsy friends. When she saw me looking, she let out a tiny whimper and quickly averted her eyes.

Good grief.

"Must you always be so intimidating?"

"I'm intimidating?"

"That is the general consensus," Alex answered. He was standing just inches away, waiting for me to let him pass.

I refused to acknowledge him. I wasn't about to be deluded yet again by the gleam in his eye or the quirk of his lips.

How did Alex respond to my aloofness? He stepped on my toes. I cursed my body for responding so enthusiastically when he grabbed onto me for support as he stumbled.

"I'm sorry," he said, face level with mine. He squeezed my knee, and I knew he wasn't just apologizing for assaulting my feet.

I briefly considered withholding my forgiveness for a bit longer. "Just don't let it happen again. Ever."

His fingers lightly brushed against my arm as he righted himself. "Scout's honor."

And thus began what I liked to think of as the Secret Relationship Game. The premise was very simple: The contestants were to have as much contact with the other player as humanly possible, while making sure everyone else believed them completely indifferent. The major plays included brief but meaningful eye contact; the accidentally-on-purpose brushing of fingers, arms, or any other reasonable body part; and an obsessive number of text messages, e-mails, and even old-fashioned, unsigned notes in the locker. Occasionally, Alex and I would reach a bonus round and find ourselves alone in the theater prop room, media supply alcove, or even the janitor's closet. The bonus rounds featured frenzied kisses, eager hands, and the abject fear someone would open the door or notice our swollen lips and mussed hair.

To someone who has never actually played the Secret Relationship Game, it might sound fun and romantic. At times, it was. But it was also heartbreakingly difficult. Every touch and kiss made me aware of how few I received and left me aching for more. We wrote back and forth to each other constantly, but I longed for a conversation. Mrs. Sole hadn't felt the need to resume the point/counter-point articles, so we didn't even have afternoons at the library together anymore.

And then there was the constant threat of being discovered. When I thought about how much was at risk, I hated myself for letting it continue. How could I be willing to risk Alex's life for a few stolen kisses? Every night I would resolve to break it off. Then, the next day, I would show up in Calculus and there he would be, looking at me without looking at me, and I couldn't do it. I wanted him. It was reckless and stupid, but I wanted him. I couldn't just give him up and walk away.

I wished on the first star of every evening for just one day to be with Alex, to talk and laugh together without having to look over our shoulder. After five weeks, my vigilance paid off.

It was a Saturday morning, which meant that I was curled onto the couch, a behemoth bowl of Cap'n Crunch perched on one knee, and Toon Disney on the TV. I was trying to helpfully point out to the endearing Dr. Doofenshmirtz that Perry Platypus was once again breaking free of his constraints and about to ruin yet another brilliant plan when someone started pounding on my front door. I hit "Pause" on the DVR and sat my half-eaten bowl of cereal on the coffee table. I was certain it was Mr. Roberts from down the road. He had a tendency to start long conversations that would begin with the weather, end with his first wife's infidelity, and hit every single topic in between. My yummy breakfast would be inedible mush before he could segue from rainfall averages to last year's tobacco crop.

"Just a minute," I called out, instantly feeling guilty for the irritation in my voice. I was supposed to be working on being more sympathetic. Mr. Roberts was a sweet man; he was just lonely. I should at least try to be nice.

I forced my face into a pleasant, friendly smile and yanked open the door.

"Well, someone is happy to see me," Alex said, looking for all the world as if he belonged on my front porch. He noted my ensemble -- hair that hung in two sloppy braids, unicorn themed pajamas, and a pair of pink and yellow stripped toe socks — with a smirk. "Good morning, Beautiful."

"What are you doing here?" My eyes darted wildly around the yard as if they expected to find Toby hiding behind a tree.

"Aren't you happy to see me?"

Of course I was happy to see him. Ecstatic even. I was also scared to death. "The treaty, Alex. I'm pretty sure you being here is in direct violation of that."

He somehow managed to make a shrug look smug. "What the Hagans don't know—"

"Won't get you killed?"

"Stop being so melodramatic. No one is going to murder me today, although I may freeze to death standing on your front porch..." He looked at me expectantly.

I could have left him out there. I *should* have left him out there. And told him to go away. And explained that I wasn't really worth all the trouble. Of course, I did none of those things.

There was something about seeing Alex standing in my foyer, leaned up against the kitschy antique table my mom bought at a flea market, that seemed right.

"So, why did I have to hear that Jase's parents were taking him to speak with a recruiting coach in Louisville this weekend from Tinsley Henson?" he asked.

"I didn't realize you were interested in my brother's college career."

"I'm not. Unlike the rest of Western Kentucky, I couldn't care less which school your brother goes to. I do care that you have this house to yourself all weekend." It took two short steps for him to reach me. His hands rested on my hips as my arms automatically wound around his neck. "I thought you might like some company."

I was going to tell him that he had his information wrong, but my lips were too busy doing something else. If I had mentioned it, perhaps Alex wouldn't have bit my tongue when he heard my name being yelled from the top of the stairs.

"Ouch!" I yelped. His teeth were sharp.

Alex's eyes were wide. "You're not alone?"

"No, Angel is here." My tongue throbbed slightly. "I'm not going to turn into a werewolf now, am I?" Dr. Smith's book, which I read from cover to cover three times, said that lycanthropy, the ability to turn into a wolf, couldn't be passed through biting, but I needed to be reassured.

"Shifters are born, not made."

At that moment my little sister appeared in the archway that led from the foyer to the kitchen. She was prepared to launch into a full-on whine about something or another, but then she realized that we had company.

"Alex!" she shrieked, running at him.

"Angel!" He lifted her up and gave her a giant bear hug, complete with a growl. It was like watching the climatic reunion at the end of one of those movies where the kid has been separated from her family because she was off on some grand adventure involving a dog or talking gerbil. Only, in real life, it managed to be even more annoying.

"Alex came by to pick up some Shakespeare notes," I said. "He was just leaving."

He sat her back down and rested one of his hands atop of her cow-licked head. "Leave? No! I haven't seen him in a million billion years!" Her sky-colored eyes blinked slowly twice as the corners of her mouth pulled down and inward, causing her bottom lip to jut out slightly. The patented Angel Donovan puppy dog face. "Can't you stay for a little while? Pleeeeeeease?"

There was no doubt that he would cave. It takes years of practice to resist the puppy dog face, with even the most seasoned of us still succumbing on occasion. "I think I could stay for a little bit longer."

"I don't think that's a good idea," I said, interrupting Angel's squeal of delight.

"Why not?"

"You know why not."

She thought about it for a minute. "Well, Jase isn't here. He won't know."

The quirk of Alex's mouth said, *My point exactly.*

"And what about when he gets home and finds out?"

My little sister placed her hands on her hips and cocked her head to the side in a familiar stance. "I'm not going to tell him. Are you?"

"Of course not."

"Good." Her victorious smile was mirrored on Alex's face. "C'mon, Alex. I want to show you something."

Angel led Alex through the house, giving him a tour of the mundane lives of the Donovan family. I tried to excuse myself to go change clothes, but Alex wasn't having it. He tugged on one of my braids and told me that he was developing a newfound fondness for unicorns when I suggested it.

After a full inventory of the first level of our house, Angel marched him up the stairs to the first door on the right. "This is my room," she said, hand on the knob.

"You don't want to go in there," I warned.

"I'm tough. I think I can handle whatever a seven year old girl can dish out."

"Suit yourself." I positioned myself against the furthest wall and waited for the show to start. It didn't take long. There was a horrid yowl followed by an almost-scream. A second later, a white blur flew out the door and down the stairs. My sister followed as fast as her little legs would carry her. When I turned back, Alex was filling the doorway.

"She has a cat," he said, rubbing an angry red mark on his neck.

"Yes, she does."

"Cats hate Shifters."

"I figured that out already." I pulled myself off the wall and took a step towards him.

"You could have warned me." He took a step into the hall.

"I told you that you didn't want to go in there." I closed the distance between us. "Is your neck okay?"

"I think it needs a kiss to make it all better."

I placed my lips just below his ear, letting his warmth and smell envelop me.

"What are you doing?" Angel's voice was like a shock of cold water.

"I was looking at the scratch your evil cat left on Alex's neck. We'll be lucky if he doesn't come down with Cat Scratch Fever."

"You were looking at his neck with your mouth?"

Crap.

She might be able to keep the news of an unexpected visitor to herself, but catching me making out with my brother's archnemisis in the hallway? She would tell anyone and everyone that would listen.

Crap, crap, crap.

I searched my brain for something - an explanation, a bribe, a diversion - anything that might salvage the situation.

"Do you want some brownies?"

Brownies? Yeah, that one so wasn't going to work.

"We have brownies?"

Or maybe it was.

"We have a box of brownie mix. I'll make them for you."

A look very akin to horror etched itself onto Angel's face. "You want to *cook* me brownies?"

"Sure I do. It'll be fun."

"I thought you were supposed to be a total zeppo in the kitchen," Alex said. He had propped himself against Angel's door frame with one long arm. He was the picture of ease, whereas I was bordering on a complete breakdown.

"I can make brownies from a box," I said, my tone a bit harsher than necessary. Couldn't he at least pretend to care that we were in serious trouble here?

"But you'll burn them," Angel whined. "You always burn everything. Even toast."

I was about to lose my cool. The idea of fratricide wasn't totally unappealing. Mercifully, Alex jumped to Angel's rescue.

"It just so happens that not only am I incredibly good looking, but I'm also an expert brownie maker," he said. "Although, I'll need some help."

Alex and Angel did not follow the directions on the box. When I attempted to point this out, Alex informed me that cooking was an art and he was an artist that didn't do paint-by-numbers. I could only assume that he considered following the tried-and-true instructions that would produce fudgey brownie goodness paint-by-number.

"How about these?" Angel asked, holding up a half-empty bag of semi-sweet chocolate chips and a similar package of peanut butter chips.

Alex squirted some chocolate syrup into the batter as he considered. "What are your feelings on peanut butter, Scout?"

"Peanut butter chips are not part of the directions," I said, gesturing with the empty blue box.

"Do you always have to follow the rules?"

"*Always,*" my ever-helpful little sister answered for me. "And she loves peanut butter."

After adding in at least ten different unsanctioned ingredients, the cooks/mad scientists declared their creation ready for the oven. We sat around the kitchen, listening to Angel detail all the first grade drama as an intoxicating smell filled the room. Alex held my hand under the table, his thumb tracing circles on mine.

The brownies were better than I ever believed food could be. We didn't even cut them into squares. Alex sat the entire pan in the middle of the table with three spoons. I was entrusted to pour glasses of milk,

I caught Angel sniffing her glass to make sure it was okay before taking a drink.

Conversation lulled as we stuffed our faces. With the exception of the occasional, "Yum," "Oh my God," "This is good," or moan, the table was silent. I was aware that Angel had been staring intently at Alex, but thought nothing of it. She had never been secretive when it came to her affection for him.

I should have realized what was coming. I should have looked at the situation from her point of view and remembered that God put little sisters on this earth expressively to torture their siblings.

She asked with the same casualness that someone might ask if you would pass something across the table or how your day at school went, but she didn't want the salt or to know about a surprise pop quiz in English. Instead, she asked Alex, "Are you in love with my sister?"

Chapter 12

A glob of brownie landed on my chest. Shock had made me forget how to feed myself.

"Is it that obvious?" Alex looked only slight abashed.

"You have googly eyes when you look at her." Angel's didactic tone and wise expression would have been humorous if I had been capable of finding anything entertaining. "Boys only get googly eyes when they're in love."

"The eyes always give it away." The two of them nodded sagely at one another. Alex's attention stayed on Angel's face, which meant that he couldn't see the way embarrassment colored my own. Of course, the fact that his neck was battling my cheeks for the reddest thing in the room made me feel a little bit better.

"She likes you too," Angel continued.

"Are you sure?"

"Definitely. When you're around she actually smiles instead of looking like this all the time." Angel puckered her lips, scrunched up her nose, and squinted her eyes.

"I do not walk around looking like I've been eating lemons." Really, where did she come up with this stuff?

Angel ignored me. "And she was sucking on your neck like a vampire. That means she *really* likes you."

Every drop of blood in my body was pooled in my face and the massive amount of brownies I ate threatened to make a reappearance. I barely heard Alex ask, "Scout, what are you doing?" over the roar in my ears.

"Waiting for the ground to open up and swallow me." My words were slightly muffled by the thick oak table I had planted my face down on.

"So, is that a sign that she likes me or doesn't like me?" I swear I could actually hear him smiling.

"Ummm....that just means she's weird." I lifted my head to glare at her. "See," she said, "lemon face,"

The two of them proceeded to discuss the finer points of my lemon face and what activities were most likely to trigger it. When I could no longer keep my expression smooth and un-lemony, I fled the kitchen in the most dignified manner possible.

Alex was immediately by my side. "Hey, you're not mad, are you?"

Yes, I am, thank you very much. "No."

"She's lying," Angel said from somewhere behind me.

Alex dropped his head and peered at me through his eyelashes. "I'm sorry if we hurt your feelings." He captured my fingers in his hand. "I think your lemon face is adorable, and I like that you only smile for me."

"Are you going to kiss her now?" Angel was practically standing on top of us with a look that could only be described as lemon-like. "I don't like mushy stuff."

"No mushy stuff, huh?" Alex stepped back, but left one finger hooked around mine. "Is holding hands mushy?"

Angel mulled it over. "A little bit, but it's okay if you're at the movies."

"How about watching a movie on TV?"

"I guess that would be okay."

Alex grinned. "In that case, I'm very much in the mood to watch a movie."

***

Watching *Toy Story* for the hundredth time gave me the opportunity to get over my humiliation and think. Alex Cole had said that he loved me. Okay, it wasn't like he looked into my eyes and actually said the words out loud, but he hadn't contradicted Angel. What did that mean? Could he really be in love with me?

What was I thinking? Of course he wasn't in love with me. He was Alex Cole, for the love of all things shiny. Alex Cole who had a face that belonged on the cover of a magazines. Alex Cole who had a body that made college girls stop and stare. Alex Cole who actually understood what was going on in AP Calc and genuinely enjoyed Shakespeare. Alex Cole who probably smiled in his sleep and was nice to absolutely everyone, even my bratty little sister. How could a boy like that be in love with me? At best, I was awkward and plain, though most days I came across as anti-social and freakish.

"Scout?" Alex squeezed my hand, snapping me out of my why-is-Alex-the-Awesome-holding-hands-with-Scout-the-Freak quandary. He motioned towards the end of the couch where Angel lay like a discarded porcelain doll - head lolled to the side, arms and legs scattered about, her unruly curls spilled out in every direction. Sleeping, she actually looked like her namesake. "So, I was thinking," he said, his voice a husky whisper. "I never did get to finish my tour of the house."

I was temporarily confused, but when his eyebrows raised mischievously I caught on.

As I led Alex into my room my stomach gave a familiar you-are-breaking-the-rules lurch. My parents didn't have Mrs. Matthews' strict No Boys Allowed in the Bedroom EVER rule, it's kind of pointless with Jase and Charlie around, but I knew they would consider this a no-no.

"So, this is my room," I said, kicking a pile of dirty laundry under the bed. "As you can see, I'm a clean freak."

Alex stopped just inside the door to examine a picture that hung on the wall. Dad had snapped it at the lake several summers ago. I was sitting on a picnic table with Angel, a toddler at the time, in my lap. She was waving with one hand and pulling my hair with the other. Talley sat on my right, an ice cream cone dripping down her hand. Jase and Charlie were on my left, giving each other bunny ears. We had spent the day swimming in the muddy water under a hot sun, so we looked a bit grimy, but we were happy. You could almost feel the perfect day vibe coming off the picture.

"How old were you here?"

"It was right before my thirteenth birthday. I think it may have actually been Jase's family celebration."

He moved on, carefully examining every picture and poster that hung on the wall. Thankfully, Zac Effron had recently been replaced by a print of Van Gogh's *Cafe Terrace*. When he paused in front of my bookshelf to read titles I felt a familiar warmth return to my face.

"This isn't what I was expecting," he finally admitted.

I grabbed a stack of library books, all urban fantasy titles, and shuffled them off to my desk. "It looks like you've got quite the supernatural fetish," he said, thumbing through a stack that was out of my reach.

"It's research," I said. "Even fiction can be full of useful facts. I've learned a lot from these books." Mostly I had learned I was somewhat addicted to mildly trashy novels that had the ability to make me blush.

"Really?" Alex pulled out a Laurell K Hamilton paperback. "And what exactly did you learn from this one?"

My face was giving off enough heat to melt the polar ice caps. "Nothing." At least it was nothing I could repeat out loud. I snatched the book out his hands before he could flip through the pages and find out exactly what that nothing was. Alex just chuckled and continued his survey of my stuff.

After making a full lap around the room, he sat on the edge of my unmade bed and plucked something from the tangle of covers. "Hiding a man in your bed? I must say, I'm quite shocked, Miss Donovan."

"Alex, meet Guido. Guido, Alex." I flopped down next to him. "Guido and I have been falling asleep in each other's arms for years."

Alex examined the battered old sock monkey. "I can see why. He certainly is handsome." In truth, Guido has seen better days. Mom, who isn't much of a seamstress, has performed various surgeries to stitch up arms, mend holes, and even reattach eyes over the years. He may have been ugly, but I loved him all the same.

"Mom took Jase shopping one day when he was two," I said. "She and Dad weren't married yet, so it had to have been either late summer or early fall. Anyways, they go into the toy store and Jase starts pointing at this sock monkey and saying 'Scout' over and over. Mom tried to explain that his soon-to-be sister was not a monkey, but he threw a major tantrum. She ended up buying the thing just so people wouldn't call Child Protection Services.

"He carried it through the mall and all the way home. Anytime Mom tried to take it from him he would tell her, 'No, Scout.' That night he brought it with him to the apartment Dad and I were living in. As soon as he came through the door he ran over, handed me Guido, and said, 'For you.'" I reached over and patted Guido's head. "I've slept with him practically every night since."

"That could be the sweetest story I've ever heard. I think I may have a new cavity." He had been shooting for indifferent and deadpan, but dimples and dry sarcasm don't go together all that well.

"Shut up. Like your brother hasn't ever done anything sappy to show you that he loves you."

"You've met my brother, right?"

He had a point. I couldn't exactly picture Liam being all warm and cuddly.

"But he's a good big brother, isn't he?" It was obvious that Alex adored and respected Liam. Surely he had done something to deserve it. Then again, we were talking about Alex. He would probably find redeeming qualities in Hitler.

"The best." He said it in a way that left no room for argument. "He's just not big on the Hallmark moments."

"It must be hard," I mused out loud, "for the two of you to be on your own without parents."

All the emotion drained from Alex's face. "We do fine."

I was at a loss as to where to go from there. It seemed like every time I tried to broach the subject of Alex's parents, he shut down. It was impossible to keep the conversation going. I felt completely inept at being alone with him as he sat with his elbows on his knees, scrutinizing Guido, who was still clutched in his hands.

"You're staring at me."

I dropped my eyes and muttered an embarrassed "sorry". Warm fingers glided under my chin, lifting my face to his.

"I wasn't complaining," he said. "Guido, however, was getting a little jealous. I thought you should know."

"Just a little jealous?" It was slowly occurring to me that I was alone with Alex in my bedroom. "I think we can do better than that." With one hand I tossed Guido onto the bed while the other pulled Alex's mouth to mine. I had only a second to be shocked by my sudden forward behavior before his lips parted under mine, pushing away all doubt and fear.

It was the first time we didn't have to worry about someone opening the door or a broom handle jabbing me in the side. Our kisses were slower and sweeter. My hands lazily trailed over his face, neck, and arms, marveling at the smoothness of his skin and tautness of his muscles. When he pushed me back against the pillows I froze up in a moment of panic. "Just kissing," he assured me. His breath was warm and moist on my ear. "Clothes stay on. Promise."

And he kept his promise, even after I decided it was a stupid one to make. When it got to the point I thought I might actually burst into flames he rolled over beside me, allowing me to finally catch my breath.

"You remember before? In the kitchen, when Angel asked me if I was in love with you?" His voice was lower, rougher than normal.

The sound of it made parts of my body that I didn't realize were voice-activated come to life.

"Uh-huh," was all I was capable of in way of response. Too much of my energy was needed to keep myself from pulling him back onto me.

"I realized that I never really answered that question." He propped himself up on his elbow and looked down at me.

God, he was beautiful.

"Oh?" I wondered if I would ever be capable of intelligent speech again. It seemed that since my tongue had found more entertaining activities it wasn't going to do something so mundane as assist me with the whole talking thing.

"I thought you should know that the answer is yes. I love you, Scout."

"You can't be in love with me," I heard myself say, my rebellious mouth finally deciding to work.

His posture went from lounging to bracing without much in the way of movement. "I can't?"

"You barely know me," I said. "I'm just the coyote's sister you're supposed to stay away from. I get the whole 'forbidden fruit' attraction, but that's not love. If Toby hadn't told you to leave me alone, you wouldn't have given me a second glance. You would have realized what a loser I am a long time ago."

It broke my heart to say everything I had been thinking out loud. I didn't want him to realize I was unworthy of his affection, but things were going too far. We were both going to end up hurt if it didn't end soon.

"You are not a loser."

"Oh, I promise you, I am. I have a very long list of character references that will be happy to confirm that for you."

"And I'm not just with you because you're 'forbidden'." The back of his fingers grazed my jaw line. "I know exactly who you are, and I love you."

"How?" I was desperate for him to convince me, for it to be true.

Alex raised himself into a sitting position in a move so quick and graceful that a normal human wouldn't have been able to achieve it. "Did you know that I'm a dream walker?"

I too sat up, though much more slowly and awkwardly than he had. "I thought only females were Seers." I also thought that we were talking about our relationship.

"I'm not a Seer. Sometimes a strong line of Seers can produce a male that has some extra talents. I can't do any of that cool brain talking stuff, but sometimes I can See things when I'm asleep."

We were facing each other, my hand on his knee, his braceleting my ankle. "What sort of things?"

One side of his mouth tugged upwards and his eyes shone brightly. "I was eight years old the first time it happened. In the dream there was an apple tree full of little green apples. The air was heavy and sweet smelling, the summer sun suffocatingly hot.

"A couple of kids around my age were playing. I tried to talk to them, but they didn't hear or see me.

"On one of the high branches was this huge, perfect apple. It was at least twice the size of any of the others. One of the girls was determined to get it. She climbed up to the top and crawled slowly out to the edge. Her hand closed on it just as the branch snapped and threw her to the ground.

"I ran over, thinking that I could help. Her arm was laying at a funny angle, and she was trying hard not to scream. I told her that it was going to be okay, that one of the boys had already gone to get help, but it did no good. I wasn't really there."

Alex's thumb ran over my wrist, tracing the scars where the doctor had put pins in to hold the bones in place. "I forced my mom to help me look for you the next day. I knew that if I looked hard enough, I would find you, even though Mom kept saying there were no apple trees anywhere near our house."

"You saw me break my arm?" It was impossible, yet he described it just as it happened. Jase had bet me I couldn't pick the big apple at the top, and I was determined to prove that I could. Talley begged me to climb down, but I was stubborn. After I fell, Jase ran back home to get Dad while Charlie and Talley stayed with me. I broke both my radius and ulna and had to wear an itchy cast for months.

"I've been dreaming of you for ten years," he said. "I could never remember what anyone else looked like, or very many details about the location, but your face and voice have always been perfectly clear."

"That's..." *crazy? sweet? creepy?* "impossible."

Alex smiled. "Shall I prove it?"

Part of me didn't want him to. The whole thing was freaking me out a little. What all had he seen? What did it mean that he dreamt of me? I was terrified of the answer, but I had to know.

He nodded towards the picture by my door. "I remember that day. There was a vine hanging from a tree that the others were using to swing out over the lake and jump into the water. You didn't want to do it because you're scared of heights."

"Falling from the top of an apple tree can do that to a girl," I said.

"Somehow they managed to talk you into trying it. You were shaking like a leaf, but you did it anyway." A grin nearly split his face in two. I covered my face in horror, knowing what was coming next. "You were so proud of yourself when you came up out of the water you didn't immediately realize that you had lost the top of your swimsuit."

"Oh. My. God." Mom had wrapped a towel around me before I knew what was happening. Jase had laughed so hard I thought, or perhaps hoped, he would rupture something. He didn't stop until Charlie pantsed him to "even the score". "I cannot believe you saw that."

"Are you kidding? That was one of the best nights of my life!"

136

"So, you've been enjoying a gag reel of my most embarrassing moments in your sleep for ten years?"

"Not just the embarrassing ones. I've seen you laugh and cry and grow into a beautiful, amazing person." His eyes, full of sincerity, were locked onto mine. "By the time I was eleven I knew I was in love with you. I was always eager to go to sleep. The mornings that I woke up without having seen you were beyond disappointing. I memorized every detail of you, from the arch of your eyebrows to the way you tilt your head and stare off into space when you're really thinking hard. I didn't know your name or where you lived, but I knew you were real. I knew that you were my destiny."

Since meeting Alex I had my fair share of surreal experiences, but this one was even more astonishing and overwhelming than the others put together. He loved me because I was his destiny? That seemed like an awful big expectation to meet.

"Did you move here to find me?" I couldn't imagine it - packing up and moving across the country to find someone you had only met in a dream.

"No, we moved..." He paused as if unsure of how to continue. "We were moving south, with no clear cut destination. Liam's Jeep broke down on the side of the Interstate. While we were waiting for it to be fixed we decided this was as good of a place as any to stay. National forests offer an ideal place for Shifters to run and hunt.

"I have no idea how I managed to not see you come into Beck's class. I wasn't paying attention to anything going on in that room until I heard your voice putting that bastard in his place." Obviously, he remembered my exchange with our Calculus teacher a bit differently than I did. "I turned around and there you were. I thought I had found you so many times before, but this time there was no doubt. I had literally found the girl of my dreams."

I replayed the first day of school in my head, trying to see it from his point of view. "And she was rude and her brother picked a fight with you."

"Well, it didn't exactly go how I had planned it. I acted like such a moron, just standing there, staring at you as if you were suddenly going to leap into my arms and kiss me. It never even occurred to me that to you I was a complete stranger

"Then, when I saw you with another Shifter in the cafeteria, I realized things were going to be a bit more complicated than I had anticipated. And, of course, your attitude towards me in the beginning was a bit disheartening." He said it with a smile, as if it were no big deal, but I felt bad all the same.

"I guess I was bit of a disappointment, huh?"

"The situation was disappointing. It still is." He pushed my hair behind my ear, and I leaned into his hand. "But you're not a disappointment. You're even more amazing than I thought you would be." His lips met mine once again. It felt as if a soft warm light spread from my mouth to the top of my head, tips of my fingers, and all the way down to my toes. When his tongue reached out to taste my lower lip, the light turned into a searing heat, melting all the bones from my body.

He pulled away from me slowly and I let my eyes drink in his flushed cheeks, swollen lips, and fiery gaze. "I love you," he said again, causing my heart to swell to the point of bursting.

I was going to say it back. I should have, but as I opened my mouth, I caught sight of Charlie's face staring back at me from a picture frame sitting on my bedside table and the words got stuck in my throat.

Chapter 13

That night I found Angel reclining in her bed against a mountain of frilly pink pillows. Elf rested on her lap until I came through the door. The sight of me sent him scurrying underneath a dresser at the far end of the room where he proceeded to hiss out a stream of vulgarities.

"Did Alex go home?"

"Yep. He told me to tell you goodnight. Again." The two of them had shared a ridiculously long exchange of "goodnights" in fake British accents before I made Angel go to bed.

I went over and sat on the edge of her bed, praying I wouldn't break it. Everything in Angel's room is tiny, pink, and orderly. "You had fun today, didn't you?"

She nodded her head, blond curls bouncing every which way. "Those brownies were so good. I think it was the candy bar that really did it. Next time I'm going to use a Snickers to see what that tastes like."

I was living with a three foot tall Martha Stewart.

"And you like Alex, right?"

"Alex is my friend. He's nice."

I took a deep breath and lowered myself so that we were eye level. I had to make sure she understood. "If you want to be a good friend to Alex, you're going to have to promise to never, ever, *ever* tell anyone that he was here today."

"Scout, I can keep a secret."

"But this is a big secret. An important one." One that probably shouldn't have been entrusted to a first grader, but it was a little late for that.

"I've kept big, important secrets before."

"Like what?" Knowing her it would be that her best friend, Kinsey Jessup, still watched *Dora the Explorer*.

Angel gave a dramatic sigh and eye roll that she had to have picked up from Jase. "If I told you, they wouldn't be secrets anymore."

How could I have gotten into a situation where so much depended upon my little sister's ability to keep her mouth shut? I should have sent Alex home the moment I found him on my front porch.

"Angel listen..." I closed my eyes and ran through the color spectrum in my head, a trick I picked up during Talley's New Age phase. "Alex means a lot to me," I finally said. "If anyone found out that he was here or that...you know..."

"You kiss him?"

"Yeah, that. If anyone found out about that I might...*we* might...never get to see him again. He would have to move really far away." Or worse.

She stretched out her arm and locked her little finger around mine to signify the most solemn vow a seven year old could make. "I won't tell anyone. Pinky-promise."

I didn't doubt her sincerity, but I did doubt her ability to follow through. Every time she opened her mouth during those next few days I kept expecting the truth to come tumbling out, but it never did. It was as if she had forgotten it had ever happened. Eventually I started to believe that she had.

Turns out, though, that my sister is just really good at keeping secrets. So good, in fact, that I had no idea what she was up to when she asked me to take her to Landing Park the following Thursday.

Lake County has more parks than people. You can't drive five miles down any given road without seeing one of those ugly brown

Corps of Engineering signs proclaiming some random field a recreation area. Most of the spots had picnic tables housed in shiny pavilions, state-of-the-art playground equipment, and other sparkly things to attract all the summer tourists. Landing Park was not one of those recreation areas. It boasted two swings, one of which had been broken since I was a kid, a rusted slide, and a wooden picnic table missing two planks. No one, with the exception of drug dealers, ever went there.

"This place is a dump," I told my sister as we walked up the gravel path. I had my hand on her shoulder, steering her along so that she didn't step on any jagged beer bottle shards interlaced with the rocks. "There is only one swing, and a slide that I'm not letting you get on without a tetanus shot."

Ignoring me, as per usual, Angel skipped over to the lone swing and hopped on. I set up station at the crumbled picnic table, where I attempted to keep frostbite from forming on my fingers. Five minutes later, just as I was ready to declare Crappy Park Fun Day over, a car came winding down the drive.

Angel reached the faded red Toyota before Alex could even get his door open.

"What are you doing here?" I asked when I finally reached them.

Alex quit spinning Angel around in circles and sat her back on the ground. She giggled as she stumbled around like a drunkard. "Ummm....you told me to meet you here?"

"Like in a dream?"

"Like with a text message."

We stared at each other in confusion for a long minute.

"Can I see your phone?" I finally asked.

Alex's inbox had messages from "Liam", "Ash" (messages I didn't read, which makes me a saint), and "Boo", who I had to assume was me. I clicked on the message with a 3:17 time stamp.

"Meet me @ Landeen Park in 1 hour."

"You thought I would misspell 'Landing'?" That bothered me more than the fact that I hadn't been the one to send the message.

"It was a text. No one uses correct spelling when they text." He took the phone from me, brow furrowed. "If you didn't send it, who did?"

I could only think of one person with both access and motivation. I walked over to where my sister was spinning around with her arms stretched out to her sides. "Angel, did you steal my phone?"

"I *borrowed* it," she said, picking up speed.

"Why did you tell Alex to meet us here?"

She finally stopped spinning and promptly tumbled onto her butt. "Cause no one ever comes out here. We can all hang out and no one will ever know. It's like having a secret club."

Not for the first time, I thought that my little sister had all the makings to be an evil genius.

The Pretty Purple Unicorn Club, named by President and Founder Angela Sophia Donovan, met as often as possible. We would talk while Alex pushed Angel in the swing or as we walked the woodland trails, Angel riding on Alex's back. When it was time to leave, Angel would graciously go wait in the car so Alex and I could have a few minutes alone. I found my affection for both the ruinous park and my little sister growing.

By the time March rolled around I was in a state of perpetual bliss. I had an amazing boyfriend who completely adored me. Okay, so he was a secret boyfriend who I couldn't be seen with in public, but thanks to Angel we got to spend several afternoons a week together. I was coming into the home stretch of my Senior year, and the homework was already starting to slack off. Calculus was even becoming easier, or at least I was starting to understand nearly half of what Mr. Beck said. And Toby had followed through with the private lessons. Every Friday I would drive down to the Base and allow Charlie's sadistic big brother to torture me. It was great. I felt stronger and more capable than ever.

After one particularly punishing session Toby left me to do repetitions with the bag as my penance for losing yet another sparring match. The front door was left open to let in the first warm, Spring-like day of the year. The breeze that wafted in smelled of rain and dirt. My iPod was cranked up, filling my ears with ass-kicking appropriate music. It wasn't long before I decided to throw form out the window and started adding a few hip shakes and shimmies to my routine. I completed a rather beautifully executed round-house kick and twirled around a couple of times, planning to hit my second imaginary opponent with a right hook. Instead, I collided into a rather solid chest.

I let out a girly yelp and would have fallen down if two strong hands hadn't caught my shoulders and held me in place.

"Who are you and what have you done with my Scout, the one who doesn't dance?" Charlie was standing so close I could smell his cinnamon flavored gum.

I stepped back, wondering how fast my heart could beat before it completely gave out. "That wasn't dancing. It was a new variant of Kenpo." Lying was much preferable to admitting that I had actually been attempting to dance. Everyone knew that when it came to getting a groove on, I was a complete lost cause. For all my supposed grace, I'm a disaster on the dance floor. Want someone to execute a perfect butterfly kick or walk the narrowest of balance beams? I'm your girl. Just don't ask me to mambo or whatever. Talley, who dances like freaking Ginger Rogers despite her size, thinks it's because I'm too much of a control freak to let myself go and move with the music.

Personally, I think that is ridiculous. My theory - that my hips are somehow misaligned and therefore won't work right - makes much more sense.

Of course, when it comes to Charlie and Jase and their incessant teasing, the reason didn't matter. All they care about is getting as much entertainment at my expense as possible.

"A variant of Kenpo, huh?" Charlie cocked an eyebrow at me, which was only mildly sexy. "I didn't realize that Bob Fosse ever contributed to the martial arts."

"You know, Chuck, it takes a very confident man to make a Bob Fosse reference."

"Are you questioning my manliness, Miss Donovan? Because I'm quite capable of proving to you what a strong manly man I am."

I pulled up one corner of my mouth in a smirk. "As if you could take me."

Charlie crouched down and began snapping his fingers as he circled me.

"Fosse and West Side Story. What's next? Do you want to get a manicure and talk about your feelings?" I teased, snapping along as the Shark to his Jet. Or maybe I was the Jet and he was the Shark.

I stepped to the right just as he lunged for me. My left leg snapped out to sweep his feet out from under him.

"Is that seriously all you've got?" I asked as he landed on the mat. I held out my hand to help him up. "I was really expecting a bit more of a fight out of you."

He may not have heard the last few words since I was flying through the air as I said them. I rolled as I hit the mat, narrowly avoiding being penned by Charlie. We were both on our feet in a matter of seconds.

When it came to fighting, Charlie relied more on strength than speed and agility. He also tended to hold back, grossly underestimating my abilities. For a few minutes I fought in a style that mimicked his own, lulling him into believed that he would be able to best me. Then, as he was delivering a right punch, I surprised him by stepping towards him, instead of backing away. My right leg snaked around and caught him behind the knees. The plan had been for him to go down. It hadn't included me sprawled underneath him on the mat, but somehow I ended up there anyway.

"Now, who is the He-Man?" Charlie put just enough weight on his elbows to keep me from being squished to death.

"You are," I said as a drop of sweat fell from his hair onto my forehead. "You're very masculine and strong and sweaty and gross."

Charlie gave me a look I knew all too well. "Sweaty and gross, huh?" He then proceeded to rub as much of his perspiration on me as possible. It really shouldn't have been the sort of thing that qualified as a turn-on, but there was a part of me that didn't seem to understand that.

"You're not exactly disproving my point," I managed to get out between yelps and giggles.

Charlie quit his assault, but stayed perched above me. All I could see was the mossy green of his eyes. "Tell me what a nice smelling, hygienically superior man I am."

"You know how I feel about lying."

He leaned in closer, which I would have thought impossible until he did it, and playfully growled at me. How did I ever think that noise was a hundred percent human? Heat was radiating off his body. If I didn't know that it was the night before a full moon, I might have thought he had a fever. I wanted to be angry at these obvious signs of his dual nature, of the truth that had been hidden from me. Perhaps I was, but that emotion was eclipsed by a much stronger one.

I lay there, staring up at a face I had know my whole life, and all I could think of was how much and how long I had wanted him. I could feel every spot that our bodies connected - his knees on either side of mine, his hands enclosed around my wrists, the gentle pressure of his right hip against my left. I was frozen in place, unable to speak, move, or look away. Then something in his eyes changed. The pupils dilated as playfulness was erased by something more intense.

"And you know how I feel about her."

My chin reflexively tilted up. The world had narrowed down to the space between Charlie's lips and mine. I wondered how they would feel, how they would taste. They were a bit fuller Alex's lips. Would that make a difference?

145

Alex.

Just like that, the moment was over.

"Let me up." I had been shooting for playful, but from the way Charlie jerked away I'm guessing I failed miserably. "I need to hit the showers and head home," I said quickly, attempting damage control. "Mom is expecting me for dinner."

What was I doing?

I was with Alex. Alex, who, against all odds, loved me. I got caught up in the moment with Charlie, but it wasn't going to happen again.

And who knows how Charlie would have reacted if I followed through? *"And you know how I feel about her."* That could have meant anything. It could have been, *"I feel like she's the sister I never had,"* or *"I feel like she's kind of pathetic and worthy of my sympathy."* Why did I automatically think he meant that he had *feeling* feelings for me? It was ridiculous.

But there was that moment when he had looked at me like he wanted me to kiss him. Like he wanted me.

No. I wasn't going to think about that.

Alex. I was going to think about Alex - the curve of his smile, the smell of his skin. I was going to think about all the ways I didn't deserve him and how I wasn't going to add to that already depressingly long list.

***

The next morning I stumbled my way to the kitchen in dire need of coffee. Most of the time I avoided the stuff. It didn't matter how much sugar, milk, and flavoring I put in, it still tasted bitter and repulsive. But I was dragging from a night of restless sleep. The Alex at the lake dream, which I continued to have on a regular basis, had featured a dark and violent storm. Cold rain soaked my clothes and branches slapped against my skin so savagely I was surprised to find my face and arms unmarked when I woke up. The worst part, though, was knowing that this time it was all my fault. I was the one who caused the storm, the one who was causing Alex, still stuck on the opposite shore, to suffer.

I didn't need Dr. Phil to tell me I was carrying around some guilt for what almost happened with Charlie.

I had a lot of time to think about the whole situation between the hours of three and five that morning since sleep eluded me. The ideal solution would have been for me to stop feeling that way towards Charlie. If I could just have normal, cousin-like feelings towards him the problem would be solved.

I was self-aware enough to realize that wasn't happening.

I had to settle for option number two: Avoid Charlie. I couldn't exactly be almost kissing him if I didn't see him. I reasoned that it would be relatively easy since he went to college hundreds of miles away. It was only the rare holiday or weekend that would require any actual effort.

As I paused outside the kitchen door, I discovered a flaw in my plan.

"She's sure that's where they'll be?" Charlie asked. I could hear him munching on something. Knowing Charlie, it was the last of my Cap'n Crunch. I had half a box left, which translated into Charlie's usual breakfast.

"Yeah, she Saw it the other day," Jase said. He was closer to the door, probably sitting on the kitchen counter. "She narrowed it down to the woods between Pelican Landing and the dock at the end of Chestnut-Oak Drive."

"We'll have to do it right after sundown." I heard something that sounded suspiciously like cereal being poured into a bowl. "Toby will expect us to meet up with him by dawn. He'll be pissed if he finds out what we're up to."

"It'll be worth it if we can get rid of them permanently this time."

No.

No, they couldn't really be talking about doing what I thought they were talking about doing.

But, of course they were. There was only one person - well, two really - that they would be trying to get rid of on the night of a full moon.

My brother was talking about doing something to Alex.

It was a good thing I hadn't eaten any breakfast yet. The way my stomach suddenly dropped would have certainly brought up anything it had been holding.

It took me a second to realize all the noise from the kitchen had stopped. The only thing I could hear was my pulse drumming in my ears.

"Scout?"

Alex had told me that on the day of a full moon he could hear every heart beating in a classroom. Jase and Charlie had to know I was there and that something was causing my heart to race. As I pushed open the kitchen door I tried to think of a reasonable explanation for why that was.

Just as I had predicted, Jase sat on the counter, his plaid pajama clad legs dangling. Charlie was draped in a chair, an empty box of cereal sat beside him on the table. My arms immediately wrapped around my chest. The thin sleep shirt I was wearing left little to the imagination.

"I didn't know Charlie was here," I said to Jase, not bothering to hide the reproach in my voice. The residual embarrassment from yesterday's incident would serve as an excellent cover for my outside the door lurking and heart racing. It even had the added bonus of not requiring any acting or lying on my part.

"We're going to camp out tonight."

Camping out. Turning into coyotes and trying to kill my boyfriend. It was all the same thing, really.

Play it cool, Scout. You can do this.

"Camping? In March?"

"We're manly men," Charlie said with a wink, causing the corners of my lips to twitch against my will.

"I've not seen much evidence to support that claim."

148

The look on Charlie's face was positively wicked. "Do you want another piece of me, Scout?" He managed to deliver the common line of trash talk so that it sounded like a come-on.

And, despite everything, I did want a piece of him. All sorts of pieces. Lip pieces. Hand pieces. And his Adam's apple. Charlie had a very nice looking Adam's apple.

I was still stammering for a response when something fell onto my head, obscuring my vision. Once I pulled it off, I realized it was one of Mom's cardigan sweaters. Jase must have reached into the mud room and grabbed the first thing he found.

"You looked cold," he said in a flat voice.

The sweater was a bit small on me, the sleeves stopping a good two inches above my wrists, but it managed to cover me up and get my hormones in check.

"What are you doing home anyway?" I asked Charlie. "Aren't you supposed to be spending your Spring Break in Miami with December or whatever her name is?"

Of course, I knew her name was January, but only because Jase had finally told me, and he only did that after I questioned him directly. Since Charlie never bothered mentioning that he had a girlfriend, I didn't feel compelled to call her the right name.

Charlie gave Jase a quick, annoyed look before telling me, a bit too enthusiastically, "We're leaving Monday. I promised Jase a camping trip first."

Yeah, I couldn't imagine poor stupid-month-for-a-name would be very understanding when Charlie disappeared for an entire night during their romantic getaway. Also, it would be a bit difficult for him to attack my boyfriend from a different state.

Charlie peppered me with questions about school as I dug through the cabinets in search of a Pop-Tart. I wanted to laugh at the absurdity of it all. We were really supposed to sit around, eat a casual breakfast, and have prosaic conversation? They were planning an assault just five minutes ago! How could they change gears so quickly?

"Where are you going?" Charlie asked as I made my way out of the kitchen with my generic strawberry toaster pastry in one hand and a cup of acerbic liquid in the other.

"I was thinking about hitting a few sales on Sunset and then heading down to Chateau Marmont to spend the afternoon lounging by the pool while Jensen Ackles feeds me peeled grapes."

"Sunset is overrated, and you hate grapes. Stay and play with me."

Was it horrible that part of me wanted to do just that? "Can't. I've got a ton of errands to run." I hurried out of the room before Charlie could respond, knowing that if I lingered he would convince me to stay.

Chapter 14

As far as Mom and Dad are concerned, I'm the good twin. Jase isn't necessarily bad, he just has a habit of attending out of control parties, staying out past curfew, and giving misinformation as to his whereabouts. On the other hand, I have our librarian's home number on speed dial. For that reason, my parents never considered that I wasn't telling the truth when I said I was spending the night with Talley.

I blamed Alex for my subterfuge. He hadn't answered any of my texts or voicemails, which left me with no other options. It wasn't exactly as if I could tell my parents that I was going to traipse through the woods looking for my boyfriend, a wolf, to warn him that my brother, a coyote, was planning some sort of attack. I'm not sure which part would come closer to giving Mom a coronary - that Jase was a Shifter, or that I had a boyfriend I failed to mention.

I studied the map one last time before getting out of the car at Pelican Landing. According to the good people at the Lake County Visitors Bureau, Chestnut-Oak was three miles due east. I decided the best option was to simply start walking in that direction and hope Alex picked up on my scent before he Changed. With any luck, I would come up with a contingency plan before the sun disappeared.

I hadn't been in the woods long when the clouds began to roll overhead, causing a premature loss of the sun as a directional guide. Since I had skipped the whole Girl Scout thing in favor of activities Jase and I could do together, my ability to navigate in the wilderness was fairly pathetic. As far as I could tell, moss grew on more than one side of a tree and the compass feature on my phone was less than helpful. I would have called Talley, whose mother insisted on an outdoor survival seminar two summers ago, but the trees blocked all reception.

The most logical thing would have been to follow the lake's edge around to the Chestnut-Oak campground. Unfortunately, the lake wasn't where it was supposed to be. I was stomping around in circles, trying to figure out where someone could have hidden a freaking lake, when the first raindrop fell. It was quickly followed by a million others. The thunder and lightning weren't far behind.

My options for shelter were pretty limited. I eventually found a place where a large tree had fallen over onto a big rock near the base of a hill. It wasn't the Hilton, or even a nice dry cave, but it blocked some of the wind and rain and could possibly prevent anything from smashing in my head.

The rain was cold. Not just cold, but icy cold. In fact, I felt certain there was sleet mixed in at times. As the wind ripped through the flimsy protection offered by my hoodie, I began to realize the fairly hopeless situation I had gotten myself into and began to pray that either the storm would pass over or that some kind person would come to my rescue.

Apparently, Alex wasn't the only one avoiding my calls. Or maybe God just didn't feel the need to answer the prayers of complete morons.

The last time I checked my still serviceless phone, it was just before two. After that, I couldn't seem to get my fingers to work well enough to dig into the pocket of my soaking wet jeans. My last thought before closing my eyes was that this was an exceptionally stupid way to die.

***

When I first heard my name I thought I was delusional, or that an Angel of Death had come to call me from this world to the next. Either way, it didn't seem worth the effort to open my eyes.

I decided to go with the Angel of Death theory when I felt my body being lifted off the ground. Apparently, he decided if I wasn't going to get up and follow him to Heaven, he would just carry me through the Pearly Gates. Of course, that was assuming I was going to Heaven. According to what Reverend Jessup taught from the pulpit every Sunday, I was good to go, but what if God wasn't Southern Baptist?

What I needed to do was to get a look at my angel. Surely a demon from Hell looked different than one of God's messengers. If it was a demon, there was still a chance I could escape, provided my legs remembered how to work, although that was seeming a bit doubtful.

Finally, my curiosity won me over and I lifted my exceptionally heavy eyelids. A pair of steely grey eyes met mine.

"Alex?"

"He's heading this way. Are you okay?" he asked with a complete lack of concern.

"I think so," I said. Or, at least, I tried to say. It sounded more like "Hubbla ho."

Another face appeared in front of mine. This one had grey eyes too, but they were filled with a mixture of worry and relief. "You're going to be okay," Alex said, his blazing hot hands caressing my face. "We've got you. You're going to be fine."

I smiled, grateful that God decided to answer my prayers after all. And with that thought, I returned to the beautiful oblivion of sleep.

***

I am not a morning person. Talley can go from sleeping to flitting around making breakfast and talking nonstop in a matter of seconds. Even Jase tends to be a fully functional human being in less than five minutes. Not me. I wake up very slowly, refusing to open my eyes and let in the daylight until it is absolutely necessary.

I was lying in bed, enjoying the feeling of being cocooned in the blankets, when Angel shifted beside me.

153

"Did you have a bad dream?" I mumbled, my eyes still refusing to open.

"The worst," said a voice that did not belong to a seven year old girl. "But then I found you, and now everything is okay."

My eyes finally flew open and darted around in utter confusion. This was not my bed, not my room, and definitely not my little sister.

"Good morning, Sunshine," Alex said, brushing a strand of hair from my face. "How are you feeling?"

My memory started coming back to me in bits and pieces. Dark woods. Violent storm. Valiant rescue. I could vaguely remember what had felt like a stinging hot shower, despite Liam's gruff warnings about watching the temperature and Alex's assurances that he wasn't an idiot. I remembered having to muster all my strength to put on the pair of sweatpants and T-shirt Alex gave me because, despite my depleted state, I knew I couldn't stand the embarrassment of either of the Coles seeing me naked. I softened at the memory of falling asleep in Alex's arms.

"Better," I finally said.

"You had me worried." Alex leaned forward to kiss me and I jerked back, throwing a hand over my mouth. His eyes flew wide open in shock, causing him to look a bit like an anime character. "What's wrong?"

"Morning breath," I said, my hand still planted firmly over my mouth.

I couldn't tell if Alex thought I was being adorable or insane; those looks were fairly interchangeable on him. "The bathroom is through the living room and kitchen, on the left. There should be some new toothbrushes in the top, right hand drawer."

I muttered a thanks and bolted. Even without the directions, the bathroom wouldn't have been hard to find. Alex's home proved to be a very small trailer, or maybe "pre-fabricated home" was the more PC term. It only took me three strides to cross the living room, but two of those put me between Liam and an episode of *NCIS* he was watching with the volume turned off.

"Sorry," I said, keeping my head down and wishing I was invisible.

"For what?" he asked, stopping me in my tracks.

He was sitting in the middle of the couch, the room's only furniture, a brown bottle clutched in one hand. I was once again struck by how he simply looked like a bigger, angrier version of Alex.

"I'm sorry," I repeated. Liam just continued to stare at me in a way I had never experienced before. I was used to indifference, annoyance, curiosity, and disdain. With Alex, I had even become accustomed to being stared at with adoration. Hatred, the pure, unadulterated form that was radiating off of Liam, was new.

To be fair, he had every right to hate me. It was my fault that Alex forced him to live here. I was the one that put them in danger from the Hagans and the Alphas.

"I'm sorry for everything." My voice was a whisper, but it was all I could manage with my throat so constricted. It didn't matter anyway. Liam was a Dominant. His hearing was so good he could probably hear my thoughts.

Apparently, my response suited him, or maybe he decided I wasn't worth his effort. Either way, he released me from his penetrating gaze and turned his attention back to a silent Abby and DiNozzo.

I practically flew into the bathroom, grateful to have a door between me and Liam. The top, right-hand drawer did, in fact, have new toothbrushes inside. It had like fifty of them, all wrapped individually in plastic.

The reflection staring back at me from the mirror was not encouraging. Dark, bruise-like circles shadowed my eyes, my lips were chapped to the point of cracking open, and a wind burn had my face a rather unattractive shade of red. I quickly learned that boys do not keep moisturizer in their bathroom, which was rather unfortunate. At least there was a hair brush to work all the tangles out of my hair. I would have felt a touch more confident going back to Alex if I had a straightening iron or some concealer, but I had to abandon that dream. When I finally made my way back to Alex's room I kept my head down and eyes averted, grateful Liam chose to ignore me.

Alex had fallen asleep. His left arm was flung up over his head and his body was turned so that my original spot on the small, twin-sized bed was left open. It looked so warm and inviting that I was already crawling between the covers when it occurred to me that my parents might not approve of such behavior.

I was frozen, half-in and half-out of Alex's bed, the angel and demon on my shoulders really going at it, when Alex reached for me. "There you are," he said, his voice thick with sleep. He pulled me down onto his chest and I made no move to resist. "I missed you."

I sighed as I snuggled into him. His body was so warm. I didn't think I would ever be warm enough again.

We lay in silence for a long while. I would have thought he had drifted off again, but his fingers were combing through my hair in a lazy, soothing manner. As I listened to the steady thumping of his heart, I took in my surroundings.

Alex's room was much tidier than my own, but that could have just been due to necessity. His bed and chest of drawers took up nearly all of the floor space, leaving just enough room to walk around. His school books were stacked on top of the chest of drawers next to a picture of an attractive looking couple. The woman was long and slender, exuding a dancer's grace even in stillness. Thick, wavy brown hair framed her heart-shaped face. The man had a ruggedness about him, like I had always imagined a rancher would look. He had obviously passed on his grey eyes to both of his sons.

The only other decorations in the room where some newspaper clippings taped to the wall beside the bed. There were five of them, and they were all of me.

"You're thinking that I'm a crazy stalker person, aren't you?" Alex asked. He must have been paying more attention than I thought.

I rested my chin on his sternum so that I could see his face. "You are a stalker," I said. "What else would you call a guy that follows you around in his sleep for ten years?"

"So you think I'm a creeper?"

I reached up and kissed the underside of his jaw. "I think that you're my hero. Thank you for coming to my rescue."

"Anytime," he muttered into my hair. "No, I don't mean that. What I meant to say was, don't you ever scare me like that again. What were you doing out there?"

"Ummm...I was coming to save you?"

"Save me? From what?"

"Jase. And Charlie." I still had trouble saying Charlie's name in front of Alex. It was due in equal parts to the pang I got in my chest, and the look on Alex's face. "I overheard them planning to do something to you last night. When you wouldn't return my calls or texts, I decided to go look for you." Really, it seemed like a sound plan at the time. "Then I got lost and that freak storm came up out of nowhere."

"The storm came from Arkansas, which is not technically 'nowhere'. They've been talking about it on the local weather for nearly two days now. You're lucky we didn't get the tornadoes they were predicting."

"You do realize that you have an unnatural fascination with weather forecasts, right?"

"Too bad I can't make some of it rub off on you," he snapped.

"I'm sorry," I said as I tried to disentangle myself from his embrace. "I didn't mean to make you angry."

His arms tightened around me, holding me fast. "I'm not mad at you. Honestly, I don't know if it's even possible for me to be mad at you." He loosened his hold and began tracing patterns along my spine. "I'm upset by the whole situation. This...*animosity* the Hagan

157

pack has towards us is ridiculous. Someone is going to end up getting hurt and for what? Turf? Pride?"

The hand on my back had clenched into a fist. "Liam thinks we should just leave, move back up north. It's the only conversation we have anymore."

"Where will you go?"

"We're not going anywhere."

I was selfish enough to be happy at his declaration. However, I was also practical. "Why not?"

"Do you want me to leave?"

"God, no." It was bad enough when he was gone in November. I couldn't imagine how painful it would be if he left me now. "But I do want you to be safe."

Alex let out a single chuckle. "It's not me I'm worried about. I know how much you care about Jase and the others. You wouldn't be able to forgive me if one of them got hurt." I thought perhaps he wasn't giving the Hagans enough credit. "And then there's you. None of us would be able to live with ourselves if something happened to you."

I could think of at least one exception. Liam would probably throw a party if I got good and battered. He would declare it a holiday if I managed to go off and get myself killed.

"The only risk to me is my own stupidity."

"If that were the case, we would have nothing to worry about, Miss Valedictorian."

"Last night was not one of my finer moments."

"You wouldn't have had a reason to be out in the woods if it hadn't been for me."

"And my brother," I added. I wasn't about to ignore the amount of blame he deserved. I love my brother, but he and Charlie were being the unreasonable ones. Their bigotry was really starting to screw up my life. "He was so certain you were going to be in the woods between Pelican Landing and the dock at the end of Chestnut-Oak, but you weren't."

"How do you know that?"

"Because you would have found me sooner." It sounded a bit presumptuous to my ears, but I knew it was true. Alex would have come to me if he had been anywhere around.

"Not necessarily," he said. "You were nowhere near Pelican Landing or Chestnut-Oak when we found you. You were only a mile south of the dam."

A mile south of the dam? Not only was that a good five miles from Pelican Landing, it was also in the completely wrong direction.

"What was that about me not being an idiot?"

His laughter was so quiet I might have missed it if my ear hadn't been pressed to his chest. "You are an extremely intelligent person, but your sense of direction sucks."

I propped myself up on my elbows. I missed the warmth of his body, but getting to look at his face made it an even trade. "But you weren't near Pelican Landing last night, were you?"

"No, we weren't."

"Why not? Where were you?" If he thought I was being too nosey he didn't show it.

"We got tipped off on Friday that there might be some trouble if we stuck around for the full moon, so Liam and I took a weekend trip to the other side of the river. The Hagans never go that far. We were driving back when I fell asleep and Saw you huddled on the forest floor turning blue." His thumb brushed my lips and I imagined that he was seeing the frozen lips from last night instead of the pink ones that tingled at his touch.

"Tipped off? How?"

"Doesn't matter," he said as he pulled my face down to his, effectively ending our conversation. His hands slid over my shoulders and down my back as I kissed his cheeks, his eyelids, his ear, and his neck. When I slid my hand up under his shirt, still hungry for warmth, he let out a moan and rolled us over so that he was positioned above me.

His lips followed the same pattern on my face I had forged on his moments earlier. My breath was coming in shallow gasps. My hands seemed to be running over the smooth flesh of Alex's back on their own accord.

Then, Alex lifted his head and started talking to the wall.

"You don't actually have to sit there and listen, Perv. You could go for a walk or a nice long drive. Maybe you could even go find a girlfriend of your very own." Alex quit addressing the wall directly and looked at me. My heart skipped a beat in response to the intense longing on his face. "Please, Liam."

Seconds later there was the unmistakable sound of a screen door slamming shut.

"Now," Alex said, "where were we before we were so rudely interrupted?"

"Dying of embarrassment?"

"Nope, that was definitely after." Alex rubbed his hand against my cheeks, which were still on fire. "You're so cute when you blush."

"You knew he was listening," I accused.

"Yes, but I didn't care." He resumed his exploration of my face.

"But I do," I said, pushing him away.

"Why?"

Besides the embarrassment that inherently comes with getting caught making out? How about knowing with absolute certainty the look of disgust that was etched on Liam's face? Or how about not wanting that vile man to have any access to any of the intimate moments of my life?

Of course, I couldn't say any of that to Alex. He thought his brother was just all kinds of awesome.

"I don't think your brother likes me." Understatement seemed to be the way to go.

"He was rude earlier. I'm sorry about that. He's just cranky because it's already starting to get warm outside. He hates the South, but not you. Trust me, once he gets to know you, he'll love you."

I doubted that. I doubted Liam's ability to love much of anything.

"He kind of scares me," I said, once again drastically understating the truth.

"That's just his Dominant wolf exterior. Underneath all the hard stares and grimaces he has a marshmallowy center. It's just going to take some time for the two of you to get comfortable with each other."

"If you say so." I still didn't believe it, but decided to let Alex keep his one big happy family fantasy.

"So, can we quit talking about the brother I just sent away and get back to the reason I sent him away?"

Alex was a pro at making me forget any fears or concerns I had. As long as he was kissing me, everything was okay. Heck, it was better than okay. I couldn't imagine an existence more perfect than one where I was with Alex, just like this. Maybe I had died in the woods and this was my Heaven.

Although, there probably wouldn't have been someone pounding on the front door of Heaven.

Alex's body was suspended above mine in terror. He tilted his head towards the door and breathed deeply through his nose before relaxing.

"Dammit," he said, pulling on his shirt as he climbed off the bed. "This can't be good."

"Who is it?" I glanced in the mirror attached to Alex's closet door and ran my fingers through my hair.

"Pack Seer," he said to me before calling out, "I'm coming, for Christ's sake."

"Should I...?" I motioned towards the closet. It was small, but I thought I could hide in there as long as Alex didn't have it crammed full of junk like I did mine.

"No, it won't be any use." He was already moving towards the door. "You might as well come with me."

I didn't really think that was the best idea, but I did follow him as far as his bedroom door. Alex took a deep breath before turning back the lock and stepping aside. My mouth hung open in shock as Talley came bursting through the door.

Chapter 15

Mamaw Donovan was fond of saying that something had made her blood boil when she was angry. I always assumed it was a figurative sort of thing, but as I watched the Pack Seer fling herself into my boyfriend's arms I decided I might have been wrong.

So, my best friend was a Seer. I shouldn't have been shocked. I mean, at this point I should have been prepared to find out that my mom was a succubus, my dad an elf, and my little sister a pixie. But, I was shocked with a healthy dose of hurt and angry. How could she have kept something like this from me? I was her best friend. Alex had lived here for less than a year and he knew more about the real Talley than I did.

Alex's arms were wrapped around Talley, holding her close. Seeing that did nothing to help with my blood pressure.

"Scout is missing," Talley said, her words coming out in a rush. "It's all my fault. I thought something was wrong last night, but I ignored it. And then, this morning, she was gone when Jase got home. Her parents said that she was at my house, but of course she's not." A tear, round and heavy, slid down her cheek. "Alex, they found her car down at Pelican Landing. The Pack is searching the woods, but the rain washed away any trail...and...and they can't find anything..."

Alex had been trying to get Talley's attention this whole time, but she was too absorbed in the drama of the moment to notice him. "Talley, she's here," he said, finally breaking through to her.

"I'm here. I'm fine." Well, I wasn't exactly fine, but I wasn't dead in a ditch. That's all that really mattered.

"Scout?" Talley rushed to me and, before I could prevent it, I was locked in a paralyzing hug. Her breath came in hiccups as she started sobbing in earnest.

For the record, it is possible to stay angry with someone you love when they're having a complete meltdown over the fact you're alive. That anger, however, cannot stop you from trying to comfort said loved one. "I'm okay. I'm fine. Everything is fine."

When she finally got herself together, Talley gave me a head to toe inspection, looking for any signs of injury or abuse. "What on earth were you doing in the woods at night in the middle of a thunderstorm? Do you have any idea how cold it got last night?"

"Really, really cold?"

"She overheard the Wonder Twins ingenious Provoke the Werewolves scheme," Alex said. "She thought she was rescuing me."

Talley gave me a look usually reserved for five year olds. "But I had that under control."

Oh, Talley had the whole situation under control. Why hadn't I thought of that?

"How was I supposed to know that?" I hissed. "How am I supposed to know anything? You certainly never told me." I wheeled around on Alex. "Or you. I mean, in all of our talks about this crazy Shifter stuff you couldn't find an opportunity to mention that my best friend was a freaking Seer?"

Alex's face was tight as he studied his bare feet.

"We couldn't just tell you," Talley said calmly.

"Why not? Am I not cool enough to be in your supernatural kids club? Or am I just too weak and fragile? Everybody has to protect poor, little Scout. Don't let her near the wolves, they might eat her. Don't tell her the truth, she can't handle it." My eyes burned as I blinked back tears. "Well, guess what. He's not going to hurt me, and I'm not some porcelain doll. I'm not weak. I don't need your protection." To prove my point, I kicked the door frame.

Charlie once punched Jase's door after one of the more spectacular rounds with his father. He had knocked the trim loose, but we were able to fix it before anyone noticed. I didn't think I kicked as hard as Charlie punched, but apparently our doors were made out of stronger stuff than the ones in Alex's house. As I felt my foot go through the faux wood I said a four-letter word that had never passed my lips before.

"Feel better?"

I couldn't bear to look at Alex, so I just closed my eyes and leaned my head against the door frame. At least the top half was still intact.

"I told you we should have told her," Alex was saying to Talley as a loud trilling noise made me jump.

Talley looked at her caller ID before sliding open her phone. "Hey, Jase," she said in an upbeat tone that certainly didn't match the look in her eyes or dried tears on her cheeks. "Listen…" Even from across the room I could hear the voice on the other end speaking in rapid, urgent tones. "Charlie, listen…Charlie…*Charlie!*" Alex moved up beside Talley and slid his hand into hers. I thought about kicking another hole in the wall. "I found her. She's okay." Charlie said something else, causing Talley to raise her eyebrows at Alex.

"She's at Joi's" Talley lied smoothly, which was almost as jarring as finding out that she was a Seer. "When I wasn't home last night she decided to come find you guys and…" Talley rolled her eyes, which was again very out of character. I felt like I was watching a Talley Cylon. "I'm sure that's it, Charlie," she said dismissively before continuing. "Anyways, when the storm came up, she ran into The Farmhouse. She decided to go home with Joi after her shift ended…No, we're going to stay here for a little while…Because we're doing fun girl bonding stuff…Charlie…I'll have her home in two hours." As Charlie continued to ramble on the other end of the phone, something in Talley shifted. She didn't even look like my friend when she said, "You are not the Pack Leader, Charles

Jefferson Hagan, Jr. I, however, am a Seer. I suggest the next time you see me, you apologize for forgetting that."

Who was this person? The Talley Matthews I knew was always meek and mild mannered. She didn't lie with casual ease. She didn't give orders. And she never slammed her phone shut on her friends.

Alex made a move to let go of Talley's hand, but she held on. "I still might need you," she said.

Talley pressed some numbers into her phone and then held it six inches from her ear. That meant she was calling Joi. Really, Joi is a fairly bright girl, she just has some issues with any sort of technology. It took her three weeks to figure out the remote when her parents bought her a new TV last year (during which QVC played in her room constantly since she couldn't change the station or turn it off). iPods freak her out, she cannot grasp the concept of Twitter or Facebook, and she has never understood, no matter how many times we tried to explain it, that you don't have to scream into a cell phone to be heard.

"Joi?"

"Talley? Oh my gosh, is that you? That's so weird! I was just thinking about you!" No need for super-senses to hear Joi on the phone.

"Can you do Scout and me a favor?" Talley looked at Alex expectantly, but he didn't do or say anything.

"Sure! Whatcha need?"

"If anyone asks, could you tell them that Scout spent the night with you last night? And if anyone calls to look for us in the next couple of hours, tell them we're too busy to come to the phone? We're ummm..." She shot another look at Alex, but he stayed silent. "We're working on this really huge surprise for Jase as like a graduation present. We don't want anyone to know about it because it would totally ruin it."

"You don't think that Jase would, like, call here, do you?" Joi had a not-so-secret crush on my brother which rendered her unable to carry on a conversation when he was anywhere nearby. The last

166

time we had a sleep-over at my house she spent the entire night staring mutely in the direction of Jase's bedroom.

"Probably not, but if he does you can cover for us, right?"

Poor Joi. We were probably giving her a major anxiety attack. Then again, it was noon, so she was on her second or third of the day.

"Sure. I can do that." She might have been more convincing if her voice hadn't been shaking.

It took several more reassurances, but Talley was finally able to end her call with Joi, somewhat confident that she had a cover story for my whereabouts. She turned her attention to me as soon as she pocketed the phone.

"I know you're mad at me right now, and you have every right to be, but we've only got a couple of hours at best to get you clean."

"Clean?" I may not have looked spectacular, but I had taken a shower that morning.

"Trust me, no one wants to know how Charlie would react if I brought you home smelling of Alex."

I lifted the Spider-Man shirt to my nose. All I could smell was a citrusy fabric softener. "You smell him on me?" Was that part of a Seer's ability? Could they smell Shifters?

"Of course not, but to Jase and Charlie you'll reek of wolf. You need a really long shower and some clean clothes."

Talley Matthews, Shifter Expert.

Yep, I was still pissed. I concentrated on drawing deep breaths in through my nose and letting it out of my mouth slowly. "Fine," I said through clenched teeth. "Let's go."

Alex intercepted me at the door. "Scout, wait." I stopped, but didn't look up. "You're not wearing shoes."

Crap. He was right. Where were my shoes? For that matter, where were my clothes?

"Liam washed everything, but you'll have to rewash it to cancel out the the eau de wolf." He did the whole stare at the feet, chew on the lip thing. "Do you want to come with me to get everything?"

"Sure." What was I supposed to do? Stand there stubbornly and demand that he bring me my freshly laundered clothes?

I followed him to the laundry room, where he closed the door and unleashed his heart melting look of sincerity on me. "I'm sorry."

"My best friend is a Seer and you didn't tell me."

"She begged me not to."

"And you hugged her. And held her hand."

"I hugged her because she was clearly upset and, in case you haven't noticed, Talley is a bit of a hugger."

"And I guess you had to hold her hand because talking on the phone requires a ton of moral support?"

Alex's eyes darted towards the living room where a voice called out, "Go ahead. Tell her." I would have wondered about Seers and super-hearing, but since I could hear her mutter, "Like I could stop you," I attributed her ability to eavesdrop on thin walls.

"Do you remember when I was telling you about Seers and I said that some of them could See what you were thinking just by touching you?"

"Yeah. Thoughts, emotions, deepest secrets." They were the Seers that most freaked me out. I liked for my private thoughts, emotions, and secrets to stay private. The idea that someone could know those things about me without my permission was not exactly comforting.

"Talley is that kind of Seer. They're called Soul Seers."

"Or, as Jase prefers, a Touch-and-See," Talley added from the living room.

"And that explains why you were holding hands how exactly?" I didn't really care which one of them answered. I assumed that Alex had pulled me into the laundry room for a private conversation, but that had proven to be pointless.

"Talley just happens to be an extremely powerful *Touch-and-See*. Most of them can only glean random images or thoughts from the people they touch. They can't control it. Little Miss Diligent in there has been conducting experiments and has figured out a way to take only what she wants and block out everything else. I don't think she's got it down to an exact science yet, but if you're thinking direct thoughts, like an elaborate lie as to your girlfriend's current location so that her family doesn't know that she's been hanging out in your bed all morning, she gets the message loud and clear."

"So you were just telling her what to say to Charlie?" It made sense. He wouldn't have been able to speak out loud without Charlie hearing him. And somehow knowing that Talley hadn't suddenly morphed into an expert liar overnight made me feel better.

For the first time since Talley arrived, Alex smiled as he nodded his head in agreement.

"And you couldn't have touched her shoulder or something?" I tried to sound annoyed, but my lips were turning up in response to Alex's newly elevated mood.

He stepped up and placed a hand on the small of my back. "You know, I'm finding the whole jealousy act very endearing."

"I'm sorry about the wall," I said. Now that my anger was diminishing I had the emotional capacity to feel very foolish over my earlier outburst. "I'll pay to have it fixed."

"Don't worry about it. Werewolf homes have a tendency to attract destruction. A little hole is nothing compared to the time Liam ripped the kitchen counter off the cabinets and threw it through the French doors."

Was that supposed to make me feel better? Knowing that Liam was strong enough to rip up a kitchen counter with his bare hands? "Oh good. Maybe he'll decide we're kindred spirits and stop hating me."

Alex just laughed and used his favorite diversionary technique. The kissing was just getting good when Talley called from the living room to remind us we had less than two hours before the coyotes came looking for me.

Chapter 16

The car was silent as Talley carefully navigated the pothole riddled road that led back to the highway. I had never actually been in the Lake View Trailer Park before. I recognized Garrett Carrow's ghetto-wannabe 1984 Lincoln parked outside a trailer that sported Transformer sheets in the place of curtains and automatically slumped down in my seat. A couple of lots down from Garrett's place I watched a girl that graduated the year I was a Freshman try to juggle her three small children as she unlocked her car. I was too busy making sure that she didn't drop the infant on its head to hear what Talley had said. "Sorry, what was that?"

"I asked if Alex was a good kisser."

Of all the things we needed to discuss she wanted to talk about Alex's make-out skills? "I don't kiss and tell."

"Since when?"

"Since you decided not to See and tell."

I thought that would shame her into discontinuing her current line of questioning, but she was relentless. "At least promise me that you're using protection."

It took a few minutes for me to answer since I managed to suck the piece of gum I was chewing down my windpipe. Talley had to stop the car and pound on my back a couple of times before I was able to quit coughing.

"We're not doing anything that requires protection!" I said, adding "thinks I'm a ho" onto my list of reasons to be angry with Talley.

"Really?" she said, finally pulling onto the main road. "Because Alex let a memory of what you guys were doing before I got there slip while I was talking to Joi, and --"

"We were making out!" Holy cow, was everyone privy to my romantic forays? Maybe I should start charging for the show.

Talley stared thoughtfully out of the windshield. "Do you love him?"

"Have you met Alex? I would be crazy not to love him."

"That doesn't really answer my question."

I sighed dramatically, collapsing back against the headrest. "Maybe? I mean, I care about him a lot. He's like fifteen shades of awesome, and when I'm with him it just seems right. He makes me happy. Like, really, truly happy. I *think* I love him but..."

"But Charlie."

The Methodist church was letting out as we drove by, reminding me I had skipped Sunday morning services to roll around in bed with a half-naked boy. As if I needed another reason to feel like a bad person. "Yeah. But Charlie," I said. "I mean, if I was truly in love with Alex, I wouldn't still feel this way about Charlie, would I?"

Talley attempted to pass the octogenarian driving 25 mph in front of us, but gave up when he made it clear he required both lanes of traffic. "Scout Donovan, I can't believe that you, of all people, would actually buy into that one true love stuff."

"Why not?" Was this another one of those 'Scout is unable to connect with real people' things?

"Your mom and dad are the best example in the world of how it's possible to truly love more than one person."

"They are?"

"Of course they are. Your dad loves Becca, right?"

"Obviously." Mom and Dad rarely fight and are always doing really sappy stuff, like holding hands and kissing each other for no good reason while they're cooking dinner. It's unnatural.

"But he still loves your biological mother, doesn't he?"

My parents don't talk about their first marriages often, but once a month Dad goes to the graveyard to put fresh flowers by my mother's tombstone. Sometimes I go with him, but not often. I feel like I'm imposing on their personal time. He talks to her when he's there, telling her about all the things going on with our lives, and how much he misses her. "Yes, he still loves her."

"Falling in love with Becca didn't make him love Jennifer less. And loving Jennifer doesn't change the fact that he's head over heels for Becca." Talley made a left onto her street. "There is no such thing as one true love. That's just fairy tale stuff."

Actually dead mermaids and unconscious girls impregnated by already married princes were fairy tale stuff, but I doubted Talley would want me pointing that out.

"So you're trying to say that I could be in love with Charlie and Alex?"

"I'm saying that you do love Charlie and Alex."

"Then I'm an idiot," I mumbled. She was right, of course. Talley was pretty much always right. Maybe I had known it all along, but talking about it made it more real somehow.

"How does falling in love make you an idiot?"

"Falling in love always makes people idiots. I just have the distinction of being a double-idiot." We were rapidly approaching Talley's house, for which I was grateful. I was ready for this conversation to be over. "On one hand, I'm in love with someone who I have to lie about and sneak around to be with because, if anyone ever found out that we're together, it could cause some sort of crazy Shape Shifter epic battle. On the other hand, I'm in love with my brother's cousin who thinks of me as the little sister he never had. And let's not ignore the fact that they're both classic B-movie monsters. If that's not idiotic, then I really don't know what is."

"You're not an idiot."

"What am I then?"

Talley threw the car in park. "You're a human, Scout. Congratulations on finally joining us." She placed a consoling hand on my arm. "Now, as a human you may experience a wide range of emotions in addition to the annoyance you are used to feeling. Do not be alarmed. While somewhat baffling and occasionally painful, these emotions are normal."

I narrowed my eyes. "You are turning into such a smart ass."

"I learned it from the best," she said with a wink.

"I'm going to pretend you're referring to Jase."

"If it makes you feel better." She started to open the car door, but stopped and faced me. "We have to go see my mother."

I re-clicked my seatbelt. "Never mind. Take me home." I would much rather face an irate Charlie than a disappointed Mrs. Matthews.

Talley reached over and undid my seatbelt. "Too late. Anyway, she'll be happy to see you. She's spent half the day certain you had been kidnapped by an online predator."

I reluctantly got out of the car. "What does your mom See?" Hopefully it wasn't whether or not you were lying, although that seemed like the most Mrs. Matthews appropriate power in the world.

"Colors and patterns," Talley said, opening the door to the garage her mother had converted into a workshop. "Not as flashy as some other powers, but infinitely more profitable."

Mrs. Matthews looked up from her sewing machine. If she suspected anything, it was masked by the tiny prisms of multi-colored light dancing across her face.

Mrs. Matthews was a seamstress who specialized in shiny. She received orders from all over the world to make outfits for gymnast, ice skaters, and drum majors. If it required sequins, Delia Matthews was *the* seamstress to hire.

"Scout, good." She stood and managed to look much taller than her five feet and four inches. "There is something I need you to try on."

She clomped over to one of the creepy mannequins that sat in the middle of the room. The workshop was strictly off limits when we were kids and I had very few reasons to visit her private sanctuary since then. It was a shock on the senses. Bright reams of fabric lined the walls in every imaginable color. An aisle of shelves held bins filled with millions of beads and sequins in various sizes and shapes. The smell of the dyes burned my nose and my ears took offense to the Bluegrass music she had blaring.

"Here, put this on," she said, handing me a strange corset looking contraption made out of a light bronze satin.

I wasn't really in the mood to disrobe and figure out all the wired hooks on the bizarre Victorian torture device, but it was preferable to arguing with Mrs. Matthews.

"Hmmm...your breasts have grown again, so I'll have to let out the top, but other than that it's fine." She reached up and, in less than ten seconds, undid the hooks I had wrestled with for five minutes. "You'll need to come over and let me do another fitting in a couple of weeks."

"A fitting for what?"

"Your prom dress," she said as she reattached the thing to a faceless mannequin.

"My what?" I looked to Talley for an explanation, but she was sorting through a Mason jar full of buttons. "That's very nice of you, Mrs. Matthews, but I'm not going to prom."

"Yes, you are."

"No, really. I'm not. I don't do school dances."

Mrs. Matthews leveled me with her eyes. "You're doing this one. Talley has a date and you're going to go along to look after her."

Talley had a date? To prom? With who? Did she tell me *anything*?

"Okay, we've got to leave now," Talley suddenly said, abandoning her buttons. "Miles to go and all that. We'll be in my room if you need us."

Talley was ushering me out the door as Mrs. Matthews called out to tell me I should come by next week to make sure the bodice was right before she moved on to the skirt. In my state of confusion I heard myself agreeing to do so.

***

I was on the second repeat of Talley's lather, rinse, repeat, repeat, repeat, repeat, and repeat instructions and still wasn't believing what she was saying to me. "James Kiplinger? Seriously? You're going to prom with James Kiplinger? You're dragging me to prom for James Kiplinger?"

"And this is the reason I didn't tell you sooner. I knew you would freak."

Of course I was freaking. I was a good friend. Good friends freak when you decide to commit social suicide and damn yourself to a night of awkward date hell.

"James is a really good guy. I mean, like a really good person. Trust me, I know people better than the average girl. He just needs some self-esteem."

"And you're the person to give it to him?"

"Yes."

"Why?"

I could hear Talley's sigh over the rush of water from the shower and the clanging of bottles as she scavenged through the cabinet. "Because only I can See what he needs, and what he needs is for someone to go to prom with him and treat him like a real person. I can do that. I'm going to do that. I'm sorry that you have to be inconvenienced, but I promise I'll make it up to you."

Crap. I couldn't argue with that.

"So, how does this Seeing thing work?" I asked as she pushed yet another bottle of fruity smelling body wash around the shower curtain. I lined it up with the others. The bathtub was starting to look like Bath and Body Works. "Like, do you have to touch flesh or could you grab onto someone's shirt?"

175

"Flesh to flesh is the best conduit, but I can sometimes get a read off someone if there is a layer of fabric between us. Depends on how strong the person is projecting."

I washed behind my ears for the sixth time. "Projecting?"

"You know, like giving off a vibe. If someone is really stressed out or upset about something they project it off of them and I can't help but See whatever it is. When I first started Seeing it was overwhelming. I couldn't walk down the hall at school without finding out someone had wrecked their mom's car, had an abortion, or made out with another guy while their girlfriend was out of town. It was too much. That's why I started working on controlling it. It's not right for me to know those things."

"It was Jordan, wasn't it? He's totally hot for guys, right?"

"Scout." That's the problem with having a good, kind hearted person as a best friend. She sucks all the joy out of gossiping.

"Fine. Sorry." I tried to remember how many times I had washed my hair and failed. Oh well, one more time couldn't hurt. "How long have you been able to See? Where you born like this?"

"No, Seers are like Shifters. We're supposed to come into our powers as we go through puberty."

"So you've been Seeing since you were, like, eleven?"

"July."

"July what?" I opened a bottle of body wash and immediately rejected it. I would rather smell like wolf than roses.

"I started Seeing in July."

I poked my head around the curtain to look at my friend who had built a fort around her out of scented lotions. "July? Of this year? You've been wearing a bra since the fourth grade and had your first period before we started middle school. I think you're a bit past puberty at this point."

Talley stopped arranging the multi-colored bottles and looked up at me, grimacing at the puddles of water my dripping hair left on the floor. "I said that we're *supposed* to come into our Sight when we go through puberty. I was a late bloomer. Everyone thought I was a squib until I had a vision over the summer." She handed me a loofah and motioned for me to continue my de-wolfing.

"I thought you were a Touch-a-Soul or whatever. You have visions too?"

"Well, Mom thought it was a vision, but then I started doing the whole touching thing. Since Seeing is an only-one-item-per-customer kind of thing, it obviously wasn't a *real* vision. Not that I can convince the boys of that."

The water had gone from hot to luke warm to tepid and was now threatening to slide into the land of flat-out cold. I had enough of cold last night to last a while, so I shut off the shower, confident that my potpourri of floral and fruity scents would mask any lingering Alex-related aromas.

"What was your vision of?" I asked, wrapping a large towel around me before I stepped out of the shower.

Talley twisted a piece of hair around her fingers and looked at the wall just to the right of my head. "It was nothing."

Nope, she hadn't developed super-lying skills over night. That was good to know.

"Still keeping secrets from me?"

"I'm sorry. I should tell you. It will help you to understand. It's just that..." She took a deep breath and looked me in the eye. "You understand that it's not a real vision, right? I can't See the future. This isn't going to happen." Her intensity was a bit unsettling.

"Not a real vision. Got it."

"I was watching one of those reality TV shows with the has-been almost-celebrities. I must have fallen asleep without realizing it because I thought I saw this man walking through the living room. I had never seen him before, but I immediately knew he was a Shifter. Something about him just seemed so animalistic." She paused and ran her fingers through her now knotted hair.

"He wasn't wearing a shirt. His chest was covered in blood, but not his. It had all came from the person that lay limp in his arms. There were claw marks across her stomach, shirt and flesh ripped to shreds." Talley rubbed her eyes as if the image was affixed to the back of her eyelids. "There was so much blood. It was everywhere. Her clothes were drenched, it was dried on her face and matted in her hair. But still, even caked in blood and completely lifeless, I knew who he was carrying." My heart hammered in my chest, already anticipating the punch line. "It was you, Scout." Talley's voice trembled. "He was carrying you."

Well, that sucked. "Good thing it wasn't a real vision, huh?"

"It's why they hate them, why they don't want you near Alex. They're afraid that if you get too close to him that he'll —"

"Gut me like a pig?"

Talley flinched. "It's not funny."

"Which is why I'm not laughing." I didn't find this even remotely funny. I wasn't worried about Alex. Alex would never hurt me, but Talley had seen a man. An animalistic man. I only knew one of those, and imagining him having a desire to disembowel me wasn't hard. "When did you have this not-really-a-vision vision?"

"July fifth." She was back to the hair twirling routine. "And before you ask, yes, that's the same day the Coles moved here."

That certainly was convenient. I sat down on the edge of the bathtub, unsure that my legs could continue to hold me. "But you can't See the future, right?"

"Alex would never hurt you."

"I know that." She wasn't answering my question and I knew why. Uncertainty was written clearly all over her face. "Does he know about this?"

"No."

"But Jase and Charlie do? And they think it's really going to happen?"

"They think it's too much of coincidence, them showing up and the vision. And then, with Alex's obvious obsession with you..." She shook her head. I wasn't sure if her dismay was aimed at Charlie and Jase's belief in the vision or Alex's feelings towards me. "I've tried to tell them, explain how much Alex loves you, that he's completely incapable of causing you harm, but they won't hear it. Well, Charlie hears it, but that doesn't really help."

"What about Liam?" I asked through numb lips.

Talley's focus shifted to the right of my head again. "What about him?"

"He's capable of ki...hurting me, isn't he?"

"I don't know."

I did. He was more than capable, he was willing.

I grabbed a bottle from the lotion fort. "I need to get dressed," I said. "I'll be out in a minute."

Talley nodded and got up to leave. She paused with one hand on the door. "I'm not a Future Seer, Scout. No one is going to hurt you."

I forced up the corners of my mouth. "I know. It's no big," I said, grateful that I was capable of lying convincingly.

Chapter 17

Finding out that Liam Cole might kill me was disturbing to say the least, but I had been aware of the possibility since August. Sure, I lost some sleep those first few nights after Talley's revelation, but eventually I was able to stop obsessing to the point of distraction. That didn't mean, however, I had forgotten.

"You know, having my guts ripped out by a werewolf is starting to sound not so bad," I said as Talley jabbed me in the skull with a bobby pin.

"Must we resort to gallows humor?" Talley used unnecessary force as she situated another long strand of hair onto the back of my head.

"Well, it's bound to hurt less. What on earth are you doing back there?"

"Trying to get this to stay in place. I swear, even your hair is stubborn."

"You don't really have to go to the trouble. What's the point? It's not like I have an actual prom date."

"Alex will be there. Don't you want to look nice for him?"

When Alex found out I was being forced into attending prom, he decided to go too. I suggested that he ask Joi, since she had recently been dumped by John Davis. I knew better than to be jealous, and I wasn't, but I did feel like a loser.

"Okay, that's it." Talley doused my head with half a can of industrial strength, only-for-Southern-women hairspray. "Go look," she said, pointing to the full length mirror mounted on the wall.

I didn't recognize the girl staring back at me. The dress Mrs. Matthews constructed looked like something out of an edgy fairy tale. She had attached layers upon layers of sheer gossamer material in a range of soft metallic shades to the crazy corset/bodice. The cut gave the illusion of a tiny waist and sizable chest, while the colors make my skin, hair, and eyes look more ethereal than freakish. Oddly enough, the messy up-do Talley had arranged on top of my head looked elegant and sexy.

"I thought you guys were Seers, not witches."

"Witches?"

"Yeah, witches. Only witches are capable of magical transformations of this degree. Well, witches and fairies. Are you and your mom fairies?"

Talley laughed and came to stand beside me. "So, you like it? Do you feel pretty, oh so pretty?"

"I did until I saw myself next to you." Talley's dress was the more glamorous of Mrs. Matthews's prom creations. It was cut to make Talley look like a voluptuous sex goddess and was dyed the exact same shade of blue as her eyes. Her hair hung in perfect, shiny spiral curls. "Poor James. He's not going to know what hit him."

A hint of red colored her creamy cheeks. "It's not like that. I'm not trying to seduce him or anything. I just want him to have one nice night, one night to feel like he belongs, in his entire high school career."

"Saint Talley," I teased.

A knock on the door prevented Talley from shrugging off the comment in her trademark modesty or delivering a speech on how we should always do the right thing, whichever she was preparing. It was okay; I had heard them both before.

Mrs. Matthews stuck her head in the door, giving us a rare look of approval. "Well, you girls look just as pretty as a picture," she said, her Appalachian accent becoming more pronounced in her obvious cheerful state. "I can't believe how grown up you're getting."

He eyes glistened in the light and I feared that she was going to shed an actual tear.

"Thank you, Mrs. Matthews. This dress is amazing. You've really outdone yourself," I said, remembering my manners.

Mrs. Matthews eyes critically trailed over me. "I should've put a bit more material up top. Your mama ain't going to be proud that you're showing off your breasts to God and everybody."

Okay, now I was blushing. Mrs. Matthews shouldn't talk about my boobs and who could see them. Ever. And she really shouldn't try to readjust the top of my dress so they were better concealed, but I was too mortified to mention that to her.

"I reckon that will have to do," she said, sighing at my bosom. "Your dates are getting tired of waiting on you two out there."

"Dates?"

"What? Is that not the right thing to call them nowadays? Are they hooker-uppers?"

"Hooker-uppers?" I didn't know what that was supposed to be, but it sounded dirty.

"Scout is going stag, Mom. That means that she doesn't have a date."

It also meant I was pathetic, but whatever.

"Well, someone should have told that poor boy sitting in my living room."

Talley and I exchanged a look of confusion before rushing down the hall. Mrs. Matthews wasn't kidding. There were, indeed, dates. James sat on the edge of the loud floral print sofa like he was prepared to bolt out the door at a moment's notice. He looked...well, not good, but better. His hair had been washed and brushed, and he wore a tux as opposed to his normal too-short Wal-Mart jeans and Nintendo T-Shirt. Of course, the tux looked two sizes too big and the angry red marks on his face were more obvious without a curtain of greasy hair to hide them, but it was an improvement.

In contrast, the other guy looked like a GQ model perched on the arm of the sofa.

"Charlie?"

"It's Hagan. Charles Hagan," he said in a rather remarkable Sean Connery impersonation.

"What are you doing here?"

He stood up and straightened his jacket. "I am here to escort you to the dance, m' lady."

"Since when?"

"Dammit. I knew I forgot something. Okay, here we go." He took a deep breath and affected a look that reeked of fake sincerity. "Scout, will you please go to prom with me?"

"Nope."

"Too bad. I'm taking you anyway."

"Listen, I know Jase put you up to this--"

Charlie executed a snort-chuckle hybrid and shook his head. "Jase didn't put me up to anything. I drove four hours, rented this stupid monkey suit, and bought some rather attractive flowers because I wanted to take you to the prom. Now, say you'll go with me."

I felt certain there were other reasons bringing Charlie to Timber this particular weekend, but I let it slide. "Let me see those flowers."

His smile was triumphant as he slid the corsage on my wrist. They really were rather attractive, for the most part. Tiny, delicate roses in every color imaginable were interspersed with baby's breath. I couldn't understand, however, why someone had stuck a clump of oddly shaped yellow flowers in the middle. "What kind of flower is this?"

"I'm supposed to be a botanist now?"

"Are you going to be snippy all night?"

"Does that mean we'll be together all night?"

Like there was ever any doubt. "I guess it won't kill me to help you relive your high school glory days for one night."

"That's what I thought," he said slinging an arm over my shoulder.

Dinner was a painfully awkward affair. Valero's, one of only two formal dining establishments within a forty-five minute drive of the school, had overbooked. The four of us crammed ourselves around a table meant for two. We kept bumping elbows and grabbing the wrong water glass. Charlie attempted to engage James in conversation, but that went over about as well as a Joan Crawford parenting manual.

The dance was held in our high school gym. I've heard rumor that some schools have prom in swanky hotels. That sounds nice. Unfortunately, there are no swanky hotels near Timber. The only place with a ball room is the state park lodge and no one wanted to fight the roaches for the dance floor.

At Lake County High the Juniors host the prom for the Seniors. They pick the theme, hire the entertainment, provide refreshments, and decorate. My first thought upon entering the gym was that the Juniors hated us. The room looked like Barnum and Bailey's had exploded. Red and white awning hung from the middle of the ceiling and cascaded down the walls. Balloon bouquets served as centerpieces for the tables along the edge of the dance floor. I noticed in horror that people were expected to have their pictures taken with a giant cement elephant. "You've got to be kidding me."

Charlie was shaking with laughter. "Jase is going to freak." He pointed towards the center of the floor where the DJ was dressed as a clown.

"Stop it," Talley said. "Lots of people are genuinely afraid of clowns. Poor Jase. This is going to ruin his prom."

Charlie and I only laughed harder.

"I guess it could be worse," Charlie said. "They could have--" I never figured out exactly how it could have been worse because at that moment he recognized the couple sitting at the table Talley was walking towards. My stomach dropped to my knees.

"Joi, you look great!" I said a little too enthusiastically. "That looks just like the dress Megan Fox wore to the MTV awards last year."

"Oh my God! I totally thought so too!" My compliment caused Joi to literally vibrate with excitement. "Wow! Who is your date? He's super-cute!"

"You remember Charlie, don't you?"

"Oh, you're Jase's cousin, right?" Joi turned to Alex, who was the very picture of dapper aloofness in his black suit and tie. "Alex, this is Charlie. He's Jase's cousin, but, you know, he's not really related to Scout, so them being here together isn't nearly as icky as it sounds." I would have to remember to thank Joi for that later. "Charlie, this is Alex."

Charlie did the guy nod thing and Alex offered a "hey" in response. It wasn't the warmest of greetings, but no one was throwing punches. That was a good start. There were only two empty seats, which left me with the option of sitting between Charlie and Alex or allowing the two of them to sit next to each other. As I slid into my chair, I pressed my foot against Alex's ankle.

"Nice flowers," he said, casually glancing where my hand rested on the table. I wondered if he noticed how I kept inching it towards his.

"They are pretty, aren't they? I didn't know roses came in quite so many colors." I could do casual conversation, right?

Alex met Charlie's eyes with a look of wry amusement. "The yellow flower is an interesting choice."

"I've never seen one like it before," I admitted. That sounded better than, *It's ugly and looks awkward in the middle of all the pretty roses.*

"It's wolfsbane," James offered timidly from across the table.

Wolfsbane? Seriously? Leave it to Charlie.

"Doesn't that like kill werewolves or something?" Joi asked.

"Depends on which mythology you're going with," James said. His voice was more confident as he discussed one of his favorite topics - weird stuff. "Some stories say that it helps identify a wolf, others that it can suppress the change. In one of the Dracula movies it was used to ward off vampires."

185

"In *Gingersnaps* it was used to make a cure for lycanthropy," Talley chimed in.

James beamed at her. It was the first time I had ever seen him smile. It could have been the first time that he had smiled in his life, period. It vastly improved his looks. "You're a *Gingersnaps* fan?"

"My mom would die if she knew, but I've watched it at least ten times." James' enthusiasm was bordering on adorable as he and Talley slipped into movie geek mode.

The smart thing for me to have done would have been to let the wolfsbane subject drop. I considered it before turning to Charlie and saying, "That was so thoughtful of you, but the full moon isn't until tomorrow night."

He didn't even flinch. "Wolfsbane, huh? I told them to stick some bergamot blossoms in there." He reached across the table to gather my wrist in his warm hands. "My flaky ecology professor said that it would put the wearer under the control of the person who gave it to them. I was going to use it to make you dance with me tonight." His mouth turned up into a wicked half-smile as one finger traced from my inner wrist to the fold of my elbow. I knew it was all just a show for Alex, but my heart sputtered and goosebumps broke out over my skin just the same. "I guess I'll have to find some other way to persuade you."

Joi did her awkward fake laugh thing. "Of course she's going to dance with you. You're her prom date."

"I don't dance."

More awkward fake laughter, which was quickly getting on my nerves. "Don't be such a Debbie Downer. It's prom. You have to dance."

Why couldn't my parents have raised me church of Christ where dancing was considered the eighth deadly sin? "I don't have to do anything," I snapped. Joi flinched, making me feel instantaneous guilt. My shoulders drooped under the weight of it. "You know I can't dance. I'm rhythmically challenged."

Alex hitched up the corner of his mouth, flashing a dimple. "Anyone can dance, Scout. You just need someone to teach you."

My brief fantasy of swaying to the music in Alex's arms was cut short by Charlie gripping my wrist so tightly he may have left fingerprints on the bone.

"Yeah, dancing is easy," Joi said. "We can show you how it's done. Right, Alex?"

"Of course." He pulled out Joi's chair for her, like the gentleman he was. To anyone else he probably looked as though he didn't have a care in the world. However, to someone that had obsessively studied every aspect of his physical form for months the pain was obvious.

The desire to go comfort him was almost unbearable. I longed to embrace him and tell him that I loved him, a proclamation I hadn't got around to making yet. Charlie's hand felt like a shackle on my arm.

Talley and James soon joined Joi and Alex, leaving me alone at the table with Charlie. As my friends danced, he kept a running commentary on the people surrounding us. I barely listened as he made cracks about Ashley's skank-alicious attire and Jordan's attempts at doing the robot. I was entirely focused on unravelling the knot in my stomach.

Charlie made several attempts to coax me onto the dance floor, but I kept shrugging him off. I was not in the mood to exhibit my less than stunning dance skills to the entire school. Instead, I watched Alex as he bounced around with Joi and Talley. I thought he might return to the table after leading Joi to get refreshments, but instead he stood around with a group of Seniors that showed even less interest in dancing than I did. After a couple of songs, he walked out the double doors.

"Where are you going?" Charlie asked before I even realized I was on my feet.

"Bathroom," I mouthed, weaving my way through the sea of bodies between me and the doors. I pushed through them just in time to see Alex slip out into the parking lot. I ran down the hall and caught up with him just as he was getting into his car.

"What are you doing?"

He jumped at the sound of my voice. "Leaving. Joi and John have reconciled, so there is no reason for me to hang around."

"You don't have to leave"

"Yes, I do."

"Why?" I reached for him, but he stepped away.

"For the same reason I can't let you touch me." He moved some loose gravel around with the toe of his shiny dress shoes.

"Is it Charlie? Listen, I didn't know he was going to do this. He just showed up in a tux with these stupid flowers and--"

"Scout, it's not your fault. It's mine. The full moon is too close. The wolf in me is dying to establish his dominance. If I stay, I'll attack him, and you won't be able to forgive me for that."

"I don't understand. You do okay being around Jase at school."

Alex looked up, his steely gaze catching mine before dropping ever so slightly to rest on the necklace that lay against my throat. "Charlie is different."

"I'll go home, too. I don't want to be here if you're not."

"No, you should stay. Have fun. Explore your options."

"My options?"

"He's in love you. He'll be good to you, take care of you. You deserve something better than I can give you."

I was silent for a long time, unsure of what to say. Alex was wrong. He had to be. I didn't know if I could deal with it if he wasn't. "I don't want options," I finally said. "I want you. You're my destiny, remember?"

Alex shoved his hands in his pocket and tried to smile. "I said that you were my destiny, not that I'm yours. I've never fooled myself into believing I could keep you."

I blinked furiously to keep the tears that stung my eyes from falling. He reached up and gently traced my jawline. "I shouldn't have done that," he said dropping his hand back to his side. "It's just so hard to not touch you." He closed his eyes, taking a long, deep breath. "Please, go back inside, Scout. Don't let me ruin your Senior Prom. Promise me you'll try to have a good time."

I reluctantly nodded my head. "If that's what you want."

"I do." He gave me one last bitter sweet smile before opening his car door. "Goodnight, Scout."

I lingered until I saw his tail lights grow dim in the distance. I went back inside, determined to have fun despite the battered state of my heart in order to keep my word to Alex. One look at my table, however, made me realize that was going to be easier said than done. Charlie was slumped down in his chair, staring a hole in the wall while Jase glowered at the dance floor.

"Where have you been?" Charlie asked without looking up when I sat down beside him.

"I told you, I had to go to the bathroom. Not an easy task in this dress."

Charlie started to say something, but Jase cut him off. "What the hell is she doing?"

The "she" he was referring to appeared to be Talley, whose hips were keeping perfect time with the Rick James song pouring from the speakers. "I think they call that dancing."

Jase's glassy eyes swung towards me. "I mean, what is she doing with that loser?" He gestured wildly towards James. "If I had known she was that hard up for a date I would have made one of the underclassmen on the team ask her out." He leaned towards me as he spoke. The smell on his breath almost knocked me out of my chair.

"You're drunk."

Jase poked his nose three times with his index finger. "Nope. I can still feel my nose. I'm good."

Well, at least I understood Charlie's mood. Charles, Sr. was an alcoholic, and not a very nice one. As a result Charlie had developed some rather strong feelings about liquor and drunks.

"What is this all about?" I asked Charlie. Jase had resumed his nose tapping intoxication test, adding in the occasional "beep-beep".

"Apparently the clown was too much for him to handle."

"What are we supposed to do with him?"

Charlie regarded Jase, who had moved on to air drumming along to a drum-free hip-hop song. "I think our first step should be to deny knowing him. Just say that he's a random stranger that started talking to us."

"Not what I meant."

Charlie sighed. "He's fine. Tinsley is driving him to Tyler's and promises not to let him drink anything else."

I know this sounds like an Adam Ant confession, but I don't have much experience with drunk people. Charlie has always sheltered me from his father, and I never had the desire to go to any of the wild parties down at the cove. When Talley and I got together our drug of choice was chocolate. Jase tried to get me to drink a beer in the tenth grade, but I refused on the grounds that it smelled like horse pee. Without my willing participation, he had also given up on the endeavor. Seeing Jase so obviously not himself was upsetting. "Have you been drinking water?" I asked him.

"Walker? No. No Johnny. Jack. Jack's a good ol' Tennessee boy."

It would almost be funny if he wasn't so pathetic. "Not Walker. *Water*. Have you been drinking *water*?"

Jase looked at me like I just asked if he ate kangaroo for breakfast.

"You need to drink lots of water to keep from getting sick. Come on. Let's go get you a bottle."

Jase, of course, argued with me. As I tried to explain the whole concept of alcohol and dehydration, Charlie slipped off, promising to bring back some Aquafina. I was grateful when Talley and James, who looked very sweaty but happy, came back to the table.

"Thank God, sober people."

"Oh, it's you," Jase said to James. "You know she's too good for you, right?"

"Yeah, I know," James said, his face seemingly stuck in this new smile thing he was trying out. "It helps to know that you're not good enough for her either."

"Oh gross! Talley is like my sister. We used to take baths together."

"We never took baths together."

"Yeah, we did."

"No, we didn't. Now get down before you fall and break your head." Talley moved to take hold of Jase's arm, but he jerked away from her.

"Don't touch me!" he snarled, stumbling off the table.

James stepped between Talley and my belligerent brother. "Don't talk to her that way!"

Jase pushed James back a step. "Are you wanting to start something with me, freak?"

James was weighing his options when a pair of hands grabbed Jase's shoulders. "Did anyone ever tell you that you're kind of an asshat when you're drunk?" Charlie asked.

"Screw you."

"Funny you should mention screwing, Dude, cause that's what it looks like Jordan and your date are doing."

Sure enough, Jordan and Tinsley were on the corner of the dance floor, grinding together in a fashion that only the most lenient of definitions would consider dancing. I had never actually watched a porno before, but was pretty sure some of them were less graphic than what I was seeing.

"That son of a--" Jase took off through the throng of bodies, pushing anyone who dared to get in his way.

"Should we do something?" I asked Charlie, my eyes glued to Jase's retreating form.

"Yes, we should dance."

"Charlie, I don't think--"

"Actually, the problem is that you think too much." His hand brushed against my face, following the exact same path that Alex had touched earlier. "Please, Scout? Please dance with me?" His voice broke, along with my resolve.

I followed Charlie to the dance floor, my heart and stomach in the wrong places. Just as we settled on a spot of our own the thumping bass ended and was replaced with familiar piano chords. I smiled in wonder as the singer's voice warbled through the speakers. "I would have bet good money this clown never heard of Tom Waits."

Charlie beamed. "He hadn't."

"What did you do?" I was acutely aware of his arms as they held me around the waist.

"I explained that I had a promise to keep to a girl." The heels on the strappy shoes I wore put me at eye level with Charlie. I was fascinated by the fact they were actually multiple shades of green, darker on the edges and getting lighter closer to his pupils. "Then I showed him how to hook up my iPod to his sound system. The guy is *old*. He has to be at least thirty. I don't think he had ever seen an iPod before."

"What promise?"

"I didn't think you remembered." Charlie looked extremely pleased with himself. "We were watching *Cinderella*, and you begged me to take you to a Ball so that you could dance with a handsome prince."

A memory tugged in the back of my mind. "And you told me that I would have to settle for dancing with you at prom."

"You've been very stubborn about letting me fulfill that obligation. I thought I was going to have to slip you some roofies just to get you out here."

"How on earth did you remember? That had to have been more than seven years ago."

He pulled me closer and I felt my heart jump from my stomach to my throat. "I've been looking forward to this dance for a long time." He leaned forward and rested his lips by my ear. "It was worth the wait. You look beautiful tonight, Scout."

I felt the familiar warmth of embarrassment in my cheeks. "I'll pass your compliment on to Mrs. Matthews, Magical Seamstress."

His breath was warm against my ear as he chuckled. "The dress is nothing without the girl inside it."

I couldn't think of a witty retort, so I just silently relaxed into his arms and enjoyed the sensation. Afterwards, Charlie tried to get me to stay on the dance floor and attempt a faster paced song, but I declared his promise paid in full and returned to our table. We stayed another hour, watching as Tinsley helped Jase out the door and sighing in relief when she called to inform Charlie that his cousin was officially the worst prom date ever, having been drunk the entire dance and missing the after party on account of passing out in somebody's hammock.

Charlie was staying at my house for the weekend, so the time honored act of walking a date to her door left him saying his goodnights just outside my bedroom.

"Did you have fun tonight?"

"Yeah, I did." I was surprised to find I wasn't lying. Sure, there had been some angst and drama, but it had its moments, like discovering James Kiplinger knew the Electric Slide. "Thank you, Charlie."

"Hey, the night is still young. Why don't you change into some pajamas and we'll watch a few episodes of *Glee*? I'll even let you sing along."

"Tempting, but I have an all-night cram session tomorrow for Monday's test in Calculus, and it's going to take me an hour to figure out how to get out of this thing and find the three hundred bobby pins Talley put in my hair."

"Here, let me help." Charlie moved behind me and started undoing the series of hooks that ran along my spine. A slight tremble when through my body as his fingers brushed against my bare back.

"Was she expecting you to wear this for the rest of your life or what?"

"I think it's Mrs. Matthews's own version of a chastity belt. She figures that any guy would grow bored after the first ten hooks. I really feel bad for James. Talley's dress had twice as many as mine."

Charlie let out a puff of air that tickled the hairs on my neck. "It's not having its desired effect," he growled. I felt a warmth deep in my abdomen as he fumbled with the last few clasps. Was it my imagination or were his fingers trembling?

"Do you..." I felt him take a deep breath before clearing his throat. "Do you need help with the hair too?"

I nodded, unsure that I could verbalize. I let out a sigh as his hands moved through my hair, gently releasing individual strands, one at a time.

"Do you love him?" he asked so quietly I wasn't certain he had spoken at all.

"Who?"

"I'm not as stupid as you think I am, Scout. I see the way you look at each other, the way you are around him."

"I...I don't think you're stupid. And I have no idea what you're talking about." My heart tripped out a rhythm that betrayed me.

He turned me so that we were standing face to face. I clutched the top of my dress in both hands, holding it in place.

"I could love you better. I'll give you anything you want, whatever it takes to make you happy. Can he say the same?"

I looked into Charlie's eyes and realized Talley was right. It was possible to love two people at the same time, but it wasn't possible to keep them both. Standing there in the dark hallway with my prom dress half-on, feeing the heat of Charlie's body warming mine, I made the hardest decision of my life.

Chapter 18

Charlie's truck was gone when I left for church the next morning. I wasn't surprised, but I was disappointed. I wanted him to be there, acting as if nothing had happened, as if I hadn't broken his heart along with everything we had together.

"Please, Scout," he begged me. I had seen that pained expression on his face countless times over the years, but never before had I been the cause of it. I hated myself more in that moment than I had ever hated anyone or anything. "Please, just think about it. You don't have to decide anything right now."

But he was wrong. And I didn't regret my decision. What Alex and I shared was preternaturally right. I couldn't give him up no more than I could give up breathing. Did that mean that I loved Charlie any less? No. It just meant I couldn't be with him.

And that sucked.

I don't know what I said, or even if I said anything at all. I do know that I ran away like the coward I am and locked myself in the bathroom, seeking solace in the sanctuary of the shower for as long as the hot water held out.

Our Sunday morning sermon focused on the sins of the flesh, Reverend Jessup assuring us that those who gave into the temptations of alcohol, drugs, and sex would burn eternally in the fiery pits of hell. I don't think I was just imagining that the preacher's eyes kept returning to the empty space on the pew next to me where Jase should have been sitting.

I spent the rest of the day hiding in my bedroom, though not so well Angel couldn't find me. She danced around my room with Guido, demanding a blow by blow account of prom night. She didn't leave me alone until we heard Jase stumble in just after noon. Angry voices floated up through the air vents almost immediately. While Dad's lecture hit the relevant points of underage drinking, breaking curfew, and irresponsible behavior, Mom seemed fixated on the fact that she wouldn't be able to return Jase's tux to the rental place. That was just too much for Angel to handle. She bounded out the door to witness the action first hand. I was half tempted to follow, but knew all I had to do was wait. Sure enough, it wasn't long before there was a light tapping at my door.

"Scout?" Jase came shuffling in, shutting the door behind him. His hair was fairly comical - half of it matted against his head and the other half sticking straight out - but it paled in comparison to his tux. Someone must have scrounged up one of those on-the-go bleach pens and used it on the pants and jacket.

"Fun night?"

"So I hear," he said dropping onto my bed. "I don't really remember anything after dinner. Strike that. I remember a sadistic clown torturing teenagers with the Spice Girls before chopping them all to bits."

"The auditory torture I remember, but the mutilation isn't ringing any bells."

"It was coming. Promise."

Jase curled up into the fetal position and threw a pillow over his eyes. When I thought he had fallen asleep, or possibly slipped into a coma, I turned my attention back to my calculus book. I was still staring blankly at the page, attempting to remember the last step that made sense, when Jase asked, "Where's Charlie?"

"I don't know." My best guess had him burning a picture of me in effigy.

Jase threw off the pillow, sat up, and winced at the light in the room. "What do you mean you don't know? What happened?"

196

"Nothing," I lied.

I wondered if Charlie would tell him. Last year, when Charlie found out Crystal Hobbs had been cheating on him with an enlisted guy, Jase pulled him through that first tough weekend with nonstop gaming and multiple assurances that he was better off without that skanky bitch.

What would he do now that I was the skanky bitch?

I felt as wretched as Jase looked. My guilt and broken heart almost convinced me to cancel my plans for the evening. I wasn't a hundred percent certain I would go through with it until Talley pulled into the driveway.

"Are you sure you want to do this?" she asked, turning down the painfully cheerful song she had been jamming to. I had my head pressed to the passenger side window, watching the new buds on the trees become a green blur against the blue sky. "He will understand if you back out. No one expects you to do this just to prove how brave you are or how okay you are with all this or whatever it is that you're trying to do."

I peeled myself off the window. "Of course I want to do this. I'm excited."

Talley's eyebrows rose skeptically. "Once more, with feeling."

"I'm not scared." I punched the power button on the radio, unable to endure another second of pop music. "I..." I took in a lung full of air. "Charlie let me know that I had options last night."

The car swerved over the double yellow line, then jerked back into our lane with enough force to slam me against the seatbelt.

"He did *what*?!?" Talley was trying to divide her attention equally between me and the serpentine road. I was too depressed to fear for my life.

"I think I really hurt him, Tal. He just looked so...*broken*."

"You told him no?"

I nodded as a single tear slipped free.

Talley let the information soak in before replying. "Well, now everyone knows where they stand. That's good." She noted my expression and amended that. "Well, it's not *good* good. Right now it's kind of sucky, but its for the best in the end."

"Do you think I made the right choice?" My voice was pathetically weak and whiny.

I was grateful that Talley took the time to think about it instead of just blurting out a confirmation to placate me. "Charlie's great, and he'll always be a big part of your life, but he's not Alex. I don't think Charlie is the wrong choice, but that Alex is more right. Does that make sense?"

"Perfect sense." It was pretty much my thoughts, word for word. I would have thought she had pulled it out of my head if she had been touching me.

"And don't worry about Charlie. You guys will get through this. You care way too much about each other to let something like this screw up a lifetime of friendship."

I whisked away any spare moisture hanging out on my face. "You're the bestest best friend a girl could ever have. What would I ever do without you?"

"Well, you wouldn't be doing this," she said, turning off the highway onto a one lane back road, "which might not be a bad thing."

After less than half a mile the road turned to gravel, tossing Talley's little car around and planting a seed of doubt in my stomach that had to be rooted out before we reached our destination.

"I have to do this."

"No, you don't. You shouldn't. It is the text book definition of a bad idea. There is probably an entire Wikipedia entry on it under the heading of 'Bad Ideas'."

"Why? Why is it a bad idea? I mean, really, what do you think is going to happen?"

Talley shot me a look that screamed, *Have you gone insane?* "You do understand that he is going to turn into a wolf, right?"

"Really? A wolf? I thought Alex was a were-fluffy-little-bunny."

198

Talley's expression indicated that she did not share my appreciation for verbal irony.

"Yes, he's going to turn into a wolf," I sighed, "but he's still going to be Alex."

"Part of him will be Alex. The other part will be a wolf. A wild, predatory animal that acts on instinct instead of logic."

"One, wolves rarely attack humans. And two, as long as there is a tiny part of Alex in there, he isn't going to hurt me and you know it."

Talley's car slowed to a snail's pace as she negotiated a spot of the road that had washed away ages ago. "What about my vision?"

"You don't have visions. You can't See the future."

"I know, but--"

"And even if you could, it's Liam we would have to worry about, and he can Shift anytime the mood strikes. Going out on the night of a full moon does not up my danger level, but seeing Alex in wolf form might help me figure out how to defend myself in the event that your non-vision vision tries to come true."

"I just have a really bad feeling about this, Scout. Please, let me take you home."

We were nearing the place where the road dead-ended into the forest. Knowing that I was going to see Alex in a matter of moments steeled my nerves.

"No, I want to do this," I said confidently. "Plus, you don't have time. You're barely going to make it to Toby's house before sundown as it is."

She conceded defeat by throwing the car into park and pulling me into a rib-crushing hug. I sent an *It's going to be okay* message her way mentally, something I was still getting used to.

"Promise me you'll be safe."

"Cross my heart, hope to die."

"Scout! Don't hope that!"

I laughed as I opened the door and gathered up my things, my mood suddenly elevated by the boy walking towards the car. "Have a

good night, Tal. Go howl at the moon." I winked as I slammed the
door shut on her wary expression.

Alex was immediately there, his mouth saying hello to mine
without the assistance of words. " I wasn't sure you were coming," he
said as Talley drove away, kicking up a cloud of dust in her wake. "I
thought you might have changed your mind."

"Not a chance." I pulled him in for another kiss. This time
when we pulled apart I held his eyes with mine. My hand brushed
his hair across his forehead. "I love you."

"You do?"

"Of course I do. How could you not know that?"

"I just thought...you know, with Charlie last night..."

"Last night I did what you asked me to do. I weighed my
options and..." I kissed the tip of his nose. "I choose you, Pikachu."

Alex lifted me into the air and spun me around, a testament to
his lycan strength. He was still laughing when his mouth closed over
mine. As I ran my hands greedily over his back I felt a muscle twitch
against my fingers.

"While this is very entertaining, it's not the show I came for," I
said, disentangling myself from his arms. I made a shooing motion
with my hand. "Go. Change."

Alex flashed his perfect dimples. "Not here." He grabbed my
hand and led me towards what could have passed for a mountain
compared to the low hills that surrounded it. "I want to show you
something."

There was no trail leading up, but that didn't bother either of
us. It was a beautiful evening for a hike. The air hung heavy with the
sickeningly sweet smell of honeysuckle. The newly green grass was
adorned with hundreds of yellow daffodils.

"So, what's with the chicken?" he asked when I handed him
the bag so I could pull myself up the rocky embankment that he
easily leapt atop of.

"Talley's idea. She said you would need food post Change, and
she didn't like the idea of you leaving me alone in the woods in order

to hunt. I only took it to be polite." I finally managed to hoist myself up to where Alex waited. "You don't have to eat it. I'll be fine while you go snag a rabbit or squirrel or whatever. I know how much you love to hunt."

I reached out to take the bag back, but he grabbed my proffered hand to drag me further up the hill. "Correction, hunting I like. You, I love. Well, you and KFC extra-crispy. So much better than raw rabbit."

We reached the spot where the trees began to thin. Once we rounded a large rock, I found myself in a clearing that had been prepared for my arrival. A blanket was spread on the ground next to a rolled up sleeping bag and pillow. A dozen white pillar candles were scattered about.

"It's our first real date," Alex said, blushing ever so slightly. "I wanted it to be nice."

I squeezed his hand, staring in awe at the view. The summit of the hill broke off into the lake, creating a scene that looked more like Colorado than Kentucky. "This is beautiful. You definitely win the Best First Date Location award."

"I'm glad you like it." He guided me over to the blanket, and then helped me take off the backpack I had been carrying.

"So, I'm curious, what did you bring?" he asked as he began lighting the candles.

"Oh, you know, frisbees, tennis balls, rawhides. I'm really excited. I've never had a puppy before."

The look of horror on Alex's face was priceless.

"A sweater, some flashlights, and my calculus book. I told my parents I was studying for tomorrow's test, and that's what I plan on doing. Not all of us--"

Alex's body convulsed violently causing a small shriek to escape my lips.

"I'm fine," he said. I had trouble believing him since he wasn't quite through shaking yet. I read in Dr. Smith's book that postponing the change was possible, but it was both difficult and painful. If a Shifter waited too long to begin the process on his own, he would begin the Change involuntarily, which never went smoothly.

"Go. Change. Now."

"No, I can wait a little longer. I'm fine. Really."

He looked the exact opposite of fine. I could see muscles shifting beneath his skin. "This is insane. You're hurting yourself for no good reason. Please, go change. I'll be right here when you get back."

I don't know if it was my plea or the second convulsion that changed his mind. He stopped to kiss me one last time on his way back into the woods. "I don't want you to be scared of me."

How could I ever be scared of him? "I won't be. Promise."

"I love you."

"I love you, too. Now, go make me a wolf."

I waited until Alex was out of sight and then went over to the edge of the cliff. The setting sun cast long shadows down below, causing the gnarled old oak tree on the opposite shore to look like a Halloween decoration.

The oak tree that looked strangely familiar.

I walked several yards along the edge, trying see it from a different angle, but something wasn't right. I crouched down and looked sharply over the edge. Much as I suspected, the hill did not drop straight down into the water. A cliff actually jutted out over a little strip of rocky beach, littered with driftwood and fallen limbs. It was a strip of beach I knew very well. I had stood on it many nights since November.

Well, that was perplexing.

I sat down and surveyed the opposite shore, matching up details from my dreams with what was there as the suns rays faded out. There was no doubt. This was definitely the spot I had been dreaming about.

Six months ago I would have chalked it all up to coincidence and gone on without another thought. In my logical, Shifter-and-

Seer-free world, dreams had no hidden agendas or underlying meanings. But now?

What did I believe now? I sat for a long time, buried deep in thought.

Alex was perfectly silent when he came up beside me. It was only the smell of Colonel Sander's secret recipe that alerted me to his presence. His wolf form was even more majestic than I remembered. Every inch of him was sleek and lean. Dark fur surrounded his eyes, making them glow silver.

"Hey, you. Welcome back." I reached out, but paused with my hand inches from him. "Is it going to be offensive if I pet you?"

Alex ducked his head and brought it back up so my outstretched hand landed between his ears. I gave it a good pat or two before running my fingers down through the soft, thick fur of his neck.

"Do you want to hear something weird? Well, it's weird to me. You might just think that I'm stupid for getting so worked up about it." I continued to stroke his fur as I babbled on. "I've dreamt of this place. A lot. And in my dreams you're always over there," I indicated the opposite shore with a wave of my arm, "and I'm on the beach down below. And even though it's obviously not very far across, we can't ever hear each other." Alex stared at me with his silvery grey eyes. "Do you think that's weird?"

Wolf stare.

Was he trying to tell me something with that stare?

"Ummm... tap your paw once for yes?"

That look was telling me something. Something that sounded an awful lot like, *You've got to be kidding me*, but he tapped his paw once all the same.

"Yeah, I thought so too." I draped my arm over his back and leaned against his neck. "Of course, I'm having this conversation with a wolf, so I guess weird is a relative term."

We stayed like that for a long time. Night settled over the lake, and the clear sky filled with a million stars. The full moon hung heavily over the nearby hills, lighting up my tiny piece of paradise.

Alex worried that I would be frightened of his wolf form, and maybe I should have been. He was, after all, a huge carnivorous animal with sharp claws, pointy teeth, and outweighed me by at least twenty-five pounds. The only thing I was feeling, though, was peacefulness. A small part of me still grieved over what happened with Charlie, and it probably always would, but I was happy with the choice I made. I was happy with Alex.

"I suppose we should really open that stupid calculus book at some point," I finally said, not happy at the prospect of leaving the perfect moment we created. Alex whined, obviously feeling the same way, but got to his feet. As I walked over to the blanket he followed obediently. I resisted the urge to tell him to sit or heel.

We actually did study for a while. I would read aloud from the book and my notes and try to talk my way through an example problem. Alex would shake his head at me when I got something wrong, a trick he could have shown me earlier.

I don't know how we got distracted. I think I made some disparaging remark about a dog's ability to do math when he disagreed with the way I was finding the derivative of f using tangent lines and Alex had responded by tackling me. Before long the night air was filled with my shrieks and Alex's snarls as he stood over me, licking my very ticklish neck. I let out a yelp as his nose nudged down the top of my shirt. "Stop that," I gasped, weakly pushing against his chest. "Your nose is cold."

I was trying to determine where exactly a wolf might be ticklish when I felt Alex's muscles tense under my hands. His head snapped up and a growl reverberated in his throat. As he stared off into the distance, he flattened his ears back. The hairs on the back of his neck stood on end.

When I began to push my way up, Alex barked at me. The sound of it drove me back to the ground and kicked my heart rate up another notch. It was a bark of warning, one that I could feel in my bones, but it wasn't nearly as disturbing as the chorus of snarls that came from behind my head.

The part of me that lived in fear, the part that cowed to teachers and hid for hours in the bathroom last night, wanted to disappear into a hole, or at least close my eyes and wait for it all to be over. Instead, I clung to what little strength I had, and craned my neck around to determine the nature of the threat. Along the edge of the clearing I saw two more canines. They were both much smaller than Alex, close to a whole foot shorter, and not nearly as bulky. They both had brown fur, although the larger one seemed to have tan highlights in his coat. His eyes were a painfully familiar shade of green.

"Alex, let me up."

The wolf above me hesitated before stepping forward, allowing me to get to my feet. Looking at the coyotes from an improved angle didn't change my estimation of their size. They were *tiny*. It was like David and Goliath. What were they thinking?

Of course, I knew what they were thinking. They were thinking that two to one was pretty good odds, no matter how much bigger that one might be. They were thinking they had speed and agility on their side. They were thinking that together they could take Alex down.

I was so not going to let that happen.

"Jase, stop this right now."

The animal that was my brother yipped at me. It was a sound that seemed to be colored with something closer to surprise or annoyance than a threat. He whipped his head to the side with a whine and looked at me anxiously. I felt a bubble of hysteria as the words, *What's that, Boy? Did Timmy fall down the well?* popped into my head.

I wasn't doing whatever it was Jase wanted me to do. Charlie gave an agitated snort and moved towards me, causing Alex to let out a threatening snarl.

Faced with an unmistakable adversary, the coyotes abandoned their attempts to communicate with me and focused on the danger Alex represented. They stalked off in opposite directions, moving further into the clearing, and positioned themselves on either side of Alex. The world seemed to slow down as I watched the animals in front of me. They all stood within five yards of one another, each of them tensed for action. Charlie was snarling and growling out the canine equivalent of mother-related comments, his curses capturing Alex's attention, but I kept my focus on Jase, knowing he would lead the attack. How many times had the two of them tried this same tactic on me over the years?

Jase shifted his weight and I bolted. We collided inches away from Alex. I felt his claws graze me as I brought my knee up into his soft underbelly, sending him flying.

I saw a flash of fur as Alex leapt past me. He landed short, giving Jase just enough time to regain his footing and bound into the forest. Under normal circumstances, the coyote would have been able to quickly put a sizable distance between himself and the wolf barreling after him, but his gait was uneven, as if one of his front legs had been injured.

Instead of leading Alex deeper into the forest, Jase circled around the clearing, darting between trees and rocks. Alex was practically on top of him when Charlie caught Alex's hind leg, dropping him to the ground. I saw blood fly as Alex wrenched himself from Charlie's mouth, yet he gave no indication of injury as he rightened himself, never favoring one side over the other.

Once again, the three Shifters found themselves in a triangulated stand-off, tensed for the next attack, an attack I couldn't let happen. There would be no winners in this fight. No matter what happened, someone I loved was going to end up hurt.

I didn't really have a plan other than *stop them*. Maybe I would have tried to reason with them. Or maybe I would have yelled and raged. I might have even smacked them all upside the head for being such chauvinistic morons. Instead, I collapsed onto my knees after attempting a single step. A pain, white hot and searing, tore through my stomach, robbing my lungs of oxygen and distorting the world in front of my eyes. The bottom half of my shirt was shredded, strips of cotton glued to my body with a disturbing amount of thick, warm blood.

"Jase." My voice was choked, full of astonishment, hurt, and fear. I slowly raised my head to meet the gaze of the three Shifters, each forgetting the others as their attentions focused on me. "Oh God, Jase. What did you do?"

The world spun. I heard a yelp. A whine. Then a growl vibrated through my body, spreading dread down to the marrow.

Alex lunged. Jase scampered backwards, but not quickly enough. Alex was on top of him, his massive body easily pinning the smaller animal to the ground. He bared his teeth with an angry snarl before striking at Jase's throat.

Charlie was almost too late, pounding into Alex's side just as his teeth sank into the vulnerable skin of Jase's neck. The two went rolling across the clearing from the force of the impact, clawing and snapping as they went. Charlie dug his nails into the dirt, gaining just enough traction to sling his body around, narrowly avoiding plunging over the edge of the cliff. He flattened himself against the earth as momentum propelled the wolf over him.

The night ripped a sound from my lungs, more piercing than a scream, more anguished than a wail. It echoed off the trees and rocks, amplifying my pain as I hefted myself off the ground and raced into the darkness of the forest. I slid on loose gravel and tripped over exposed roots as I made my way down through the trees, but I kept moving. Limbs smacked against me, leaving cuts and whelps on my face and arms, but I didn't care. I was only vaguely aware of the searing heat in my abdomen and the hair-raising sound of howls loud enough to be heard over the roar in my ears.

I stumbled through the dark, frantically seeking the thin stretch of beach, my throat growing raw as I called his name over and over. My chest constricted when I finally saw his body, naked and human, crumbled on the ground.

"Alex!" I fell to my knees beside him, ignoring the tiny stones that bit into my skin.

His breaths were quick and shallow. A ragged shard of wood protruded just below his left shoulder.

"Scout?"

"Shhh... I'm here. You're going to be okay. Everything is going to be okay." One of my tears landed on his cheek. I wiped it away, along with some of the blood that had spilled out of his mouth.

He tried to speak, getting out a word with every other gasp of air. "Scout, I--"

"Shhh.." I brushed my thumb across his lips. "I know. You don't have to talk. It's okay." I stroked his face tenderly as I spoke to him. "I love you. I love you so much." I bent down and pressed my lips to his, but for the first time he didn't kiss me back.

I held onto him as the Laodicean moon leeched the warmth from his broken body. I watched his eyes fill with fear as he struggled with his final breaths and laid witness to the emptiness that followed. Even after he was gone, I couldn't let go. I curled my body into his, struggling to tell him how much I loved him, how much I would always love him. I bathed him in tears and blood, and when I had none left to give, I finally surrendered to the darkness.

Chapter 19

Opening my eyes seemed like an impossible task, so I didn't even attempt it. People spoke in hushed tones around me, but I couldn't distinguish one voice from another, much less individual words. Strong cleaning chemicals strained to mask the decidedly more human smells underneath.

"Scout?"

I knew that voice. It took a couple of tries, but my eyelids finally managed to pry themselves away from one another. Everything was slightly blurry and surreal. The television blended seamlessly into the cabinet that faded into the wall that was attached to the head of a middle-aged woman with curly brown hair, petite features, and sky-colored eyes.

"Mom?"

Crap, that hurt. My throat was raw and bruised, my tongue triple its normal size.

"I'm right here. Everything is going to be just fine."

"Where--?" Had someone washed my tonsils with a Brillo pad? I didn't know it was possible for a throat to hurt so much.

"You're in the hospital. There was an accident."

Hospital? Accident?

I remembered being in the woods with Alex. He had let me see him as a wolf, and then--

Oh God.

"Alex! Mom, Alex! We have to help Alex!" I bolted up, but immediately slammed back onto the pillow. Someone was screaming, a blood-curdling, ear-splitting sound that filled the tiny room.

"Scout! Don't try to move!" Mom placed her hands on my shoulders to restrain me, but it was unnecessary. I couldn't move if I wanted to. The pain blazing in my stomach was all-encompassing. Mom glared at the portly woman in Sponge Bob Square Pants scrubs I hadn't noticed being in the room. "For the love of God, give it to her before she busts her stitches out!"

And then the world went black again.

***

Our final play in Shakespeare was to be *Romeo and Juliet*, a rather unimaginative grand finale, in my opinion. With the exception of that really pretty version with a pre-balding Leonardo DiCaprio, I pretty much hated *Romeo and Juliet*. The plot never made sense to me. Two teenagers kill themselves in the name of love after knowing each other for a couple of days? I didn't get it.

Lying in the Vanderbilt University Medical Center, I finally understood. Alex and I had known each other less than nine months, yet I had curled up with him on the ground that night with the intent of dying by his side. Instead, I ended up in a hospital room where my parents took turns watching over me - Mom continuously checking the monitors, IV drips, and pillow situation while Dad stared blankly at the television. I spent my time watching the rain pound against the tiny window, disappointed that my shattered heart still managed to beat.

I had four lacerations stretching from just under my right breast down to my left hip. Two of them were deep enough to have nicked some muscle. I had forty-eight stitches across my abdomen and three more in my shoulder where I had fallen against a tree branch. That, I vaguely remembered. I couldn't, however, figure out how I managed to break two of the bones in my left hand.

The main concern, according to my mother, was the amount of blood I lost. During the course of my two day drug-induced coma I received eleven units, which was apparently a lot. I didn't need anyone to tell me they weren't sure I would pull through; the haunted look in my parents' eyes told me that much.

I wondered if they could see how much I wished I hadn't in my own.

My parents never asked me what happened or why I was in the forest in the first place. They never spoke of Alex. They made sure I was as comfortable as possible and honored my every request, save one.

On my second day of semi-consciousness my mother announced, beaming, that someone was there to see me.

"Mom, please. No visitors."

"They aren't visitors; they're family." She opened the door and ushered Jase and Angel into the room.

It was unfortunate they had unhooked the heart monitor that morning. If it had still been displaying my heart rhythm for the world to see Mom would have been calling for a crash cart instead of slipping out to get herself some lunch.

They stood just inside the door, Angel timidly huddled against Jase's legs. There was no evidence that he had been in a fight, which was to be expected. When Shifters go from one form to the other the process repaired any damage to the bones or tissue that must tear apart and reform to complete the Change. In the event of a major injury - like Jason Hagan's gunshot wound or Alex's fall - a Change would be triggered as a last ditch effort for survival.

I couldn't bear to look at Jase. I wanted to talk to Angel, to attempt to ease some of the fear I could feel radiating off of her, but I couldn't do that with Jase in the room. I could barely breath with Jase in the room, so I ignored them and went back to my new hobby - silently counting the water droplets that clung to the window. I was on droplet number forty-six when he broke the silence.

"I'm sorry."

He was sorry? For what? Trying to eviscerate me or being an accessory to the murder of my boyfriend? It didn't matter. Apology was not accepted.

"Charlie is in the waiting room. He refuses to leave, not even to eat or take a shower. You have to talk to him."

Droplet number eighteen, my favorite, decided he couldn't hold on any longer and fell towards the ledge, taking several unnumbered friends with him.

"I don't have to do anything." I took a deep breath, congratulating myself on being able to get out a whole sentence. "I want to be alone with my sister."

"Scout--"

"Please."

I was as much shocked as relieved that he actually left. When I head the door click shut, I turned to Angel. Her hair was braided down her back, but several unruly curls had worked their way free, frizzing out around her cherubic face. She looked small and scared.

"I like all of my pictures," I said, nodding towards the wall in front of my bed. Every time Mom came back from the hotel where my family was staying she brought a stack of drawings Angel made for me. I had her hang them on the wall so that I could see all the *Get well soon*'s and *I love you*'s every time the drugs wore off enough for me to wake up. My favorite was the first one on the second row. In it she had drawn two blond girls and a boy whose smile was so big it couldn't be contained by the round circle of his head. In his hand he had a plate of brownies. "You're becoming a really good artist."

Angel didn't say anything, but she did come over to the side of my bed. Her eyes would slide from my face to my stomach and back up again. Her bottom lip quivered.

"Do you want to climb up here and snuggle with me?"

"I'm supposed to be real careful not to hurt you."

"You won't hurt me." I patted the empty space on the bed with my cast. "Look, you can lay right here. We'll just be sure not to touch my tummy, okay?"

She was exceedingly cautious as she climbed up beside me. The jarring of the mattress did cause a few stabbing pains to shoot through my midsection, but I managed not to scream. When she finally settled in I pulled her head down onto my shoulder. She smelled of hotel shampoo and cookies. I watched as tears pooled on the bridge of her nose before plunging onto my hospital gown.

"Mommy said that Alex went to Heaven." Her voice trembled as she spoke.

"That's right. He went to be with his mommy and daddy."

"And they'll take care of him and won't let him be lonely?"

"Of course they will. He's in a better place now."

Angel wiggled around so that she could look at me. "You're not going to leave me and go to Heaven too, are you?" Her voice hiccuped as she started crying in earnest, her tiny face screwed up into a mask of heartache. If you had asked me an hour before, I would have said it was impossible for my heart to break any further. I would have been wrong.

"I'm not going anywhere." I awkwardly patted her back with my broken hand and covered the crown of her head in kisses. "I'm going to get better and come home in just a couple of days."

"Promise me," she sobbed. "Promise me you won't die."

"Angel, sweetie, I can't promise that. No one can make that promise."

"Promise me!" she wailed.

And so I slipped my pinky finger around hers and promised to stay where I was, in my very own version of Hell.

***

The next time I came to a new visitor was occupying the chair where my parents normally kept vigil. Talley twisted her hair around her fingers as her unblinking eyes flitted down the page of the novel balanced on her lap. From the blush on her cheeks I assumed she was to the kissing part.

"Hey," I said. My voice was still weak, especially when I first woke up.

Talley jumped up and tossed the book aside without even marking the page. "I'm so sorry. Have you been awake long? Do you

213

need anything? Water? Ice chips? Are you in pain? Do I need to get a nurse?"

"I'm fine." I swallowed and reconsidered her offer. "Actually, ice would be awesome."

Talley darted down the hall, reappearing seconds later with a styrofoam cup and plastic spoon. She made like she was going to feed me, but I fixed her with a look that caused her to hand it over. When her fingers touched mine she jerked back and apologized. She did that a lot now that I knew about her Seer abilities.

"It's fine," I said for perhaps the hundredth time. "I trust you."

That was apparently the wrong thing to say. Talley's face completely crumbled.

I braced myself, certain Talley was going to tell me she had told Jase and Charlie where to find me. I had been refusing to admit that was the most rational explanation for how they found us because I knew once I did, I would have to pass some of the blame for Alex's death onto Talley, leaving me without a single friend.

"I've already Seen what happened that night." The world weighed heavy on her shoulders. "I didn't want to, but they made me do it to protect the Pack. He had to know what happened. I'm so sorry, Scout. I know I promised never to get inside your head without your permission, but--"

"It's okay," I said, cutting her off. "Mi brain es su brain."

My own memories of that night were still jumbled, but it was getting clearer all the time. Some things, like the stick protruding from Alex's flesh, seemed to be seared permanently into my brain. Sometimes the image would suddenly float in front of my eyes, blocking out everything else. Other times, I would be gripped with a sudden paralyzing fear out of nowhere, my heart hammering in my chest, my brain screaming for fight or flight without any finite source of danger. And then there were the nightmares. I wondered if Talley was able to sleep peacefully.

"I'm sorry you had to See that," I said.

"I'm sorry you had to live it." She sat down on the edge of my bed. I placed a hand on her arm, both to comfort her and to let her know that I was still okay with her touching me. I watched as tears made rivulets down her cheeks, her face mirroring the window.

"Tal, did you tell them where we were?"

I couldn't help it. I had to know.

"What? No. Of course not." She grabbed one of the sandpaper grade tissues from the nightstand and delicately wiped her eyes. "We were doing a distance test to see how far away they could get before I lost their voices. They were supposed to be heading south, *away* from you. I have no idea..." She dabbed her eyes again. "Toby asked, of course, but they won't say what they were doing there."

"Couldn't you just..." I squeezed her arm to illustrate my point.

"Jase hasn't gotten close enough for me to touch him since July, and Charlie..." She cleared her throat in as ladylike of a manner as possible. "No. I haven't been able to get anything."

She stared out my window for a long while. I wished that her power worked both ways so I could know what she was thinking. My medication was wearing off, and since I was still holding onto Talley's arm, she realized it the same moment I did. "Here," she said getting up, "let me go get someone to give you something for the pain."

"No, not yet. It's not that bad." I had learned that pain was relative. For about five minutes I thought my throat was the ultimate in suffering. Now, even though it hadn't healed much, I barely noticed it. Compared to my injuries, it was just a nuisance. And compared to the hollow ache in my chest, physical pain was nothing. "I want to talk more before I slip off into the deep, dark abyss yet again."

Talley glanced at the door, and then sunk into the chair. "What do you want to talk about?"

"What does everyone think happened that night? Where do they think these scratches came from?"

"It was a nice night, so we decided to study outside, like a camping cram session." I wondered if the speech sounded so rehearsed every time she told it. "You went in the woods to pee. We heard you scream and found you on the ground, bleeding. I saw a flash of an animal disappearing into the woods. Alex had taken off to get help, but he must have gotten confused, because he ran right off the cliff. I tried to make you lie still while I went for help, but you wouldn't listen. You went looking for Alex, which is how you ended up losing so much blood."

"And how exactly did you explain the fact that Alex was naked?"

Talley dropped her eyes. "He wasn't. He had taken off his shirt to stop your bleeding, but he was wearing pants."

"But he wasn't wearing pants. Did the emergency crew just happen to not notice that?" When the realization hit of what she must have done my stomach heaved. I couldn't hold back a strangled scream as white hot pain burned in response.

Talley jumped up and made for the door. "You need medicine."

"No. I need answers. What really happened?"

"You know what happened."

"I mean, how is it that everyone thinks you were there the whole time? How did you know that something was wrong?"

"The guys thought they were too far away for me to hear them, and really they were. But then things started going wrong. I couldn't hear anything at all and then Jase was in my head, screaming that he hurt you and needed me. I took off without even telling Toby where I was going."

She came back over and resumed her position on the edge of my bed. "It was an accident, Scout. They never meant to hurt anyone."

I let out a single hysterical laugh. "An accident? I was there, Talley. They attacked us."

"They attacked Alex, you got in the way."

What the hell was this? Talley was defending them when Alex was *dead*? "I was supposed to just sit there and let them kill him?"

"They just wanted to scare him off. They never meant to kill him."

She believed what she was saying, which was even more infuriating than if she was covering for them.

Her phone trilled as I attempted to sort my emotions. She automatically looked at the caller ID and gave me a conflicted look.

"Go ahead. Take it." We were done anyway.

She walked over to the window, whether to get a better reception or to have a more semi-private conversation I wasn't sure. "Hey, have you got anything yet?...Sunday afternoon?" She looked at me and turned back to the window. "Yeah, she may be out by then...Listen, I'm actually at the hospital. Can I call you back to finalize things later?"

After she hung up, she came over to stand at the end of my bed. Something about the look in her eyes briefly quelled my anger. "That was Tinsley. She wanted to let you know that he has set a time for Alex's funeral. We're going to do it Sunday afternoon. Your mom said you should be able to leave by then."

"Why is Tinsley making funeral arrangements?"

"You remember that aunt Alex had in Montana?" I nodded. "Turns out, she doesn't exist. In fact, none of the contact information they provided the school is correct. Since we have no way of reaching the next of kin, the Senior class took up money to pay for a funeral. As class president, planning the actual service became Tinsley's job."

"What about Liam? I mean, I know they don't have much money, but he's still his brother. Shouldn't he be making funeral arrangements?"

Talley examined the bags hanging from my IV pole as she spoke. "No one has seen Liam since he carried you into the emergency room."

"Since he did what?"

"After Alex fell, Jase and Charlie started howling for help. Liam was hunting close by. He was already carrying you out of the woods when I got there." Her eyes met mine once again. "It was just like my vision. You were laying across his arms, blood everywhere."

Something was off. Wrong. There was too much that didn't add up. Too many questions without answers. Too much to process. Fortunately, the nurse came with her syringe of liquid oblivion, saving me from trying.

***

I did, in fact, get released from the hospital on Sunday morning. The doctor was hesitant, afraid of infection, but Mom agreed to continue IV antibiotics at home. She explained that I had a funeral to attend.

We got to the cemetery just before the service started. I was wearing a light black cotton dress that was two sizes too big so it wouldn't agitate my sutures. Dad pushed my wheelchair along the uneven ground as gently as possible.

The entire school turned out for the memorial service. I doubted even half of them had actually known Alex. They thought they were grieving for the boy who died, but really they were just mourning their long held sense of immortality.

Everyone stared at me as we made our way to the front. My hospital room had been filled with cards, flowers, and balloons from fellow classmates, yet every time I looked over the crowd eyes darted away like cockroaches scurrying from the light. The Scout Donovan who stood at Death's door was a beloved friend of the entire Senior class. Scout Donovan, the survivor, was merely a spectacle, a topic of conversation.

I briefly wondered if it should bother me.

Since Alex was not active in any of the local churches, the service was conducted mostly by the high school administration and staff. Our principal, Mrs. Tavers, started by talking about the tragedy of losing someone so young. Several of Alex's teachers got up and spoke about what a good student he was and his positive attitude.

Mrs. Sole was the only one that talked about him like she actually knew him, although most of her speech was unintelligible through the sobs. After the eulogies, Jane Potts did an emotionally draining acoustic version of "When Soul Meets Body". The service ended with a prayer led by another senior, David McGowan, who was heading to seminary in the Fall.

And then it was over. The whole of Alex's life had been reduced to a generic grave side service attended by people who never knew him in any way that mattered. I wanted to scream at the injustice of it all.

"Baby, do you want to go say good-bye?" Dad nodded towards the casket where several people had gathered, most of them leaning on one another for support.

I did want to say good-bye. I wanted at least one person who knew him, who loved him, to stand by his casket and acknowledge the life that was lost and could never be replaced, but there were so many people. People who watched me through the entire service, waiting for some response. People who wanted to see me break down, wanted to witness my grief. What were they saying about me? About my relationship with Alex? About what happened that night?

Why on earth did I care?

"Yes, please."

The group of mourners parted as Dad wheeled me forward. I saw groups of people turning to look at me. For the first time in my life, I truly didn't care what they thought. If they wanted a show, fine. I would give them one.

The casket was, of course, closed. I was grateful. I had already seen his face pale and unmoving once before, I couldn't stomach doing it again.

There was a photo sitting on top. Normally it would have been a Senior picture, but Alex had never got around to doing those. Instead, it was a candid shot, obviously taken from a cell phone. He looked like a kid at Christmas, joy seeping from every pore. I had already forgotten how beautiful he was when he was like that.

I stretched out my hand and placed it on the casket, ready to say my goodbyes, but the words got stuck in my throat. I stared at the plain wooden box, my thoughts and emotions in chaos. I knew it was impossible. I watched him die; he was gone. Yet I was certain, beyond a shadow of doubt, that the casket was empty.

If I hadn't been sitting down I would have collapsed.

I was so absorbed in my thoughts I didn't notice I was no longer alone.

"He was in love with you, you know." Ashley Johnson was wearing what I'm sure passed as appropriate funeral clothes in her book - a black mini-dress, four-inch heels, and Jackie O glasses. "He's looking at you in that picture. Normally he looked so bored, but the moment you were around he lit up like the Fourth of July." She swatted her hand at a tear that trickled down from beneath the glasses. "God, I'm such a horrid person."

Why was she talking to me? Couldn't she see that I was in the middle of something? I wanted her to go away so that I could think.

"I took that picture," she said with a tear saturated voice. "I took lots of them. Pictures of you two together when you thought no one was watching. Pictures of you sneaking off into closets and empty classrooms.

"Do you know how hard it is to live in your shadow? How hard it is to look at your perfect family, your perfect best friend, your perfect grades and know that nothing in my life will ever live up to that? You have always had everything and then you took him too."

It was as if she was suddenly speaking Mandarin. What was she prattling on about? And why would she think that I cared? I needed her to leave me alone.

"I just wanted to take something away from you, to knock you down a level. So I took pictures to gather proof. Jase would have never believed me if I just told him outright. He hates me. You made sure of that.

"On prom night I gave Jase the pictures and told him how I overheard your plans to meet the next night. He was livid. He started rambling about full moons and suicide attempts and God only knows what else. Charlie, however, was completely sober and unmoved. He gave me my pictures back and told me to go have inappropriate relations with myself."

The waterworks started, mascara tracks ruining her flawlessly made-up face. "When Tinsley called to tell me you were in the emergency room, I was happy. Happy." She let out a short bark of a laugh, loud enough that several people turned to look at her. "I thought Jase had come looking for you and found you with Alex. I thought...I thought you two had gotten into a fight, a real knock-down, drag-out fight with all of your karate kicks and judo chops. I imagined you with a black eye, maybe a broken arm. And then they said that you weren't expected to live through the night, and I *knew* it wasn't Jase, but still I felt so guilty. Like it was my fault that coyote attacked you."

I had to be emotionally numb. That was the only way to describe it. I didn't feel angry or horrified or pity or any emotion that would have made sense. I felt nothing. Nothing at all.

"Remember that time I got the stomach flu when you were staying at my house? You stayed up with me all night, holding my hair back every time I puked." The sun peaked out from behind a cloud reflecting off the snot that ran out of her nose. "You were a good friend, and I screwed it up. I miss you."

I couldn't even pretend to feel the same. "Do you still have those pictures of Alex and me together?"

"They're still in the Gucci clutch I took to prom."

"Can I have them?" I hoped what my mouth was doing looked more like a smile than a grimace. "I don't have any pictures of him."

"Of course! I'll even put them in an album and everything!" The thing about Ashley was that she was easy to comfort, always had been. Her guilt was instantly assuaged by my request, our friendship restored in her mind. That wasn't to say she wouldn't try to sabotage my life yet again tomorrow, but for now she was pacified.

Ashley started to babble on about something or another to do with what I had missed at school over the past week, now oblivious to the open grave not five feet from where we were standing. I was resisting the urge to push her in when Talley appeared at my elbow. She tactfully got me away from Ashley, noting that I was beginning to burn under the midday sun, and escorted me towards a small crop of trees.

The moment we separated ourselves from the masses, a man cut across the cemetery towards us. When Talley saw him she whispered a profanity under her breath, putting me on guard.

He was solidly built, possibly in his forties or fifties. He might have passed for attractive at some point in his life, but now he just looked worn out. A scar ran from his right temple down to the corner of his lip, mangling his bushy eyebrow as it passed through.

"Harper Donovan?" His accent was unusual. I thought it could be Eastern European or maybe even Russian.

"Yes, I'm Ms. Donovan."

"Ms. Donovan, I am Stefan Vasile." He extended a hand towards me. I instinctually wrapped mine even tighter against around my injured stomach. "I understand you were quite close to my nephew, Christopher."

"Christopher? I don't know anyone named Christopher."

"I am so sorry. I am forgetful." He recovered from the awkwardness of the unreturned handshake by stuffing his hands into the pockets of his suit. "When the boys ran away they assumed new names. I believe you knew him as Alex."

"I knew Alex." My voice held steady, my breath even.

"Perhaps you can help me. I am looking for his brother. The two ran away after their parents died in a house fire, and we've been desperately looking for them ever since. And now, with little Christopher gone..." He trailed off, looking forlornly where the funeral service had been conducted. Most people had left, only a few stragglers lagged behind. "It would mean so much to the family if I could bring his brother home. Do you have any idea where he could have gone?"

I met the dark brown eyes of the man who was not Alex's uncle and repaid Liam for saving my life. "He was always talking about how much he loved living in a warmer climate. If I was you, I would look south."

"South? Are you sure?"

"He tried to talk Alex into moving to Florida on more than one occasion."

"That's...interesting. Thank you, my dear. You have been most helpful."

"I hope you find him," I lied.

"Don't worry. I know we will."

Before he made it to the line of dark cars parked in the drive he whipped out a cell phone, talking rapidly in another language. I couldn't tear my eyes away from him. It wasn't until he got into his car and drove away that the tension began to seep out of me.

"That guy was in serious need of a mustache to twirl," I said, turning slowly back to Talley. Moving took a great deal of personal effort. The stress of the day, coupled with the handful of pills Mom made me swallow before the service, was starting to have an affect on me. I was tired, sore, and groggy.

"Huh?" Talley's head whipped around. She moved to block my field of vision, but was too slow. I saw him, standing on the edge of the wooded area that surrounded the cemetery. My heart stalled as the wolf's grey eyes met mine for the briefest of moments before he ran into the forest.

THE END

Acknowledgements

Writing your first novel is a terrifying and crazy-making experience. I wouldn't have made it through without the help of Crystal Blackwell, who read every single chapter as I wrote it, and then every single draft that followed; Alyson Beecher and Erin Lowery, the world's best online writing partners/support team; Jennifer and Kelly, friends who love me enough to tell me when something doesn't work; Tori, Kitty Kat, Meg, Jake, Victoria, Emily the Jorge, and Emily the Bobbit who made sure Scout didn't sound old or lame; Pottsie for making sure my characters kick butt; Terri Kirk, super-librarian and beta-reader; and Sarah Pace-McGowan, the Grammar Goddess who taught me the difference between "whelp" and "welt". The biggest thanks of all goes out to my mom, who in addition to doing the good mother thing of encouraging me and believing I could write a novel when I had sizable doubts, gave Scout her stitches and blood transfusions. And thanks to *you* for reading this book. Seriously, it means a lot to me that you did.

About the Author

Tammy Blackwell is a Young Adult Services Coordinator for a public library system in Kentucky. When she's not reading, writing, cataloging, or talking about YA books, she's sleeping. You can follow her on Twitter (@Miss_Tammy), write to her at tammyblackwell.ya@gmail.com, or visit her at www.misstammywrites.blogspot.com.

9 781460 918685